Colour Studies

Shelagh Meagher

Torriver Press

This edition published 2015

ISBN 978-0-9880374-2-7

Book design by eBook DesignWorks.

Be silent in that solitude,
Which is not loneliness—for then
The spirits of the dead who stood
In life before thee, are again
In death around thee—and their will
Shall overshadow thee: be still

—*Edgar Allan Poe,*
'*Spirits of the Dead*'

Also by Shelagh Meagher

Pearls in the Ashes

Gumption:
The Practical Woman's Guide to Living an Adventuresome Life

The Spirit of the Garden

Thank you

I first wrote *Colour Studies* seventeen years before it finally saw the light of day as a published book, when I was living in Italy with my family. It took the intervening years to learn how to tell the story well enough to put it out into the world. Way back in those days of the first draft, I ran into an American woman selling her art in a piazza in Florence: Angie Elizabeth Brooksby. We chatted. She did beautiful work. Somehow she agreed to teach me everything I needed to know about painting, for the purpose of bringing this story to life. I remain amazed and grateful for her generosity and patience. Any errors in explaining technique or details are purely mine; Angie is deservedly renowned as an artist and certainly wouldn't make such errors herself. She now lives in Paris and I in Toronto, but the large painting she made for me of the Ponte Vecchio back then still has pride of place in my living room.

The other person who made *Colour Studies* possible is Glen, who took me to live in Italy in the first place. Without him, this book would never be.

To Vanessa Wells for editing and to Renee and Mark D'Antoni for the book design inside and out: thank you so much for the polish you gave the final product.

Chapter One

*O*F ALL THE DRESSES that lay strewn on the bed together like collapsed lovers, the one that particularly caught her attention was bursting with racemes of purple lilac on a white background. On impulse, Sarah held it up to herself and looked in the mirror. The dress transformed the image that stared back at her into someone vaguely familiar but definitely not her. For a moment she could see, wrapped in the dazzling fabric, a perfect reflection of what her grandmother must have looked like wearing this dress. Captivating, flirtatious, a woman who loved to dance. Sarah grasped one edge of the full skirt, holding it wide, and imagined herself whirling, the fabric flying around her legs in a ravishing swirl of colour. Then she noticed her chewed-down fingernails and unbrushed hair, and the image abruptly vanished. The smell of camphor from the open storage bag was sickening in the hot room, despite the window being flung open wide. Blotting up the sweat on her chest with the front of her T-shirt, Sarah put the dress back on its hanger and hung it from the curtain rod in the window to air it out.

An orange tomcat watched her unblinkingly from the doorway.

"It's not exactly my style, is it Beppe?" she said to him. "I'm going to keep it anyway. Just that one." The cat remained motionless. "Is that a stare of disapproval, or are you cross about not getting your supper right away?"

The rest of the dresses were still in a pile on the bed. It was tempting to ignore the whole mess until later, but that camphor smell was revolting. She stuffed them back into the storage bag, dragged it down the stairs and set it outside the back door until she could figure out where she might get rid of dresses that were at least half a century old. Besides the garbage.

The kitchen offered some respite from the stultifying heat of an Italian August. This room was the heart of the house in many ways, the best place for just sitting around. In the summer its thick stone walls and brick floors sucked coolness up from the earth, and a large chestnut tree shaded it from the midday sun while still allowing plenty of light through the large windows. A long, wooden table, marked by its service to many past lives, stood solidly in the centre of the room. At the far end, in front of a fireplace that took up almost the entire wall, sat an overstuffed easy chair, a magnet for settling down with a book in winter or for a midday nap in summer.

Beppe had padded down the stairs after her and Sarah tossed a handful of kibble into a small clay bowl for him. His ravenous crunching and the gulp of her own swallows as she downed a glass of water sounded loud to her in the stillness of the house, a rude interruption of the gentle, steady hum of cicadas outside. She poked around in the cupboards for something to nibble on. Cream crackers. Packet soup. A can of tomatoes. She had to get to the market to stock this place properly.

Settling on the cream crackers, she ate them unthinkingly while wandering around the kitchen, taking a mental inventory of its contents. Beppe scurried after her, licking up bits of cracker that dropped on the floor as she went along.

Despite the appearance of the house as being a casual country home, an artist's getaway, Sarah's grandmother Katherine had always maintained high standards in its furnishings. In the china cupboard everything matched, with a full and mostly intact set of Spode blue and white Italianate china accompanied by wine glasses that had been hand blown by a friend in Florence. In one of the drawers there were various linen napkins in lively colours, all of which had been carefully ironed before being put away. Paper ones had had no place in Katherine's house. Sarah grabbed her grocery list and scribbled *paper napkins*. She couldn't remember the last time she'd ironed a thing.

The other pantry drawer, always a bit hard to wrestle from its hole, held a twelve-piece set of antique English silver cutlery. It was tarnished from months of neglect and humidity. Katherine had so many things that required special care. Sarah picked up a spoon, the weight of it surprising after years of using stainless steel, and looked again at the familiar insignia engraved on the handle. A crest with two crossed flags and a falcon. As a child Sarah had thrilled to think of the silver, freshly crafted, in the hands of some aristocratic family in a castle. She and her sister had made up stories as to what calamity might have befallen those first owners to make them sell their precious silver. Now Sarah found herself wondering, for just a moment and with some guilt, what the set might fetch today if she got that desperate.

She put the spoon back in its place and shut the drawer. All these things of Katherine's were pretty lovely. Having started out with the notion that she ought to be changing things around to suit herself, Sarah felt faintly disturbed by the fact that there was little, actually, she wanted to alter. An old clothes bag removed from a wardrobe didn't constitute much of a revolution in the way the house was set up. But maybe it didn't matter. She had lots of time, after all, to make changes as they occurred to her. This was supposed to be her home now.

◊ ◊ ◊

The phone rang, its insistent bleep-bleep penetrating the dark sludge of Sarah's sleeping brain. She considered letting the answering machine pick it up, then decided that choosing to ignore the first call she'd received since moving in would set an anti-social precedent she might fall into full-time if she weren't careful. The cheerfulness of the voice at the other end of the line further shocked her groggy system.

"Hi, it's me. I didn't actually wake you, did I?"

"Lily. Hi." She let her sister's voice pull her up into the day. "You did. What time is it?" She fumbled at the bedside table for her watch.

"Nine o'clock."

"Sure doesn't feel like it."

"It's not like you to linger late. Did you have a wild night or something?"

"A wild night isn't exactly like me, either." Sarah yawned loudly.

"People can change."

"Well, I haven't." God, she felt exhausted. Why was she so tired? There'd been some kind of strange dream last night…what had it been about? Misty fragments of a man and a dark sky slipped around her mind, just out of reach.

"So how's the house?" Lily asked, bringing her back to the morning.

"It's good."

"Only good? I thought you'd be in heaven."

"It's odd, being here without Gran. I feel a bit like an intruder."

"I guess it would be strange, but that'll wear off after a while. Have you started painting yet?"

"I've only been here a few days."

"Sounds like a no."

"I wouldn't call it a no, exactly. I've done the prep work. The studio's all cleaned up, there's canvas ready to go and everything."

"So you're still procrastinating. Roger was wrong, you know. He's a prick. You're good. Really good."

Sarah smiled. That was her Lily. They had been each other's ports in every storm they'd weathered growing up, and Lily was one of the few things in England Sarah missed. "When are you going to come visit me?"

"When I win the lottery. Then I'll move out of Mum and Dad's house to a flat of my own, and I'll take bucolic holidays to your little country place whenever I want a break from the whirl of London." Lily's failure to get out from under their parents' roof was a chronic but unresolved family concern.

"There'll be cheap fares starting November," Sarah offered.

"Maybe by then you'll have some paintings for me to see."

"Don't worry. I am going to get started."

"And a handsome Italian man or two would be nice. Seen any good ones around?"

"All the handsome men are at the sea in August. Anyway, this house is in the middle of nowhere, remember?"

"Sounds like hell."

Sarah laughed. "That's why I'm here, and you're there."

"To each her own. Have you seen Annalisa?"

"No. I know I should have visited by now, but I've been enjoying pottering around on my own. I hope she doesn't know I'm here or she'll be really miffed."

"She's pretty cool, I wouldn't worry. But she will know that you're there. She always knew everything."

"Don't tell Gran."

"Of course not. Look, I'd better ring off now or Mum will have a fit when she sees a big long distance bill. God forbid they should get a Europe plan. Does your cellphone work there? Or the internet?"

"My phone works if I go to the top of the hill, by the rock. Otherwise it depends on which way the wind is blowing. And no, Gran didn't install internet service, are you joking? She's resolutely pen, paper and land lines. I don't even know if I can get it, outside of buying a satellite dish I can't afford. There's internet access at the café over in Camugnano. It may be the start of the twenty-first century in London, but it's still rustic here."

"I'll say. Well, I just wanted to know how you were getting on. Now go and paint."

"Aye-aye, Captain."

Sarah smiled to herself as she hung up the phone. It had been good to hear from Lily. She was far away, but she was still there. Sarah was not completely alone.

◊ ◊ ◊

The painting studio, originally a sitting room but commandeered for art on account of its superior light and space, was the brightest room in the small house. Its entire front was a wall of window that looked out across the broad valley before it. Most of the room's interior was left open, so an easel could be positioned anywhere the light was best throughout the day. Off to one side was a small sink for cleaning up, and neat, sectioned areas for separately storing freshly primed canvases, those in progress and those temporarily abandoned.

With the windows opened wide, a scent like baking herbs floated in on the outside air and mixed with the pleasing smell of linseed oil inside. Sarah lifted the lid on the wooden box that held her paints. It was an exquisite, handmade box of cherry wood with a small brass clasp, a present from Roger in the early days. She hated the fact that she loved it so much, feeling it had been tainted by the dreadful mess of their relationship, but she couldn't stop finding it beautiful. She sorted through the tubes inside, checking each one in the hope that something was still usable, and replaced spent tubes with the stock of new ones she'd brought with her. The names of the colours sounded like poetry—Alizarin Crimson, Cerulean Blue, Viridian Green. And the earth tones, warm and rich: Ochre, Umber, Sienna. As she squeezed selected colours from their tubes onto her palette, Sarah imagined them in the landscape she intended to start that morning. A mixture of fear and excitement filled her. She had loved this once, and had come to it as easily as the wind meets the sky. But that had been a couple of years ago. Perhaps her talent had left her. Perhaps it had never existed.

Then it occurred to her, the way to begin. She would grind a special colour from powdered pigment, as she and Gran used to do from time to time. There was a meditative element to the laborious, time-consuming process. Gran had always presented the making of colours as an almost religious ritual, a gesture to summon and honour the gods of creativity. Rummaging in the cupboard, Sarah found the remains of what used to be an extensive supply of luxurious Zecchi pigments, as well as the smooth, marble grinding stone and glass mortar. *Something for the sky*, she thought. *French Ultramarine with Cobalt Violet*. She transferred precise portions of each powder onto the stone using a delicate porcelain measure, poured a little linseed oil into the well she had created in the middle of the powder, then lifted the mortar. Its cool, curved handle felt perfect in her hand as she began the rhythmic, circular strokes that would blend the pigments evenly into the oil.

There had been a poem they had always recited, to keep the strokes even. It was Katherine's favourite from *A Child's Garden of Verses*:

> *O wind, a-blowing all day long,*
> *O wind, that sings so loud a song!*
> *I saw the different things you did,*
> *But always you yourself you hid.*

Sarah began to chant under her breath. She stopped for a moment, added a touch more violet and a few more drops of oil, scraped the accumulated paste off the sides of the mortar, and began anew.

> *I felt you push, I heard you call,*
> *I could not see yourself at all—*
> *O wind, a-blowing all day long,*
> *O wind, that sings so loud a song!*

The finished colour gleamed, rich and inviting. *Well, that's one thing I can still do,* she thought. She loaded a thick gob of the paint onto a brush and held it over the blank canvas like a hot swimmer poised to dive into a chill lake, wanting the relief but dreading the moment of first contact. Then she forced her hand forward and pulled the brush across the canvas in a broad sweep. There it was, an arc of deep, purple-blue night sky slicing through the fresh, white surface. She had started.

◊ ◊ ◊

Mid-afternoon she stepped back from the easel and frowned. She'd avoided looking too critically at what she was producing until that moment, not wanting to think about what she'd find if she let herself pause. That had been a good idea; while she'd harboured a tiny dream that it would all magically come back to her, the reality was as she'd feared. She was out of practice and it showed.

The sky was breathtaking but the other colours lacked a subtlety she once would have captured. Outside the window, the real valley was a soft mosaic of parched, deep greens in the woodlands, the sheenless brown of ploughed earth left exposed to the sun, and golden fields of ripened grain. In Sarah's version, the greens were a bit too lush and the browns too lively, making the scene almost garish. Practice would improve that, she assured herself, trying not to let disappointment squash the victory she'd felt at having produced the canvas at all. Her talent hadn't gone completely, it was just sleepy. If she poked at it enough, surely it would wake up again.

It had better, because going back to her painting was part of the deal she had struck with Katherine. "I'll give you the house on the condition that you paint again when you're there," Katherine had said. "The house cannot be owned by anyone who doesn't paint." So Sarah had agreed, the house had become hers, and now she had to stick to her promise.

While she cleaned her brushes carefully she could hear echoes of her grandmother instructing her on how to take care of them, all those summers when Sarah was growing up. She sighed. It hardly seemed right, painting in the house alone. Katherine was sitting in her nursing home back in England right now, maybe thinking about her, willing her to make the most of this opportunity. Envying her even. Gran had loved this house so much. Sarah would call after supper to let her know she'd started painting.

She put the brushes in their worn and splattered coffee-can holders and ambled through the kitchen to the back door, grabbing the last apple on the way. Having eaten almost nothing all day, she vowed for the hundredth time to start taking care of herself more conscientiously, then quickly rationalized her current slip on the basis that getting that first, crucial painting done had been far more important than a balanced lunch. For now, her priority was a walk up the hill behind the house to her favourite spot on the ridge.

The farmhouse was a simple structure made spectacular by its setting. In an area of Italy where the Apennine mountains north of Florence give way to the more manageable slopes of Emilia Romagna, the house was perched high up on a hillside and commanded a breathtaking view of the entire valley before it. At the back, it settled itself into a slight curve in the slope which, along with a handful of mature, surrounding chestnut trees, gave it a comfortable, nestled feeling like a cat that has found the perfect spot in an inviting pillow.

The worn path that started at the back door led upwards through rough mown fields, hayed by the neighbouring farmer for the few cows he kept. Sarah climbed slowly, the crisp sweetness of the apple in her mouth contrasting with breaths of air so limp with heat it felt as though the oxygen had been sucked right out of it. When she reached the top, she turned to look out across the sweep of hills and valleys that extended in all directions, each undulation greyer than the one in front until the horizon swallowed the last. The vast, great beauty of it caused her heart to lurch with a longing almost like love.

She turned to a flat rock the size of a double bed and laid her hands on its sun-baked surface, taking its warmth into her palms in greeting, then climbed up to stand on top. The Rock at The Top of The World had once been the site of marvellous castle games, where princesses Sarah and Lily were rescued by daring local princes, through liberating sword fights and spell-breaking kisses.

She felt traces of its magic, even if it did seem a bit smaller than she remembered and it had been years since it had hosted a prince. *And what a prize I'm looking like for a prince,* she thought. In her determination to start that morning she hadn't taken a shower, brushed her hair or washed her face, and the clothes she wore were the same old T-shirt and cut-off tracksuit bottoms she'd slipped on straight out of bed. Both top and bottoms were spotted with paint, as were her hands. A quick check of the soaked armpits of her T-shirt confirmed that she smelled as well. Sarah laughed up at the clear, blue sky. It felt good to be a painterly mess at the top of the hill. The world's princes could go rescue someone else today.

The twilight air seemed weirdly alive as she stood in the doorway to watch the fleeting passage of dusk. There was a sense of mystery that accompanied this hour, an apparent suspension of time that occurred as the remains of the day's light clung briefly to the air before being swallowed by the night. An extraordinary hue of deep purple-blue bruised the sky. As it deepened, the first stars began to shimmer like match heads struck to flame in the darkness.

A warm breeze, heady with lavender and cricket-song, swirled a light cotton dress around Sarah's legs. She glanced down at the touch of material against her skin and saw to her surprise that she was wearing the dress of lilacs, although she couldn't remember having put it on. She held it wide and watched the material sway provocatively. It reminded her of dancing. She rarely danced. Roger didn't like to.

A figure appeared in the dirt roadway below. He hurried up the slope, and the fluttering of pleasure she felt at the sight of him confused her. Although she didn't recognize his face, she understood that she knew him intimately. Then, as she stepped out of the doorway to meet him on the terrace, her vantage point shifted. She could feel herself standing there, but at the same time she floated strangely disembodied above the scene, looking down on herself as though she were another woman altogether.

Sarah watched the two lovers embrace and felt for herself the pleasure of the man's familiar touch. His arms became a cloak around her, enveloping her in a sweet, warm darkness. The rhythm of his heartbeat drummed softly inside their cocoon as his kisses and hands moved over her body.

It was from her place above that she started to sense a whistling sound like a rising wind and saw the lavender stems bend to touch the ground. Inside the cloak she was still overwhelmed by his presence until his heartbeat suddenly sped up, breaking the spell. Faster and louder it began to bang, like the sound of frightened, running feet, with the wind whining and screaming in pursuit.

All at once the man burst into a thousand blackened fragments, leaving Sarah exposed to a night that had turned cold. At the core of her, a ball of pain grew until it forced her mouth open to vent itself as a long, anguished cry. The tortured sound rose, and with it the fragments whirled into a maelstrom above her head. She ran back to the house, clinging to its doorframe desperately as the maddened air whipped at her dress.

Then, abruptly, consciousness.

Sarah sat bolt upright in bed, the echo of her sobs ringing in her ears as she awoke. Her hands were still clutching twisted wads of the sheets as she strained to catch any noises that might be out there in the darkness: a gust of wind, the sound of feet. All was silent. She sat in bed a few minutes more, calming herself slowly. She'd had this dream before. The depth of love she felt in his arms and the sudden, horrific loss of him felt vaguely and dreadfully familiar. She got up and crept down the stairs to the front door. As she stood in the doorway she saw a bright, full moon illuminating the empty terrace, the slope to the house, the roadway below and the broad valley. No one was there and nothing moved save a slight breeze that rippled her own cotton nightdress around her legs and brought with it a hint of lavender. She shivered despite the warmth of the night air and walked back into the house, locking the door carefully behind her.

Chapter Two

THE SITTING ROOM at the back of the house was where Katherine kept all her books. It was a cozy space, somewhat overwhelmed by things that had formerly lived in the larger, sunny studio room crammed into its confines. The far wall was lined in books, with an upright piano awkwardly in front of them. Taking up most of the opposite wall was a long sofa, over which hung one of Katherine's paintings. It was a landscape typical of what Sarah thought of as her grandmother's style; spare in its graphic detail and bold in its colours, a slightly abstract representation of the natural world, with a restrained emotional quotient. A painting that was pleasing to look at but kept you at a distance.

Sarah was hunting the bookshelves for escapist reading, something to stop that damned dream from preying on her mind. There was a haunting and unusually vivid quality about it that just didn't want to leave her alone, a niggling mystery about the man whose identity she couldn't quite put her finger on. A perfectly clear image of him floated back into her head, the irresistible feel of his arms around her, his handsome Mediterranean features, and the scent of something—what was that? Not the faint lavender that had been in the air: no, it was something lovely that clung closer to him. Her heart picked up speed at the thought, and she shook her head. This was ridiculous, fantasizing about some dream lover. Concentrate on the books.

The shelves were organized, but not in a way that was easy to decipher. Some books were grouped by author, others by subject, and some by the first letter of a key subject word. A dog-training manual was tucked in beside Dante, which led to various works of Italian poetry and on to *Pottery for Collectors*. On the next shelf down were several books about reincarnation and concepts of the afterlife, which seemed odd given that Katherine always claimed to be an atheist. In the far corner, tucked nearly out of sight, was the less esoteric part of the library that Sarah had been looking for: dozens of paperbacks of the type sold by airport newsagents. Perfect for distracting the mind.

Getting to them was challenging, in the tiny space between the piano and the shelves. She grabbed the first ones she came to and backed out again. What was a piano doing in this house, anyway? No one in the family knew how to play it. It had always just sat there, ignored. Sarah set her books down on top of it, ran a finger through the dust covering its rich mahogany surface, and raised the lid to reveal the keys. They were of real ivory: yellowed, cracked, and chipped with the memory of fingers probably long dead. Sarah sounded out a simple scale and was surprised to find the piano almost perfectly in tune. Why would Gran have bothered? In the bench was a pile of music, most of it as yellowed as the keys, a combination of classical pieces and popular songs from an earlier time.

Sarah closed the piano up again and glanced at the tracing her finger had left across its top. One more thing she needed to clean. Ignoring it, she turned her attention back to the books.

Of the four she'd managed to get from the shelf, she'd read two already. A third was about Russian spies, a topic that didn't interest her in the least. The fourth looked about right. It was thin enough not to be too much of a commitment, and thick enough to keep her occupied for a while, with a storyline involving some polo players in America. It held a promise of lust, treachery and excess, and that sounded good to her. She left the others on the dusty piano and brought the winner into the kitchen, where she laid it on the easy chair as an incentive. Later, if she'd accomplished enough, it would be her reward.

◊ ◊ ◊

The gravel road crunched dry and dusty underfoot as Sarah wound her way down its curves towards Annalisa's house. She'd considered being lazy and taking the battered Citroën Katherine had left with the house, tempting as it was to avoid the walk back up, but she decided to enjoy the slow route instead. Memories were everywhere. The farmhouse where hunting dogs, trapped in their pen, would hurl themselves in a frenzy of barking when she and Lily walked by, startling them anew every time. The climbing tree that marked the halfway point in the trek to Annalisa's, an old cherry from which they lobbed fruit at the neighbourhood kids, or were lobbed at in turn. The farmhouse with the calico cat who seemed to always be pregnant or nursing. Sure enough, there was a calico lounging in the shade of a quince bush beside the drive. A second generation, doomed to continue producing more cats than were wanted.

Then Annalisa's house came into view, the first of a small cluster of crumbling buildings that served as the village of Guzzano. The village was little more than a narrowing of the road as it threaded its way past the doorsteps of the few houses that clung to its edge. Annalisa's two-story home, stucco peeling to reveal the stones beneath, was much like the others except that it was larger and had a hectare of land running off the back and one side of it. In that space were an old shed housing two goats, a coop for a handful of chickens and their rooster, a pen with rabbits, a dovecote, a large vegetable garden and a small fruit orchard. Everything necessary for culinary self-sufficiency most of the year.

Sarah had been invited for the midday meal. There had been no mention of how long it had taken her to get in touch. She paused before the screen of furry, nylon ropes that hung over the open front doorway to keep out flies without stifling whatever breeze might come up. "*Salve, Annalisa—permesso?*" she called out. It didn't matter how well you knew a person, you always asked permission to enter. Katherine had drummed that into them from an early age.

A short, wide, egg-shaped woman appeared in the front hallway, wearing floppy rubber sandals and a simple dress that had once boasted a bold floral pattern in galling colour choices, mercifully subdued through countless washings to a faded version of its former glory. *"Tesora!"* she cried, falling on Sarah with hugs and kisses.

Then she held her visitor at arm's length to begin her appraisal. "Too skinny," she assessed. Her dark eyes, resting now in the crinkled, puffy sockets of an old face, still held an ageless vitality. "No colour, either. You need to go to the sea, to get the sun. It's good for you."

Sarah warmed to the sound of Italian in her ears once again. It had been worth keeping the language up over the years she'd been away. She bore Annalisa's scrutiny in good humour, prepared for it. "So why aren't you at the sea, then?"

"Beh, me" the old lady answered with a dismissive wave of her hand. "I'm a creaky old ancient now, the sun is past being able to prolong my life." She turned and went back into the house. "Come in, I have to tend the stove." They walked straight to the kitchen at the back of the house. "Sit," Annalisa commanded, pulling out a chair for Sarah at the big table and pouring her a glass of red wine without asking.

"Is Franco still making this?" asked Sarah. It was light and almost frothy— *vivace* they called it in Italian—but highly drinkable.

"Yes. His son tried to get him to make grappa last year, but Franco knows what he knows, and he's sticking to it."

The two place settings looked inadequate on a table that could easily seat ten and had hosted many more. The times in her childhood when Sarah had come here with Lil and Gran to share a meal, it had been hard to find enough space along with all Annalisa's family members squeezed around it. Three generations of Tondi, and often cousins as well. "We're a pretty small party for this table, just the two of us," Sarah said.

"It looks this way too often these days. I guess you know my Bruno died last year. Our children have all moved away to the big cities and they're too busy to come home to eat more than a couple of times a month."

"I'm sorry to hear it."

Annalisa brought a wooden spoon to her lips to sample a fragrant tomato sauce. "Not bad." She added a tiny amount of salt. "Things change," she continued, "and I manage. My great-nephew—you remember the story of my brother Filippo's son, the one who moved to the United States and married an American? Well their son, Luca, is back and he visits me often enough. He lives in Florence but he comes here to get away from the city."

"Luca?" Sarah cast about in her memory but couldn't sort out which of many cousins he was. "Have I met him?"

"I doubt it. He grew up in America. Filippo only came back once, when Mama died. And his son never visits. But now Luca's come home."

Even though he was born and raised in America, two generations removed, Annalisa still thought of his move to Italy as coming home. "That's nice for you," Sarah said.

"He's an architect, with a good job. And he's a good-looking boy, too."

"Everbody in your family is good-looking."

Annalisa grinned. "Especially my side. The Morettis pass along their looks." She heaved a huge pot of water onto the stove and set the flame under it to high.

"Can I help with something?" asked Sarah, although she knew it was pointless.

"Of course not." Annalisa waved her hand about, dismissing the very idea. "Luca visited your grandmother a fair bit when she still lived in the house. You would have met him if you hadn't been living in China all those years."

"Indonesia."

"All the same. But that was kind of him, don't you think?"

"It was." Somewhere in the back of her mind Sarah recalled Gran having written her about 'a charming young nephew'.

"Maybe he should visit you, too."

Annalisa was facing the stove so Sarah couldn't see what kind of look was on her face, but she suspected there was the sly smile of the matchmaker who senses an opportunity.

"I'm not looking for that kind of company at the moment."

Annalisa had turned around, brandishing a wooden spoon in her hand like a school matron about to rap Sarah's hands if she didn't behave. "You have to move on, you know. That bad Englishman…"

"Roger."

"Yes. You need to get over him."

"I am, thank you." She should have known her grandmother would share her history with Annalisa. There was no hiding. "Truly."

Annalisa grunted, unconvinced, and turned back to her cooking.

"But back to you," Sarah continued. "Are you getting on all right?"

"Well enough. I can still do everything for myself, except reading. I have cataracts and they make it hard, it gives me a headache. Luca says I can have them removed but the idea gives me goosebumps. They aren't bad enough for that yet. But I miss my books."

"I can come read for you, if you like," Sarah offered. "It would be good for my Italian. Something light, though. I doubt I could do justice if you set me onto anything demanding."

"How about a good romance novel?"

"Perfect."

"If you really have the time."

Sarah found it hard to imagine being pressed for time in Guzzano. "I'll have to take a break from painting occasionally."

"Well then, I'd like that. How are you finding the house?"

"It's good." That tepid answer, again. Sarah wondered why she wasn't more thrilled.

Annalisa came over to the table, her pots burbling to her satisfaction, and eased her weight into the nearest chair with a satisfied sigh. Nearing eighty now, the dynamo was starting to slow. "You know, I wasn't certain if Katherine would actually give it to you in the end. I thought she might choose to die in it and have it sealed over like a crypt when she was gone."

"It's very dear to her."

"Too dear. That place was an obsession."

"Well maybe, you know, it held a special place in her heart because that's where she felt most creative. She set conditions; I had to promise to paint." Sarah gave a short laugh. "Gran might give up her house but she doesn't like to give up control."

Annalisa scrutinized Sarah as if weighing her words before deciding to speak. "It's possible to love something too much. That house, she loved it more than anything alive—except you, maybe —and that can't be right."

It was true, now that Sarah thought about it, that Katherine had spent her time at the Guzzano house alone. Sequestered, almost. Sarah couldn't remember ever having seen her grandfather there when he was alive. She assumed he'd preferred London. And Sarah's mother Victoria, Katherine's only child, had often complained about how she had been regularly abandoned as a child to the care of the London housekeeper, while Katherine went off to indulge her passion for Guzzano and painting. Only in the summer, when Sarah and Lil came to visit, was the place alive with other people.

"I always thought she liked the solitude so she could paint," Sarah said.

"But tell me, how much painting can a person do?"

"I guess I'm about to find out."

"Well don't hole yourself up like a hermit. You're young and need to get out and about. Luca will help with that."

Sarah let the assumption slip. It was no use protesting when Annalisa got an idea about something.

When the food was ready, they sat down to a gargantuan feast of antipasti, a savoury, tomato-based pasta, several meat concoctions, and a salad of fresh greens. Sarah wasn't certain what she was eating by the time she got to the meat stews and didn't want to ask. She maintained some squeamishness about consuming the common fare of donkeys and rabbits, and found she could enjoy the taste and worry less if she simply didn't know. There was enough food on the table for five people by Sarah's standards and there was no indication it had been murderously hot all week; Annalisa had cooked as though it were winter.

As they waded through the meal, Annalisa picked up their conversation where they'd left off earlier. "Solitude," she said, then paused as she considered the concept. "Even when I was young and village life was the norm, Guzzano wasn't a very exciting place. Now it's near dead." Annalisa heaped another helping of stew on her own plate, then gave more to Sarah, heedless of whether she actually wanted it. Sarah thought she might explode.

"Maybe living in Guzzano is going to extremes," said Sarah, "but I like the idea of having some independence for a change." She had always lived with someone else, first her parents and then Roger. Striking off on her own this way felt full of possibilities. "The house gives me a chance to start again."

"That's what Katherine said she hoped for by giving it to you."

"And I like the house a lot. It speaks to me."

Annalisa looked up sharply. "Speaks to you?"

"Not literally, of course." Sarah laughed. "Just that I've had many happy times there, and that makes me feel good about the place."

"A happy past is fine, but now you need to build a happy future." Annalisa looked at Sarah's unfinished stew. "You're not finishing that?"

"It was delicious, but really, I'm so full."

"No wonder you don't have any meat on your bones."

"I'm just built like this."

"Like your grandmother." Annalisa picked up Sarah's bowl and took it to the back door, where she scraped the leftovers into a battered metal bowl on the ground. "The neighbour's dog will come over at some point to eat it." She put the empty dish in the sink, then triumphantly pulled an enormous plum tart from its hiding place under a linen towel and brought it to the table. "I hope you left room for this. We can wait a few minutes, though."

Together they cleared the dishes and set out clean plates for the tart. Sarah felt her mouth salivating over the smell of it, despite being so full she could barely move. She let Annalisa cut her a bigger piece than she would have liked.

"How is Katherine doing?" Annalisa asked.

"It's hard to say, since she's so good at pretending she's fine." Sarah took a bite of the tart. "Oh my, but this is good, even if I don't have another inch of space in my stomach."

"There's always room for fresh plum tart."

"I think the new medication Gran's been getting since she came back to England has helped with the pain." Sarah shook her head, remembering. "She certainly had enough energy to boss everyone around at my mother's house." It had been a nightmare, in fact, when Katherine had been set up temporarily in the spare room while they were waiting for her place at the nursing home to be made ready. Her demanding presence had turned the house upside down.

"Katherine and your mother never did get along, even when Katherine was in good spirits. So unfortunate. A mother and daughter should be close."

"I confess I was happy to have the excuse to escape Mum and Dad's house and come here. But I'm feeling a little guilty that I didn't wait for Gran's transfer to the nursing home. She moved there yesterday."

"Katherine, of all people, would understand your preference to be here."

"She's the one who told me to get going, so I took her at her word."

"And your mother? What does she think about you being here now? She can't have been entirely happy about you following in your *nonna*'s footsteps."

"It hasn't completely estranged us, I don't think." When Sarah and Lily had become old enough to travel to Italy for holidays, their mother had reluctantly let them go at Katherine's insistence, but she never went there herself. She'd tried it once and refused to go again, referring to it as 'that spooky holiday house'. Sarah and Lily had adored their summers there. Katherine was liberal with them, allowing them freedoms they would never have managed at home and, through her permissiveness, rankling their mother further.

"It's too bad Mum didn't take to the place," Sarah said. "I never completely understood why not."

"Katherine wouldn't let her be a part of it."

"I never really understood that, either. And Grandpa, too. I never thought about it when I was younger, but I guess Gran was pretty territorial about the place."

"She was. Coffee?" Annalisa asked, and stood up. Sarah sensed this conversation, for some reason, was at an end.

"Yes, please."

"Let's have it out front where it's cooler." She set the flame going under the little espresso pot and motioned for Sarah to leave the kitchen. "Go on."

"Don't you want some help cleaning up?"

"Of course not. What do I have to do all day anyway? You're my guest: you sit and relax. Go, and I'll bring your coffee in a minute."

Sarah took the long route through the front parlour, reacquainting herself with the old house. The worn, '50s-era sofa and wingback chair, the little brown coffee table built like a tray with upturned sides—nothing had changed. She paused before a tall shelf holding a few books and dozens of photographs showing various generations of Annalisa's extended family. Sarah hadn't looked at them much when she was younger but she examined them now. An endless array of relatives, many of whom she'd met during her summers at the house, graced the shelves. There were cousins and second cousins and others who were once removed, so many extensions that were still considered 'close family' that it was hard to keep track. One group shot included Sarah and Lily with a dozen Tondi-related children. They were always referred to as 'the cousins' in one big group, not as anyone's individual offspring, because collectively they had formed a single indivisible unit. It had been like a private club in which they played wildly in the freedom of summer vacation, inventing innocent games when they were all small, then graduating to kissing games and whispered indoctrinations into the facts of life as they got older.

On a higher shelf were sepia-toned photographs of the old-timers in their prime. All gone now except for Annalisa, looking more beautiful in her photo than one would ever guess at this point in her life. To one side of her was a picture of a solid bulk of a man with a rifle in his arms and a hunting dog at his feet. That was Bruno; she recognized him from her earlier visits. To the other side was a more formal portrait. Filippo, perhaps? He looked stern. Sarah recalled the oft-told story of his one precious son, inheritor of most of the family land and most of the buildings, who had had the audacity to reject both his birthright and his country for a foreign woman. It had been considered a real treachery by most of the family. Sarah felt the story was very romantic.

Along with Annalisa, Bruno and Filippo was a fourth photograph, and Sarah froze when she saw it. The handsome young man in a soldier's uniform was undoubtedly the man from her dream. She took it down from the shelf and held it, unable to take her eyes away from the hint of a smile and a gaze both intense and playful, as though daring the cameraman to do something outrageous. Sarah felt once again the touch of his hand through her hair, his breath on her cheek. The terrible pain of his loss.

Annalisa walked into the room. "Who is this?" Sarah asked, her voice coming out in whisper.

There was a moment's pause before Annalisa answered. "That's my other brother, Gianluca. He died in the war."

"I guess I've seen this photograph before." That would be it, Sarah thought. She'd retained this image of him for years without realizing it and, now that she was back, her mind had put him into that strange dream. But it was so vivid.

Annalisa stared hard at the photo, as though remembering. "It's always been there."

"He's quite arresting."

"He was certainly that." Annalisa sighed. "That was all so long ago. Come, let's have our coffee before it gets cold," she said, turning towards the door abruptly without waiting for an answer.

Sarah had a hundred questions, but Annalisa was clearly not interested in letting her ask. Could his death still be so disturbing, more than a half century later? Sarah set the photograph back in its place and followed her outside.

Two wooden chairs and a tiny table were set up against the front wall of the house, in the slice of shadow that arrived there by midday. The road was so close by it would be possible, while seated in the chairs, to kick passing cars if any were to make their way through the village. It was unlikely any would. All down the road, most houses had similar arrangements, as though the road were a large communal parlour. A few folk were out, reading or just sitting and resting. They each nodded a greeting, then went back to their own thoughts.

Sarah sat down. "Tell me about the cousins," she said. "Frederica, Giuseppe, Carlo, and the rest of them. Your grandchildren especially, of course."

Annalisa described the lives of everyone in the clan: where they were living, what they were doing, whether the women could cook well, whether the men were good workers, who had babies. The cousins were scattered everywhere throughout Italy and in a few other countries as well. Some had children already. It was strange for Sarah to think of people she had played with being mothers and fathers. Motherhood still felt to her like something that was a generation away.

She was glad to hear that Carlo, at least, was single and living in Florence. He had been around more than most when Sarah and her sister had stayed at Katherine's house, and he had often been the daring prince in their rock games. Although he had mostly wanted to save Lily instead of her, he was good fun and she remembered a real closeness the three of them had shared.

"What's he up to these days?" she asked.

"Making money, mostly. He has some kind of computer business." There was a slightly disparaging edge to the words.

"Nothing wrong with making some money."

"No, there isn't, although his mother would like to see him spending it on something worthwhile like a house so he can marry and settle down, instead of fancy cars and the like. At his age he should have a wife and babies."

"He can't be more than thirty, can he?"

"*A punto*, you see? Exactly my point. Thirty already. But he's a good boy, really. Visits his mother regularly."

Sarah smiled at the standard measure of a son's worth. "Will you give me his phone number?"

"All right. He's not as good company as Luca, but he'd be someone else for you to know." Annalisa made no effort to hide the fact she was backing a particular horse.

"Thank you." Sarah rose. "I should be getting back now." It was just possible she had digested enough that she could make it back up the hill without collapsing. She wanted to do some painting, even if it was only a bit of colour testing. Something every day, no matter how little, she had promised herself. Otherwise she wouldn't allow herself to read that juicy book. "Thank you for the wonderful meal and the company."

"Anytime. You just tell me when you want fattening up and I'll cook for you." Annalisa went into the house and came back with a scrap of paper with a phone number on it. "Carlo's number," she said. "But Luca is coming here the day after tomorrow."

Sarah allowed herself a small smile. "Then you'll have good company again." She kissed Annalisa on both cheeks. "*Ciao, cara,*" she said, and turned towards the long climb back.

Day 1—Highfield Residence, England

They've put me away in this hellhole because I'm dying and it's not going fast enough. Palliative care, they call it. From the Medieval Latin, palliare, to cloak. They cloak my pain and my creep towards death with medicines and bright smiles. I might try and stay alive just to spite them. I've been given a notebook with pink flowers on the front. It looks like bad wallpaper and it's been suggested to me that I write in it, to keep my mind active. Well my mind is already active, thank you, but I have another purpose in mind. I've decided, dearest, that our story shouldn't go to the grave with me, so I'm going to write it down.

I remember so clearly the day I came to the house for the first time, in the summer of 1939. The winding drive pulling me along to see what it revealed next, the way the house sat nestled into the hillside as though it was the comfiest place on earth. The blue wooden door, weathered to a subtle translucency that let the wood shine through with centuries of stories. I knew I'd come home before I'd even opened that door.

I was very young then, only twenty-one years old but already married for two years. Everyone thought I was crazy to want to come to Italy at that time. Young women didn't go off without their husbands, for a start. And the political situation was volatile, with Britain and Italy making up one minute and arguing again the next, and Hitler and Mussolini being so cozy together. But there were technically no obstacles to me travelling there, and all the rest of it was of no import to me. I just wanted to paint and to escape London and the confines of my narrow life. Friends of ours owned the house then, and offered to let me stay there. Well, they were my friends, really, not James's. His friends wouldn't have dreamt of offering me a painting getaway.

But he did eventually agree to let me go. I think he understood that it was my intention regardless of his approval, but I wanted his agreement, and he wanted to pretend he had let me. That was the nature of our marriage: a bond built on a mutual desire for civilized agreement regardless of how we felt about things. How we felt, we kept to ourselves. It made for a peaceful relationship.

I wonder if James ever regretted that particular agreement.

Chapter Three

By MONDAY AFTERNOON, Sarah was patting herself on the back for her efficiency. She had got up early to go to the market in nearby Camugnano. She had managed to produce another test block of colours in preparation for creating a new version of the first landscape painting. Then she'd moved on to cleaning the house. Sure, she might have been more proud of herself if she had produced an actual painting instead of just creating a third test block, but who could paint seriously with a house in this condition? Katherine had had a local woman do the cleaning who must have decided that her client no longer had the vision to notice details such as grimy windows or a terra cotta floor that had layers of dirt waxed solidly into the pores of the tiles. Now it was up to Sarah, who couldn't afford the luxury of having someone else do it, to put it all to rights.

There was something very satisfying about being down on her hands and knees, scrubbing the floor with a brush. It was like an act of ablution for any doubts she still had about taking the place on, or the rightness of her being there. She flung open all the doors and windows and went at the task with the zeal of someone possessed, ignoring the sweat that dripped off her.

A portable stereo in the kitchen blasted out popular opera arias loud enough to make Beppe go outside for peace. Sarah sang along with them at the top of her lungs. A closet singer, she had a decent voice and loved to use it at full volume when no one else was there to hear. "*O lo lo laaaaa*," she sang, unable to recall the lyrics. As a favourite aria came to an end, she howled out the final high note, albeit an octave lower, with far more zest than accuracy. Then, in the momentary silence between songs, she heard a knocking at the open front door.

"Hello? Sarah? Are you here?" It was a man's voice, deep and husky, the seductive sound of dark bars and low whispers. Whoever it was must have heard all that crowing she'd been doing with the last song. The next one began and she lunged for the stereo, quickly turning it off. She took a calming breath before stepping out into the hallway.

Silhouetted in the open front doorway against the bright, afternoon sky stood a lanky, slack-hipped figure that made Sarah's heart stop. *Gianluca from the dream,* she thought, panic holding her rooted to the spot. Then her eyes adjusted to the unaccustomed light and she saw that, of course, he was not Gianluca. He was every bit as attractive but in a different, blonder way.

"Hey, hi—sorry—did I startle you?" he asked her, since she still had not moved or spoken.

American voice. Annalisa's prize, the Moretti from America. A shaky little laugh escaped Sarah as the adrenaline drained from her body. "A little, yes. I was, um, absorbed, as I suppose you heard." She walked towards him. "I don't expect people to show up here."

"Yeah, apologies, I didn't mean to barge in." He grinned. It was infectious despite Sarah's misgivings about his arrival. "Great voice, though." He extended his hand in greeting. "I'm Luca Moretti—Luke if you prefer."

Annalisa hadn't wasted any time in sending him over. "Sarah Powell." Sarah brought her hand forward automatically, then remembered she was wearing rubber gloves and hastily pulled the right one off. When she gave him the resulting hot, wet hand to shake, she wondered if the rubber might not have been better. To his credit, he didn't flinch.

"You look like Katherine. Especially the way you tilted your chin up just now. She always does that when she's not sure about something, too." He cocked his head, assessing. "You can send me away if you're busy."

"I was washing the floor." She was busy, actually, and a bit irritated to be interrupted, but more irritated to be reminded of how much she looked like her grandmother. People had been telling her that for years. The eyes, the chin, the same trilling laugh. So, although he was beginning to look a little awkward still standing in the doorway, she couldn't quite bring herself to invite him in.

He held up a plastic grocery bag. "Annalisa made some pesto for you."

That clever Annalisa, she had even sent him over with a good excuse to be there. Sarah took the bag from him. "That was kind of her." She peeked around him to check the driveway. There was no car except her own dusty Citroën. "You walked up here in this heat just to give me some pesto?"

"I like to walk. And I wanted to meet you."

"Annalisa can be very forceful."

"She didn't send me here, if that's what you mean. I will admit she made a point of telling me you were here—many times. But I like to think that visiting you was my idea."

Sarah studied his face. He had a lovely wide smile that was really quite beguiling and very white teeth. American teeth, all gleaming with health, to match those clean American good looks. She supposed he would have to be invited in now that he had made all that effort to get up the hill, just to see her. He would be thirsty. He would need to be given a drink. "Would you like to come in?" she finally asked.

"If you're sure I'm not interrupting."

Sarah had a sudden vision of how she must look to this neat, linen-clad, clean-shirted, relentlessly pleasant person who appeared to be unaffected by a steep climb in sweltering heat. She was dishevelled, sweaty, paint-stained, suspicious. Like a madwoman. "I could use a break," she said, poking at her hair as though that might make some difference. "If sweat and dirt don't bother you."

"Not a bit," he agreed at once, taking a step into the hallway as soon as she gave him a bit of space. Sarah found herself noticing how good he smelled. Freshly scrubbed and vaguely herbal.

She led the way back to the kitchen, dropping the rubber gloves on the floor beside the bucket as she went past. "Would you like something to drink?"

"I sure would, thanks."

Sarah opened the refrigerator door triumphantly, proud of her recently stocked kitchen. "Take your pick."

Luke peered in. "That limonata would be great."

As Sarah tucked the pesto into an available space and took the limonata out, Luke went to the cupboard. "Do you want some, too?" he asked, removing two glasses like someone who had done so, from that shelf, many times. *Katherine must have had him waiting on her hand and foot*, Sarah thought, disconcerted by his familiarity with what she now thought of as her kitchen.

The two drinks poured, Sarah handed him his and raised her own in toast.

"Cheers. Would you like to go sit on the terrace? We might catch a bit of breeze there if we're lucky."

Outside, they settled themselves into a pair of large wicker chairs. There was, in fact, no breeze. It was as oppressively hot as it always was in the middle of the afternoon, despite the thick shade of the old wisteria pergola. Sarah was about to blot her chest sweat in a gesture that had become habitual, but stopped herself.

"Are you enjoying being back here?" Luke asked.

"It's good. It's been a while."

"You have a great house. The first time I ever came here, I felt at home. Funny how some places strike you that way, isn't it?"

It was. Why did he find it so easy to feel that way when Sarah was still struggling? It wasn't even his house but here he was, lounging in his wicker chair—sprawled almost—looking as though he'd just got back from doing chores.

"You used to visit my Gran," Sarah said.

"Yeah, I'd come and play the piano for her. We had fun."

"Fun? Wow, that's not something I tend to associate with Gran. We're close, but our relationship is more of a master-pupil one."

Luke laughed. "She does like to command, doesn't she? But I guess since I was entertainment she let me off the hook a bit."

"So you're the reason Gran had that old piano tuned."

"Actually, it was already perfect. Annalisa sent me up here the first time and she must have called to tell Katherine, because when I got here Katherine opened the door and said, without any preamble, 'I've been expecting you. Do you play the piano?'"

"Gran is good at knowing what she wants."

"I'll say. It was like a ten-second job interview. Then she dragged out all this music from when she was younger and had me play and sing."

"You sing, too?"

"Not as heartily as you do," he answered, grinning. Sarah felt herself redden.

"I wasn't planning on an audience."

"But you have a good voice," he insisted. "You sounded as though you were really enjoying yourself."

"I *was* enjoying myself, when I thought I was alone. I'd never sing like that with someone listening."

"That's a pity. You like opera?"

"Oh, I'm the worst kind of enthusiast, an utter pleb. I know all the choice arias by heart but tunes only, not the words, and I have no idea about the rest of the operas they come from. Real opera aficionados frown on people like me."

"No different, really, than knowing only the most popular songs from musicals, without knowing the whole thing."

"Guilty there, too, I'm afraid."

"Now you're on my ground. Which songs are your favourites?"

"I don't know if I want to confess that."

"As long as it's not 'Memories' you'd be safe."

"It's worse, maybe. And older."

Luke looked thoughtful. "Katherine liked South Pacific. 'Stranger in Paradise' was one she had me play a lot."

"Then can I blame it on her?"

"Ah-hah! That's your favourite? I would have guessed 'Happy Talk'."

"You're pulling my leg now, aren't you?"

"'Happy Talk' is a great song! Unapologetically upbeat. Katherine has the music for the whole show here."

He was leaning forward now, his piano-playing hands splayed on his knees, his blue eyes bright and guileless as he enthused about a cheerful fifties tune most people had long forgotten. Sarah could see why her grandmother had liked to have him around. He had an energy about him that sucked you in even if you didn't think you wanted to be.

"Is that actually your favourite song?" she asked.

"One of. There are so many to love." He looked around with a contented sigh. "What a view. Katherine must be happy that you're here. She talked about you a lot. The continuity of passing this place on, it seemed really important to her."

"She talked about me?"

"A bit."

"You said 'a lot'." God only knew how many embarrassing things Katherine had told him about her. It was unfair. Sarah knew almost nothing about Luke.

He smiled. "No worries, she only ever told me good stuff. And she showed me the nude you did at art school, the one upstairs. I really liked it."

He'd been in Gran's *bedroom*, for god's sake, admiring a nude. Not Gran, at least. And it was Sarah's bedroom now, which felt even more disconcerting. "It's just a Modigliani rip-off. A school exercise."

"It still looked good to me. What are you working on now?"

Sarah waved her hand about vaguely. "Oh, some landscapes. Simple things. I've only just started back after a bit of a lull."

"Can I see them?"

The idea of showing anyone her work, once relatively easy, now threatened to bring on a panic attack. In any case, there was only one canvas. How could she deal with the small fib of pluralizing her output?

"They're not quite ready yet," she said.

"Maybe when they are, then."

"Did Gran show you any of her work?" she asked, to distract him. "I've been looking, but I haven't yet found any of the sort of thing artists usually leave around. You know: old work, half-finished stuff, things that maybe didn't sell. She seems to have cleaned it all out pretty thoroughly."

"Try the hall closet upstairs. She had a bunch in there."

Another surprise. Was there any bit of this house he hadn't seen, or was he familiar with every square inch? "That's an odd place to store paintings. Why not in the studio where they belong?"

"You've got me. When she showed them to me she said they were very early paintings, so you've probably already seen them. I wanted to buy one of them, but she wouldn't let me. She said they weren't to be sold to anybody, they had to stay with the house."

Maybe Katherine had felt they weren't good enough to be brought into the open. But if they were so poor, why had she shown them to Luke? It was strange. "Thanks for the tip. I'll take a look later."

They talked amiably for a while longer. Luke told her about growing up in Seattle, his passion for buildings, and about exploring the other half of his heritage in Italy. He had an easy way about him. An 'even keel,' Katherine would have said. Sarah was less forthcoming; she sidestepped all her years with Roger and didn't go near the topic of how she had stopped painting. Perhaps Luke already knew all that, from Gran. But if he did, he was discreet enough not to mention it.

Sarah sent him home after an hour or so. She had a floor to clean. And she didn't want this pleasant, handsome, even-keeled man interrupting her plans any further. That's what she told herself as she scrubbed the floor, despite the bits of their conversation that floated back to her as she worked, and that lovely grin, and the smile that both those things brought to her own face.

When she was finished admiring the gleaming results of her efforts with the floor, Sarah went upstairs to bathe. Late afternoon light slanted across one long wall of the hall, accentuating the heat despite the open window. As she passed the closet, she remembered the paintings. Could Gran really have left them in there?

Sarah felt a twinge of inexplicable apprehension as she opened the closet door. It was a deep closet with clothes hung on a rod across the front, masking the depth that extended back into the angled roof of the house. She drew the clothes aside: another batch of old things to inspect and probably toss. In the shadows she could make out boxy shapes. She tried the light-pull but the bulb was out so she opened the door until it lay flat against the wall, trying to let in as much light as possible. As she stepped inside and paused to let her eyes adjust, a cold shiver travelled up her spine. It felt like being in the wardrobe in the Chronicles of Narnia. Only creepier.

Sarah stood there for a minute more, telling herself she was being ridiculous. The shapes at the back were clearly canvases, and she wanted to see them. Taking a deep breath, she plunged in and retrieved them as quickly as she could, then lined them up, one by one, against the hall wall. There were five of them altogether. Because they hadn't been carefully stored, merely tucked away one against the other, time and heat had cracked their surfaces. That must have been deliberate. Gran knew what would happen to paintings kept that way. But why?

When she stepped back to look at them better, Sarah saw an intensity that took her breath away. She had never seen anything like their power in her grandmother's other work. They started with landscapes, but had human figures superimposed over top, amorphous lovers floating together in a variety of embraces. In every one of them, the same colour infused the sky, like a kind of bass note that remained regardless of what played over top.

At the third one from the left, Sarah gasped. Only half of the man's face was visible in the painting, but her mind had filled in the rest of his features in a flash, recognizing Gianluca immediately from her dream. A single eye would have been enough to tell her who it was. Suddenly the hallway seemed not just warm but unbearably, oppressively hot. With the back of her hand she wiped away beads of sweat that weltered up on her forehead.

Calm down, she said to herself. What's the panic? Katherine had bought the house after the war but, being friends with Annalisa, she would have seen the photo. He was good-looking, so why not use him if you're doing a series about lovers? Artists modelled their characters from photos all the time.

And yet, when she looked at those paintings, Sarah felt as though she were being pulled over a precipice towards emotions too frightening to face. *I'm probably just tired and hungry*, she thought. *I got carried away with cleaning, a stupid idea in this heat. I'm going to take a shower, then eat some pasta with that nice pesto Luke brought, have a nice glass of wine, and ignore these paintings until I'm sane enough to look at them without getting all spooked.*

Under a tepid shower, Sarah scrubbed away the day's grime, then stood there letting the water beat down on her head and shoulders. She tried to clear her head of the jumbled thoughts swirling through it. She wished she were a better meditator. The incessant chatter in her mind seemed to defy being tamed in such a way, as though her thoughts were unruly children who would not listen to her demands for order. Blah blah paintings, blah blah dreams, blah blah American with white teeth, blah blah embarrassing opera moment. Et cetera.

She gave up, towelled off and put on a clean pair of cut-offs and T-shirt before heading down to feed herself. The pesto was perfect, as she expected. She ate out on the terrace while playing out responses in her conversation with Luke that could have been much more clever or, at least, perhaps more sensibly guarded.

When all this and the washing up were done and she had no more urgent tasks she could use to postpone the moment, she went back upstairs and stood in the hall staring at the paintings. She felt calmer this time, but that frisson of energy—not quite sinister, but still disturbing—hovered at the edge of her senses. There was a magic about these paintings, and her own visceral response told her they went together somehow with the dream, like keys and a lock. But did she want to open that door?

As she stood in front of them, something about the colour of the sky twigged in her mind. She grabbed the painting that was so clearly Gianluca and took it downstairs to the studio, propping it beside the one landscape she'd painted since coming to the house. In it was the sky she'd rendered using the special paint she'd mixed from Katherine's powdered pigments. Sarah had developed the colour before seeing the paintings upstairs, but there it was: the identical shade of purple-blue swept across the top of the canvas as though it had been conjured there by the same hand.

She picked up the old painting and saw that her hands were shaking. It was all so weird. She swallowed hard and took the painting back upstairs. Carefully, she put them all back in the closet just as she had found them. Whatever this was about, she didn't want to know.

Coming back down into the kitchen, she poured herself another glass of wine, took Beppe onto her lap in the big chair for comfort, and read about oversexed polo players and willing women until the images of the paintings began to fade from her mind enough that she could sleep.

Day 5—Highfield Residence, England

In Camugnano, at the time, life was pretty much as it always had been. The Fascists had been indoctrinating everyone for years, but deep in the countryside people tended to continue to live in their own ways. After I had been there about a week, I spotted Annalisa at the market in Camugnano. What a beauty—a swirl of stunning contrasts with her dark hair pulled back under a bright red scarf, the warm Italian bronze of her skin against the white cotton of her blouse, eyes that guarded and beckoned at the same time. I wanted to paint her, so I just asked her if I could. I remember how suspiciously she looked at me, as though I were out of my mind. My Italian was terrible, just a bit from what I'd studied at school. "Io," I said, pointing at her and making painting gestures, 'voglio fare pittura'.

In a small agricultural community like Camugnano, having a foreign stranger offer to paint a woman's portrait wasn't exactly an everyday occurrence and I almost thought she'd run from me.

But in a place where little happens, such an offer can be too interesting to pass up. That was the start of it. One chance encounter at a market, a thought about a painting, a map to my house pencilled on the back of a paper bag filled with carrots. I didn't really expect her to show up. I didn't expect any of it, least of all where it would all lead.

Chapter Four

IN THE DAYS THAT FOLLOWED, Sarah established a routine for herself and managed to stick to it. The mornings were devoted to painting, resulting in two colour studies of the original landscape and the start of a new scene. In the afternoons she did something for the house or went to read for Annalisa. Each day she was careful to eat at least a couple of things that were good for her and to get a bit of exercise, even if it was only an evening stroll. These small acts of self-discipline gave her a satisfying sense of control over her life. Luke had gone boating with friends and Sarah thought about him with the kind of pleasure that accompanies the possibility of romance, before it becomes real and acquires a greater sense of need. She knew he'd call her when he returned.

The almost complete lack of a social life, if she didn't count reading to an old lady, felt both liberating and worrisome. She was glad enough to be away from her parents, and the friends she'd once believed she had in London had not stood her previous absence well, so there were few people to miss besides Lily. But as the initial euphoria of being free started to wear off, she had an inkling of just how isolated she was in Guzzano. It was fine when it still felt like a holiday, reading junk and settling in. Now she understood there was work to be done in building a life in this secluded place. She would need to find a way to get out and meet people, or end up like a scene from *The Shining*.

The terrace was at its best in evening. Worn flagstone, weedy in the cracks and worn to a soft polish over the years, had been set to the west of the house so as the sun began its dip to the horizon, its progress, and the shifting tones of the sky in response, played out in full view. Sarah looked up from her book as the light began to shift. The sunset would be a good one this evening, with wispy clouds already picking up pink tones and spreading them like a watercolour wash throughout the sky. If she went quickly into the kitchen, she could get a glass of wine and a snack, then come back out and watch the show.

She set a tray on the kitchen table for her supplies. Wine. Crackers. Cream cheese. When she went to get a spreading knife from the pantry, she found that the silverware drawer was sticking even more than usual. She tugged and it moved minimally, just enough to get a grip on the drawer itself instead of only the tiny handle. She went at the drawer with both hands, pulling hard. It suddenly gave, sweeping right out of its hole, clearing the pantry, crashing to the floor, and scattering the cutlery with a great clatter. Beppe, who had been sleeping in the easy chair, skidded out the door in a panic.

"Damn! Bloody drawer."

Sarah stood among the strewn silver, surveying the damage. The fall had broken the back off the drawer and she went down on her knees to inspect it. As she picked it up she could see that it wasn't just a flat back, but rather a thin box that had been set at the back as a secret compartment. She examined it closely. It was hinged along one edge and a tiny clasp closed its lid. Her heart pounding, Sarah undid the clasp and opened the lid slowly. "Double damn," she breathed in a whisper when she saw what was inside.

The image of Gianluca looked up at her from a faded photograph. Gianluca, Annalisa's dead brother, the man in Sarah's haunting dream, the man in the paintings, great-uncle of the current Luke. Here he was again. But what was he doing hidden away like this?

As she lifted the picture gently to reveal what lay below, she found a dozen letters on thin parchment, carefully folded. Sarah opened the first one and saw that it was creased in the way that paper becomes when it has been folded and unfolded again countless times, the creases destroying some of the words. The beautiful, flowing Italian script was a letter to Katherine. 1939. Before the war. Sarah's eye darted to the signature line. *Sei l'amore della mia vita*, it said. *Gianluca*.

You are the love of my life.

Good god, Gianluca had written Katherine love letters. She might have bought the house after the war, but somehow she had known Gianluca before it. Known him very well.

Sarah sat holding the letters and wanting desperately to read them but hesitating. It felt like peeping through a keyhole at something that should remain behind the closed door. Still, the letters had offered themselves up to her in a way, jumping out of the drawer like that. And she had the distinct sensation that she was already part of the story somehow, her dreams drawing her into it whether she wanted to be or not. Why hadn't Gran taken the letters with her when she went into the nursing home, anyway? Were they another thing that she believed belonged to the house?

Sarah took a deep swallow of wine, ignoring the cheese and crackers, and the sunset as it deepened outside the window. She sat down at the kitchen table, picked up the first letter, took a breath and began to read, translating as she went.

September 10, 1939

My beloved Catarina,

> *I can't believe it has only been two weeks since you went back to London. I have been trying to forget you and go back to my life here, as I know you must go back to your marriage, but it is proving hopeless. I find it so difficult to believe what we have done is wrong when it feels so right. You are the love of my life, I am sure of it, and if the circumstances of our lives make it impossible to spend them together, I can only wonder at the reasons why God would play such cruel games with us.*
>
> *The war that is breaking out around us worries me; Mussolini says he is not involving us in the German conflicts but many of the people*

here think that he only says that for now and that because he is aligned
with Hitler it will not be long before Italy, too, is a part of it. We were
taught to look up to him as boys. Now many of us wonder if his actions
are still good for us.

If you are thinking you will come here again (please be thinking
that!) it may soon become more difficult. There are so many
obstacles in our way.

I am writing this in my room at Guzzano. I look in the direction of
the house up the hill and remember our time together, and yearn to
be with you once again. I want to lie together in the old iron bed, to
watch you paint, to gaze at the sunset together and to make love in the
meadow under a starry sky. All these pleasures exist now only in my
memories, and it is not enough. I am completely selfish. I want only
and above all to be with you.

Please say I am not alone in my love! My heart will never be the
same: it is closed now to anyone but you.

You are the love of my life,
Gianluca

Sarah laid the letter on top of the others, drained her glass of wine and got up to pour herself another. Was this why Annalisa had been so reluctant to talk about her brother? What a mess the whole thing must have created. Why had Gran come here in the first place, a relatively new bride, without her husband? But she had, and she had met Gianluca, cuckolded her husband for the summer, then returned to London. She hadn't returned willingly, Sarah imagined, if Gianluca's photograph and letters had been saved all these years, and Gran had become besotted with the house enough to buy it.

Unable to resist the siren song of the other letters, Sarah sat back down and read on.

My Dearest Love,

What great joy to receive your latest letter. I am to see you again! I cannot stand to count the days until you will be here. I will come to the house as soon as you arrive and stay with you every moment you remain. It has been an agony to wait for your response. The post is so slow, and I did not know even if your friend would deliver the letter I sent to you, although you said she is trustworthy.

I am sorry you are so sad there. I wish I could take you in my arms and console you, but of course I am the source of your problems. Is it wrong of me to persist in wanting you? I know my love makes your life very difficult, but I cannot stop it. I remember when you told me you felt our love was irresistible: a predestiny we could never avoid. I feel it, too. Annalisa tells me I am mad and worries what this will do to us both.

I hope you have no trouble in your journey. There are uneasy feelings here, and the police are sometimes making things awkward for foreigners, especially the English.

Whether I am mad or not, there has never been a happier November in my life than this one I am about to spend with you. I give you—

All my love, always,
Gianluca

November 5, 1939

Dearest Beloved,

The cancellation of your visit left me in the deepest anguish, even though I know it was for the best. James is right to protect you from the dangers that are everywhere on the continent these days and although I am filled with jealousy at the thought of him, I am also glad that you have someone there who seeks to keep you safe.

I am torn apart by my desire for you and rant against the fates that keep us separated. What is to become of us? You know that nothing could make me happier than to see you become my wife, but you already have a husband. Even if you would abandon him for me, there are so many other problems. Hitler takes more territory, piece by piece, and no one stops him. Mussolini is in awe and I am certain Italy must soon become involved. I can only hope that if we are drawn into the fighting, it will end quickly. Only then will you and I be free to choose to be together. So many obstacles—I fear it may be another lifetime before my dream is fulfilled.

I should feel guilty about wanting you but it is not possible for me to feel guilt. I am too full of love for you; there is no room for anything else.

I wait, impatiently as always, to hear from you.

All my love, always
Gianluca

The rest of the letters were similar, declarations of love and dreams for a life together after the conflicts were over. Even without having Katherine's replies to read, Sarah could tell by the tone of these that her grandmother had been fully prepared to abandon her husband when the opportunity to be with Gianluca finally arose. There was no further mention of James in the remaining letters. Their focus was solely on the reunion of the two lovers.

Like many others separated by the conflicts, they would have had no idea how long it was all to last; at that point the full breadth of war hadn't yet unfolded. The last letter in the pile was sent near the very beginning of Italy's official involvement.

June 29, 1940

Beloved Catarina,

All the most terrible things I feared have happened. We are now at war, the Germans have captured the north of France and there is no longer any way for you to come here.

There is worse; I have been conscripted. I depart for the army camp tomorrow. I do not know where I will be sent to battle, but I am sure it will be soon. This is a great weight on my heart. I go unwillingly—how can I fight in a war in which I do not believe? I am also fearful, but the most difficult thing to bear is to be parted from you so completely, with no idea how long it may be before we can be together again. This is my greatest sorrow.

Whatever happens, know that you are the most incredible thing that has ever happened to me. Your love is a precious jewel I hold in my mind. My memories of our time together will be my comfort in the terrible times ahead, and dreams of being with you again will be the force that drives me to go on.

I am giving this letter to Annalisa to send to you. I hope it arrives; she says she has a route for it to go safely.

Hold me forever in your heart, and know that you are here in mine. In this way I will be with you always.

You are my dearest, greatest, only love —
Gianluca

Sarah wondered how long Gianluca had survived after that last letter. From the absence of any others she figured that, for him, it had been a very short war before he lost his life in the vanguard of the millions of others who were also to perish.

She imagined her grandmother feeling imprisoned in London, a strong-willed tigress pacing against the confines of her small cage, powerless to alter the events around her. Katherine's absorption with the house made more sense now. And was this why Sarah had never seen her grandfather here? Had he ever come? Did he know about Gianluca? It occurred to Sarah that her grandmother had lived as a kind of a bigamist, with one living husband and the other, her husband in her heart, present as an unshakeable memory.

There was something else missing from Gianluca's letters. Sarah's mother, Victoria, had been born in July 1940. She must have been James's baby, conceived around the time Katherine was supposed to have travelled to Italy again but couldn't. It didn't seem that Gianluca knew about the pregnancy. Would Katherine have given up not only her husband but also her child to be with the man she truly loved?

Sarah picked up the scattered cutlery and put it in what remained of the drawer, on top of the kitchen table until she could get a chance to fix the back properly. Late into the night, she re-read the letters and searched the house for other clues about the affair, caught up in her discovery. She examined every drawer for hidden spaces, checked the backs of cupboards and wardrobes, and combed the library shelves for signs of a diary. In the end she found nothing more than the letters and photograph that had already fallen into her hands.

She sat in the big chair in the kitchen, finishing the last of the bottle of wine and musing about how her grandmother's simple act of coming to Guzzano one summer had altered so much. How it had led to Katherine's purchase of this house, and her alienation from Victoria, how that alienation had tainted Sarah's own relationship with her mother, and how the house had finally come to be the place in which she now resided, trying to salvage the course of her life. One small act determining the direction of all these things.

Sarah went up the stairs, ready to put herself to bed. As she went past the door of the hall closet, however, the image of the paintings beckoned to her. She turned on the light, having replaced the bulb in her earlier ransacking of the house for more clues, went to the back, and took the paintings out, lining them up against the hall wall again.

They were complex work, using a great deal of veiling over nearly monochromatic underpaintings that let the two subjects, lovers and landscape, coexist in a sympathetic weaving of images. Katherine had shown her the technique in some of their summer painting sessions, but to Sarah's recollection had usually painted landscapes where the final colours were laid down immediately, *alla prima*, without much layering. It was as though she had spent her greatest creative effort on these five paintings, then stowed them away, along with the technique that produced them.

Sarah picked up one in which the couple were entwined in a sea of blossoms, in a meadow under a star-filled sky. The blossoms were caught up in the curves of the lovers, blurring the point where the landscape left off and the people began. As she looked at the painting, Sarah felt both great joy and profound sadness. She wanted to look but it frightened her at the same time.

Putting the other four paintings back in the closet, she took the meadow scene and brought it downstairs to the kitchen where she hung it, unframed, on an existing nail. Just because it had to stay with the house didn't mean it had to stay in the cupboard. Maybe if she saw it every day, in fact, she would come to find it less disturbing. Sarah smiled sadly at the image of the two lovers entwined in a summer meadow under starry skies. It was just as Gianluca had wanted.

The grass of the meadow was still warm from the heat of the day, filling the air with its rich green smell as stars began to twinkle overhead. Scattered around the two lovers on the blanket were the remains of their sunset picnic: fruit, cheese, tiny flowers that had been picked in the last of the light and presented to her with a flourish. She raised her head from its resting place on Gianluca's chest and sat up to reach some grapes, ate one, then turned back to offer him some. When she turned to him, however, she found not his warm, waiting body but only its impression left upon the blanket. Looking up, she saw his image hover briefly at the edge of the forest before it disappeared into the darkness.

She tried to rise and follow but a powerful force, heavy and invisible, pinned her to the ground, becoming heavier the more she struggled to free herself. The soft blanket beneath her disintegrated and the grass turned hard and brittle, pricking her flesh, the languor of moments before replaced now with a rising panic. Her body was leaden. She saw herself, no longer stretched out on the grass in human form but as a great, stone statue that had fallen over years ago and remained there, limbs broken, too heavy to lift back into place. The grass turned to weeds that grew over the rubble, obscuring it. She called out, over and over, pleading with the figure in the woods to rescue her, but her only answer was the wind growing strong and fierce, blowing out the stars and sucking the sound from out of her cries.

The stars disappeared. A coldness penetrated her body so deeply it made her bones ache, and her cries became whimpers as her stone face hardened, trapping her in a rigid tomb from which she knew she would never escape. She had never felt so hopelessly alone.

Then searing, sudden wakefulness. Sarah found herself lying not in the meadow but in her bed, staring into the darkness of a starless room, her sheet a damp and tangled mass, her face covered with tears and her heart filled with the greatest sorrow she had ever known. She remained there, unmoving and unblinking. She didn't have to go to the window to see what, or who, was out there. Now she understood. They were in here; in the house and in her head.

Katherine and Gianluca.

◊ ◊ ◊

When she got out of bed the following morning, Sarah felt more hung over than she had in years, whether from the bottle of wine or from her latest nightmare she wasn't sure. She negotiated the stairs gingerly, silenced what sounded like deafening cries from the cat by giving him an extra large breakfast, and downed two aspirins with a full glass of water before putting on enough espresso for four to brew. The meadow painting screamed at her from its place on the wall and she took it off its nail, setting it on the floor with its face turned away. So much for exorcising its influence over her by the act of hanging it. The nightmare had been even more debilitating than the first one, the intimacy sweeter and the subsequent loss more dreadful. She was going to read something cheerful before bed tonight.

Grabbing her megadose of espresso, Sarah clutched the mug in both hands and went to the sitting room. On a round side table sat a small cluster of photographs in simple silver frames: Sarah and her sister Lily grinning self-consciously as teenagers; their mother looking grim; and their father, Charles Powell, whose stiff expression when faced with the camera gave the impression he was standing in front of a firing squad. The softer image of her grandfather, James Steele, stared out from an early black and white photograph. Slightly older than Gianluca, handsome but contained in his suit, he looked as though he might be doing math sums in his head as his picture was being taken. The forlorn and out-of-date group of photos took on a new light now that Sarah knew about Katherine's past. A typical display, but had Katherine ever looked at them with any sense of longing, or only with a vague regret?

The phone rang and Sarah went to answer it in the hallway.

"Hello?"

"Oh good, you're home. Since I hadn't heard from you lately I thought I'd better take it upon myself to call you instead of waiting any longer."

Sarah had called Katherine only once, to see how she'd settled into the nursing home. It had been a call full of complaint and envy. "I'm sorry, you're right. I should be calling you more often. I've been painting." It was true enough. *And reading love letters, and looking at secret paintings, and dreaming about your old lover,* she thought.

"Painting what?" Katherine asked.

"Landscapes. I'm a bit rusty but it's coming."

"Only landscapes?"

"For now, yes. Abstracted somewhat, in the way—" Sarah began to explain, before being cut off by an impatient Katherine.

"But only landscapes?"

"I felt I needed to start where I felt most confident."

A prolonged silence, heavy with what Sarah took for judgment, hung on the line. Then Katherine spoke.

"Are you mixing paints the way I taught you?"

"Yes."

"The key is to keeping mixing longer than you think is necessary."

"I know. I use the poem we used to chant. The one about the wind."

"Right. Good."

Was that a tiny smile Sarah could hear in her voice? "The light is so good in the studio," Sarah said. "It's a really special place to paint."

"Yes, well, that's why you have the place."

"I'm taking good care of it."

"As you should. Has Luca come by yet?"

"Uhmm, yes. Once." *When I was scrubbing floors and smelled like a gym sock,* Sarah thought. "He's away now though."

"He'll be back. You need to take good care of that, too."

Sarah bristled. Among the various commandments with respect to the house—caretaking, no renovation (as if she had the money for that), returning to her painting—tucking into Luke hadn't been mentioned until now. "Oh, well, we'll see how that goes. I'm really here to paint, after all."

"Hmph," Katherine grunted. "Don't get complacent about how lucky you are."

"Of course not." How tempting it was to ask about the letters and the paintings. Tempting the way putting your fingers in a candle flame is tempting. You have an idea that there's a way to do it that won't damage you, but you're not entirely certain how. Better just to stay away.

"Are you settling in all right at Highfield?" Sarah asked.

"I will never feel settled in this dreadful place."

Sarah remembered the beautiful photographs of lawns and woods, and the mellow Victorian brick of the residence itself, in the promotional materials. But she hadn't gone to check it out with her mother. Could it really be that bad? "The photos looked lovely."

"It's a waiting room for my appointment with death. How lovely could it be?"

The conversation was quickly veering into something like their first call. Sarah changed the subject. "Annalisa says hello. I've been reading to her, and she's been feeding me."

"She's a good soul."

"And a good cook. She's trying to fatten me up."

"That's her mission with everyone." Katherine sighed: a long, tired wheeze. "That's it for me today," she said abruptly. "Call me more often."

"I will, I promise. Love you, Gran."

"There's a good girl."

The handset clattered back into its cradle on the other end of the line and Sarah felt a rush of relief coupled with guilt. *I really should be more gracious*, she thought. Of course Gran was grumpy. She had a right to be, under the circumstances.

Walking back into the sitting room where her coffee was growing cold in its mug, Sarah looked again at the photos and wondered if, when Katherine had been in the house alone, the one of Gianluca had had its own special place in a silver frame. Or had he always been tucked away, with the letters and the paintings and all the secrets they contained, out of sight if not at all out of mind?

Day 9—Highfield Residence, England

My portrait of Annalisa still graces the parlour of her house. For all those years later, I still enjoyed seeing it there and remembering the sittings. Despite the language barriers, we managed to talk, as young women do, and after the painting was done we continued to meet almost every day. That first invitation to dinner with her family was a big deal; a gesture of trust not only in my ability to say more than two words, but more importantly in our friendship.

Oh, that dinner. It feels like it was just a moment ago, my darling, it's still so clear to me. I was wearing my nicest dress, the one with the lilacs on it, and was standing in the kitchen when all the brothers started coming in, fresh from the fields. Every one of them good-looking, and then you came through the door and they all disappeared from my view. You'd washed at the outdoor tap and had water in your hair and on your shirt, not yet changed for lunch. The water made your shirt cling to the muscles of your chest and I felt myself staring, unable to take my eyes away. So muscular and masculine compared to the soft, white-bodied gentlemen I knew in England, and the soft, white-bodied gentleman who was my husband. When you shook my hand, a bit guarded but curious, I felt a shock of energy surge straight to my heart.

Your family thought it very peculiar that a young married woman would travel away from her husband for such a long period. And there'd been all the anti-English propaganda Mussolini had been spreading since the disagreement over Ethiopia. Suspicion mixed with fascination and Annalisa's friendship (along with the painting, which everyone agreed was very good) barely nudged me into a position of acceptability. You found that intriguing, didn't you?

A minor breeze lifted the late afternoon air as Sarah sat down with Annalisa at the small street-side table that had become their habitual reading spot. They were about to start on a new book.

"This looks interesting," Sarah said, picking up a well-thumbed paperback from the table. On the cover was an illustration of a swooning young woman dressed in old-fashioned riding clothes, limp in the arms of a rough but devastatingly good-looking man. Horses lingered about in a pastoral background.

"I think you'll like it," said Annalisa. "It's one I read ten years ago, but I'd love to hear it again."

"What's it about?"

"If I tell you, it will ruin the story for you."

"Just a hint, then."

"A man and a woman, and love, and stupidity."

Sarah smiled. "Sounds like the last one we read."

"Ah, but the ways a man and a woman can be stupid about love are infinite, don't you think? And each one of them a unique story."

Stupidity had certainly been a consistent theme in Sarah's own romantic life, she had to admit. With what she now knew about her grandmother, she wondered if she wasn't the proverbial apple falling not too far from the tree. Or perhaps Katherine been overpowered by fate, a victim of bad timing? Sarah shook her head. To silence the many questions in her head, she began to read.

The story, as Annalisa had promised, was a whopper. Gabriella, heiress to a chocolate fortune, is thrown into a bush by her spirited horse and is rescued by Massimo, the son of the keeper of her father's country estates. Gabriella falls instantly in love. Massimo rebuffs her obvious feelings for him even though he's tormented by his own, secret desire for her. It is a time of changing social values, but there is still no way he's going to meet with her father's approval and he's too proud to even put himself in that position.

As she read, Sarah glanced occasionally at her audience and found her to be rapt with attention, her eyes focused on the wall of the house opposite as though the whole thing were unfolding there in front of her like a movie. It had always amazed Sarah that the level-headed Annalisa enjoyed these stories about the follies of love. At the end of chapter three Sarah closed the book. "I don't think I can do any more today. It's tiring to read the Italian, with the heat and all. I always found reading Italian more difficult than speaking it."

Annalisa nodded. "I have the easy part, I only have to listen. What do you think of it so far?"

"Gabriella and Massimo seem an unlikely match, but it's absorbing."

"Love is often unpredictable. She's an idiot and he's unaccountably full of himself, but never mind," Annalisa assessed. "It's still a good story."

An easy silence settled between them. In the quiet Sarah noticed the soft purring of the chickens at the side of the house and the occasional cooing of a dove.

"It's cooling off now," Annalisa noted after a while. "You can feel summer is ending."

"You can? It still feels sweltering to me."

"It is still sweltering, but there's a change starting. It always does around now, and soon there will be storms to take away summer's heat."

"Thank god. I thought it would be cooler, living in the hills."

"Compared to Florence, this is cool. Come winter, you'll be remembering these days fondly."

"No doubt." Sarah fiddled with a thread that had come loose on the hem or her shorts. There were so many things she wanted to ask Annalisa, but she was unsure about broaching any of it. Annalisa had known about her brother's affair with Katherine. She'd helped him send his final letter to her, after all. But what if she didn't want to talk about it? When Sarah had seen Gianluca's photograph for the first time, Annalisa had cut off her questions peremptorily. Maybe she had worked hard to put the whole thing out of her mind, and would be upset if Sarah were to drag it back out into the open now. Maybe Sarah wasn't so ready to talk about it either, truth be told. It wasn't an easy thing, to discover that your apparently circumspect grandmother had done something scandalous, and had cherished the memory of it enough to buy the house where it happened.

Annalisa looked questioningly at her. "You seem distracted today. *Tutto bene?*"

"*Si, si, benissimo,*" Sarah said automatically. Then, seeing that Annalisa was unconvinced, she added, "I've just had a little trouble sleeping, that's all."

If she couldn't bring herself to talk about the letters, then getting into the reasons for her sleeplessness was worse. Telling Annalisa that her dead brother was the feature performer in some highly sensual, albeit nightmarish, dreams was too embarrassing to contemplate.

"Is it the heat?"

"No. I mean, not exactly. I'm not sure."

Annalisa squinted at her, assessing. Did the old lady somehow know everything, just as Lily had joked? Including what Sarah was holding back?

"You should try a chamomile infusion before you go to bed," Annalisa suggested.

Some herbs in hot water seemed a weak defence, but Sarah didn't say so. She was willing to try anything that might help get her nights back to something calmer.

Annalisa went into the house and returned with a small plastic bag containing the dried and crushed herbs. She pressed it into Sarah's hand and held it there. "I grew this myself so it's much better than anything store-bought."

"Thank you, Annalisa," Sarah said, hugging her. "You're the best." Then she turned and braced herself for the long climb back up the hill.

Day 10—Highfield Residence, England

The first time you came to my house, it was to fetch Annalisa. At least that's what you said. But she wasn't there and yet you stayed. Just a glass of water after the long climb. Then a look at my paintings. Then the whole afternoon slid by inexorably, our hearts falling towards each other with the momentum of dense, hurtling planets propelling themselves through space and time.

That first visit had a kind of innocence about it. We didn't quite, fully realize then how little power we had over those planets, how inevitable our collision. But it didn't take long.

Chapter Five

LUKE CALLED ONE MORNING, just as Sarah was settling into the hills of a painting. Despite having told herself that she really didn't want a man in her life at the moment, her heart skipped a beat at the smoky sound of his voice on the phone.

"Sarah, hey. I just got back from the boat last night."

"Hi," she said, hoping he couldn't hear her pleasure too loudly. "Did you have a good time?"

"Yeah, it was great. But I'm happy to be back."

"Are you in Guzzano, or Florence?"

"Guzzano."

"Oh, good." It popped out involuntarily, before she had a chance to pretend she didn't care that he was near. She could almost hear his mouth break into a smile on the other end of the line.

"Would you like to go out to dinner tonight?" he asked. "There's a good trattoria in Camugnano."

She made a quick appraisal of her condition: unwashed, but she could take care of that if she finished what she'd set out to do with her painting quickly and didn't bother wiping down the baseboards with ammonia the way Katherine had told her, to keep bugs away. That time would be much better spent showering and making her hair nice. Some makeup, even. Sarah caught herself thinking this and chastised herself for letting a simple invitation make her behave like a schoolgirl.

"Is that too little notice?" Luke asked when she still hadn't spoken.

Sarah laughed. Maybe she was being juvenile, but it had been a long time since she'd felt wanted and it felt good. "Oh yes, because my social schedule out here in the middle of nowhere is very demanding. I need much more notice."

"So...?"

"It's fine. Tonight would be fine."

"Great! Pick you up about eight?"

"Fine again."

Sarah spent the rest of the day humming little tunes: tiny, defiant songs of happiness that refused to be intimidated by her constant declarations to herself that she was being silly. She changed in and out of her only two dresses several times and almost put on Katherine's lilac-strewn number, then thought better of it. Definitely not her. She settled for the pale blue shift of simple cotton and tried to stop fussing. Was she going to let herself act as though a casual dinner date were her first prom? He was almost a total stranger, for heaven's sake, and probably had all kinds of massive flaws that would irritate her beyond endurance.

But it didn't feel that way.

The restaurant was an intimate place with roughly stuccoed walls and simple wooden tables covered with paper toppers. Luke had reserved one that was set towards the back in a cozy spot. They ordered their food and a jug of house red, which came with little tumblers instead of stemmed glasses. Luke raised his to her. "Here's to getting to know each other. I'm really glad you said yes to coming out."

It was a little unnerving, how open he was. None of the usual holding back or playing it cool. He was facing her across the table, leaning towards her, glass held up and looking as though he really meant it. She clinked her glass to his, acutely aware of her own instinctive reserve.

"Tell me about your trip," she asked. "Was it a sailboat?"

"Nothing that strenuous. We were cruising around Elba on a small yacht that comes with a cook."

Sarah tried not to be intimidated by the idea of the yacht or the cook. "That's a bit of all right," she ventured.

"I met the guy who owns it a few years back when I was working on a country house for his father in England. I was just the junior on the project. An errand-boy, really, part of learning the ropes. Richard was kinda in the same position for his dad." He chuckled. "But without the pay. We became buddies."

"Nice."

"Yeah, sometimes you just get on with somebody right away. His wife's fun, too. They have the *Turtledove* berthed in La Spezia this summer. A sweet break for me, being so close by."

"Certainly is. Do you go out with them often?"

"I've been out a few times this year. Cruising around like that actually bores me after a few days. There's no real destination." He paused, frowning. "That sounds pathetic, doesn't it? Complaining about something so luxurious. Can I take that back? It's a great getaway."

"No, sorry, no taking stuff back when we're getting to know each other." She pretended to write a note on her hand. "Bores easily," she mumbled.

"Guilty. Do you like boats?"

Sarah thought about the little rowboat she and Roger had used almost every day in Indonesia, if the weather was fine, to explore the shoreline and find interesting flotsam for his very individualistic sculptures.

"There's a bit of a difference between yachts and boats, in my world," Sarah began, "but I know I like boats. I lived in Indonesia for a few years before I came here. The water was beautiful there, not at all like the grey mass we call the sea in England. We—I—had a little rowboat, just a tiny thing for getting about on the water in small, quiet bay near our house. I liked to set anchor and lie in the bottom looking up at the sky while the waves bobbed me up and down. It felt like nothing else existed, just my little boat capsule and the sky." It had become, in fact, not just an idle pleasure but an indispensable refuge in the few short weeks she had tried to endure after the other had moved in with them. Before Sarah conceded defeat and ran. Roger and the other would be rowing around the bay now.

Luke broke into her thoughts. "You might get a bit of that feeling if you were on the *Turtledove* and we launched you in the dinghy," he said, laughing. "Indonesia. What were you doing there?"

"Long story." She glanced at Luke and saw someone who looked as though he might understand her if she told him things. But not yet. "The short version is that I was enticed there by a misplaced love and it took me a ridiculous amount of time to realize I had to leave."

"Love of a guy or love of the place?"

So maybe Katherine hadn't told him too much about her after all. Or was he just testing to see how much she'd tell him herself? "A guy. The place was the part worth loving, as it turned out. But not the guy."

Their first dish arrived, a plate of antipasti with local salami selections, tiny pickled vegetables, lardo, olives and bruschetta. Sarah went for the lardo first, slicing off a great gob and smearing it on a thin crostino. Its fatty, salty greasiness was perfect. "God, I love lardo. It's so disgusting but so delicious."

"You gotta love a girl who loves lardo," said Luke, making her blush. He sampled a small, hard disc of salami. "The Italians sure know their way around a pig."

Sarah nodded. "I'm really liking this restaurant."

"Have you never been in here before? Katherine said it's been around since before the war."

Before the war. She wondered if Katherine and Gianluca had ever eaten there. Is that why she'd mentioned the place to Luke? She had never taken Sarah and Lily there. "What do you know about your great-uncle Gianluca?" Sarah asked.

"Not much. My grandfather—his brother—well you know my dad left Italy and married my mom, and that didn't go over very well, so we didn't see my grandad enough to hear a lot of stories. We didn't see him ever, in fact. So all I know is that Gianluca's the brother who died in the war."

"The family sounds as though they had a lot of expectations of their sons."

"In those days, yeah, I guess so." Luke looked at her quizzically. "Why do you ask?"

It occurred to Sarah, belatedly, that of all the relatives she could have mentioned, it might seem pretty strange that she would bring Gianluca up. "Oh," she said, waving her hand about vaguely, "I saw his photograph the other day at Annalisa's, and something about it just caught my attention."

"He was a good-looking guy. Must have been quite the ladies' man."

You don't know the half of it, Sarah thought to herself. *He's pretty impressive in a dream.* "Yes," was all she said out loud. "Do you think your father ever regretted moving away?"

"I think my father has been very happy to be married to my mother. And he did well for himself in America." Luke shrugged. "I'm glad he emigrated. Now I have access to both worlds, my American one and my Italian one."

"Do you have a preference?"

"Well, the food's better here." He pushed a square of the lardo her way. "If you take the last of the lardo can I have the last olive?"

The waiter came with steaming bowls of pasta, redolent of tomatoes and fresh herbs. Luke speared a piece with his fork, closing his eyes as he chewed. "Man, this is good." He opened his eyes again and tucked in heartily. "Seriously though, I love the States but I had the sense when I moved here of having come home. Not in Florence so much but specifically here, in this landscape. In Guzzano." He smiled a little sheepishly. "I probably sound like a million other Americans looking for themselves in the Old Country."

"Everybody needs a sense of home."

"So where's yours?"

The answer to this question eluded her. During the days, it felt possible to call her new house home. But at night, the presence of Gianluca and Katherine in her dreams made it hard to stop feeling like an intruder. Not that she could explain that to Luke. Not only was it a secret, but it sounded ridiculous.

"I'm trying to make one here," was the best she could say.

"You've got a great house, for a start."

"I thought it would be easy, but somehow it's not."

"Is that because it still feels like Katherine's territory? All the stuff that's hers, all those memories."

"Yes."

"Maybe you just need to give it time."

"That's my plan."

"Good." Luke smiled. "If you went back to England it would be really hard to see you."

He had this way of finding cracks in her armour and sticking a compliment in to hold the crack open before she could seal herself off again. She let him get away with it. "And is that *your* plan?"

"It is."

"It's not just because you like my house."

"Damn, you've found me out."

"I might still let you visit. If you're good."

"What's involved in being good?" Luke was looking at her so intently she felt her stomach flip-flop.

"I'll be making that up as I go along. Woman's prerogative."

"I thought changing their minds was the prerogative women always claim."

"That, too."

"Then it'll be interesting trying to keep up with you," he said, and Sarah found herself thinking she wouldn't mind him doing that at all.

After dinner they headed back to the house in Luke's car, a serviceable but completely unassuming Fiat Punto which he drove with the gusto of someone piloting a Ferrari. It was clean inside. No food wrappers on the floor, errant shopping lists or other debris, and the dashboard was pretty clean considering the dust of the area. Not like her Citroën, which Katherine had left perfectly tidy but had been accumulating bits of Sarah's detritus with every use.

Opening her window as they drove off, Sarah breathed deeply of the night air. "Smells like rain," she said. "And the sky's really dark over there, in the west. I'll bet we're going to have a good storm tonight." She dangled her arm out the window, playing with the air that streamed along the side of the car as they shot along the winding road.

"The area could use some water."

"It would help clear away the haze that's been building up around here lately. I'd like my view back so I can see what I'm trying to paint."

"You've been doing more work?"

"Oh, well, a few things." Sarah started to backpedal, but it was too late.

"Do I get to see them yet?" Luke asked. He seemed genuinely interested. Could it be safe to show him?

"They aren't much. A few colour studies of one composition, and two other smaller things," she began, then stopped. Don't start berating your work before he even sees it.

"I'd just enjoy seeing whatever it is you're up to, even practice stuff."

"All right."

In the fifteen minutes it took to return to the house, Sarah had vacillated a dozen times between looking forward to showing him her paintings and being gripped by anxiety. She was trying to stay on the positive side as they walked through the front door. "Would you like a grappa? I'm going to get one for myself."

"Great idea," he said, following her to the kitchen.

As Sarah was getting the drinks, Luke stepped towards Katherine's painting, the one Sarah had left turned towards the wall. He peeked at the hidden side. "I see you've brought my favourite painting downstairs. Strange way to hang it, though."

Sarah reddened. "Hm, well, it was on the wall properly, but it gave me such a weird dream I decided I needed a little break from it," she explained with a small laugh. She handed Luke a filled glass.

"It's a powerful painting."

"It is indeed. Are you sure you want to see mine? They're not the stuff of dreams, just interpretations of the landscape around here."

"Of course I do."

Sarah led the way into the studio and turned on the overhead lamp. Her finished work was lined up against the wall, providing limited but visible proof that she could paint, just in case she started to have doubts again. There was a small painting of the house, shown from below, and another of a lone tree in a field. The original landscape with its overly lively colours stood beside a second that was glowing and golden, and a third that was muted the way the true colours tended to be at that time of year. Although the composition itself was barely altered, the mood of the painting changed dramatically with each rendition. She had changed the colour of the sky in the second two as well, not wanting that purple-blue hue to haunt every painting.

Luke stood in front of the canvases studying them intently, his hands in his pockets and his body in its habitual casual slump, while Sarah waited nervously to one side, silently sipping her drink. "You have a great sense of colour," Luke said. "I love the way you can make the painting change just through that. It's not like I'm an expert or anything, but I like these a lot. How long did you say you'd been off?"

The sigh of relief that escaped Sarah's lips was barely audible as she replied. "It was a slow drying up, but I stopped completely for about two years."

"That's a long time to be away from it."

"It feels even longer."

"Imagine what you'll be able to do when you're back in good practice."

Sarah's ego, which had been cringing in a corner, started to creep back out into the open. "I've been trying to imagine exactly that. It's not always easy."

"Why did you stop for so long?"

Sometimes she had trouble remembering exactly why it had seemed so necessary. "I guess my creative spark went out for a while. But I think I might be getting it back."

"Sure looks like it to me."

"You think they're good?"

"Really good."

"You're not just saying that."

"Why would I?"

Sarah blushed. "I don't know; maybe, a little, to win me over?"

"Ply you with compliments to get you into bed, you mean?"

Sarah felt the blood rushing into her face. "That's putting it very, uh, bluntly."

"You don't seem that simple to me."

Best not to let him know how well it had been working so far, then. As Sarah looked at him there was something about his expression, teasing yet truly affectionate, that reminded her of Gianluca. Suddenly, overwhelmingly, she wanted to kiss him, seized by the conviction he would feel the same to her as the dreams: breathtaking, liberating, perfect.

Instead, she led him from the studio and turned towards the parlour. "Would you play the piano for me?" she asked. "One song, some favourite of my grandmother's. If you'd like to."

She put her hand lightly on his arm and he responded by grazing it with his fingertips. A butterfly touch, startlingly intimate in its familiarity.

"How could I say no?" he said, and it took Sarah a moment to remember what she had asked him. He sat at the piano bench while she leaned against the instrument to watch him play. He was clearly pleased at the prospect. "OK, I'm going to do the song that Katherine had me play for her even more often than 'Stranger in Paradise'." A tinkle of notes cascaded down from the treble clef to be answered by a rising set from the bass clef, setting a mood of sentimental romance. "*Mi ricordo, mi'amore, la tenerezza della tua pelle,*" he started singing, in a voice so rich and full of promises it had Sarah instantly mesmerized. He continued, his eyes sometimes closed, sometimes on the keys, occasionally on her. He switched back and forth between an Italian and an English version of the words.

"*How can the sky retain its blue, or leaves their green, their colours cannot mean a thing,*" he sang on, then ended on a long, low note sung to the accompaniment of a brief and plaintive piano riff and a minor chord. Luke let the sound fade, then looked up and smiled at Sarah's openly stunned face. "Whaddya think?" he asked.

"You didn't tell me you were actually good," she accused him. "No wonder Gran had you here crooning away all the time. I know that song, too. At least, I know the tune of it. Gran used to hum it constantly."

"It was her big fave." Luke started playing the first few bars of 'Stranger in Paradise'. "Do you dare?"

"Absolutely not." Sarah shook her head for emphasis even as she was thinking it might, in fact, be quite fun.

"Oh, come on. I've heard what you can do, remember?"

Sarah remembered all too well how loudly, and badly, she'd been wailing opera when he'd first come to her door.

"Down your grappa and try a few notes. *Take my hand...*" he began.

The remaining grappa burned its way in one shot down the back of Sarah's throat. "*I'm a stranger in paradise.*" Her voice came out as a barely audible squeak.

"Nice start. Got a volume control in there?" Luke patted the bench beside him and Sarah sat obediently, wondering why on earth she was agreeing to any of this. He started the piece again. "All together now—*Take my hand...*" He looked at her encouragingly, that wide smile lighting up his face.

This time her voice gained some confidence as she took up the tune and Luke sang intermittent harmony. It wasn't exactly an uninhibited performance, but she was amazed, at the end, that she had managed it at all. Luke turned to her, his face very close. She felt the heat emanating from his body.

"Exquisite," he said softly. He bent his head, his lips an inch away from hers. A question, waiting patiently for an answer. Sarah felt a rush of anticipation tinged with recognition; she knew exactly how it would be between them. An image of Gianluca flashed through her mind and melded with the warm flesh and blood of the man who was kissing her now in a deep and hungry foray.

Upstairs, the loud bang of a loose shutter smashing against an outside wall sounded like an alarm bell, making Sarah jump. "Damn, the storm!" she cried, breaking away and leaping up from the bench. "The windows are open upstairs. The place will be soaked." She ran out of the room and up the stairs to pull the windows closed in her bedroom, with Luke right behind to close the spare room.

Breathless at the top of the stairs, she heard a plaintive mewing and dashed back down again to the kitchen to open the door. Beppe flew in just ahead of a rain-laden gust of wind that she forced back out with a determined slamming of the door.

Laughing and flushed from the frenzy, she turned to Luke. "Phew! That was close," she said, leaning back against the kitchen table to steady herself. Rain began to pelt against the windowpanes and the wind rattled the shutters. Luke came to stand in front of her, slipping his arms around her waist.

"I guess this means I'm stuck here for a while."

"Mmhm," she murmured, kissing him. "You might be stuck here all night." Their mouths met again in exploration and their hands followed, roving slowly over each other's bodies.

Luke drew his fingers through the gloss of her hair, down the ridge of muscle that defined her neck and up over a small hillock of thin cotton to find an expectant nipple. He moved lazily, wordlessly, as though each inch of her was worth dwelling over. Then he lowered the zipper at the back of her dress and slipped it off her shoulders, exposing glistening skin to his searching lips and fingertips.

She felt completely uninhibited with him, giving herself over to a touch that knew where to go and what to do. Vanquishing the buttons of his shirt, she caressed the smooth skin of his back with her hands, pressed her lips to the warm pulse in his neck, then found his mouth again. Her unzipped dress fell to the floor and Luke slipped down to his knees, following it, pulling her panties along the same course in one simple motion, burying his face in her belly, his rough chin razing against the silky white skin there. He continued along his downward course until his tongue slid into the cleft of her, and her body turned liquid at the swelling pleasure of it. She let the feeling grow in her until she thought it would spill over the edge at any moment, then she pulled him upright, damning the finickiness of buttons as she assaulted his shirt and trousers. "Now," she whispered, urgent and demanding, her fingers fumbling with his zipper.

He stood naked and pulled her to him, their skin meeting hot and slippery down the whole length of their bodies, the promise of his hardness pressed against her stomach. When he lifted her up onto the kitchen table, she lay back and opened herself up to take him deep inside.

Luke kissed every sweet and sensitive spot still within reach of his lips, moving slowly until Sarah's body responded with a sudden surge of desire and she quickened their pace, wanting to consume him utterly. His hands were strong on her hips as the taut bubble in Sarah grew and a cry of release escaped her lips from somewhere deep inside. She felt Luke stiffen with one final push as his own low groan filled the air above her. He lowered himself to his elbows, spent, his sweating chest against her breasts.

Sarah slipped her arms around him, her fingers delineating each notch in the ridge of his spine one by one as they both recovered their breath. Luke raised his head to kiss her.

"I've spent a lot of time imagining this, since the day I first met you," he confessed.

Sarah smiled slowly. "Was the kitchen table a part of your fantasy?"

He nuzzled her neck. "You're the one who said "now," so I obeyed." Easing himself out of her, he helped her upright, then lifted her up and carried her with him to the big chair, where he sat himself down with her cradled in his lap.

"More comfy?" he asked, stroking her hair and kissing the top of her head. "I'd carry you all the way to bed, but honestly I think those stairs would do us in."

"There's plenty of time to move as far as the bed." Sarah nestled into him, her head resting against his shoulder as her fingertips played absently on his chest. With the clamour of their own noise having subsided, she became aware once again of the sounds of the storm buffeting the house, the crack of thunder and the howl of the wind accentuating by their contrast the tranquility of her place in his arms.

Luke spoke. "You know, that first afternoon when I came here, this idea came into my head that making love to you wouldn't feel like a usual first time. That it would be more intimate. Like we already knew each other." He paused, running his fingers down the length of her arm. She could feel his heartbeat through his shoulder, a slight quickening, a question as to whether this confession was acceptable.

"And it was," she said. "I don't know why, but it was." It had felt, she thought, as though the lost pieces of a puzzle, half finished, had clicked into place.

They sat awhile more in silence, their hands picking up the rhythm of exploration once again, idly at first and then with more focus, until Sarah felt a stirring in his lap under her and stood up, taking his hand and leading him up the stairs.

Day 17–Highfield Residence, England

I've been hearing a tune in my head all morning. My favourite from when you played the piano for me and sang those popular, romantic songs that didn't even need translating to understand their meaning. You know which tune I mean—you'd get that raspy catch in your voice every time you sang the words 'tenerezza della tua pelle' and my insides would liquefy. Even this decrepit body feels a wisp of that old thrill when I remember how we were back then.

But we were not just about lustful longing. It was something deeper than that. You were a man of polar extremes. Of the earth, hard and tough and male, yet possessed of an artistic sensitivity in your perceptions of the world and all that was in it, and a greater tenderness than I could ever have imagined. By comparison, James was predictable, an embodiment of the middle course.

I wonder, often, how it would have been with you after twenty years, or forty, or sixty. Would that tenderness have remained after the passion had subsided? Would I still melt at your touch?

Chapter Six

THE STRAINS OF SOMETHING UPBEAT and modern drifted out of the windows towards Sarah's shady place under the tree as she put the final touches on a painting of the house. It was pleasant working to Luke's accompaniment. The music set a buoyant rhythm that her brush seemed to pick up, so the work came more easily than it had before. As she packed up her supplies and headed back to the house, she thought about how much a part of her life Luke had become in just a week. Their time together had grown without calculation. He was still in Guzzano on holiday, and while at first they'd maintained the pretense that he was staying at Annalisa's, by dusk he would be drawn back to Sarah. A few clothes were brought over. A razor and toothbrush appeared in the bathroom. A box of Cheerios, his favourite cereal, was added to the pantry.

Occasionally Sarah wondered how she'd got so deep so fast, when her objective had been independence. When the thought came up, however, she brushed it aside. She wanted to enjoy the pure, giddy feeling that marks the beginning of love. Anyway, she reasoned, when Luke returned to work in Florence she would have plenty of time to herself again. Meanwhile, she was happy and productive. Her earlier preoccupation with Gianluca had shrunk to a few infrequent thoughts, and she'd stopped having the dreams.

In the studio, Sarah put the painting on an easel to dry and cleaned her brushes. When she'd finished she went into the sitting room and interrupted Luke's playing by putting her arms around him from behind and kissing the top of his head. "I'm done," she announced.

"OK." He stood up. "That makes four finished paintings, right?"

"Yes, if we only count the livelier version of those three colour studies. I think it's better than the other experiments."

"So now I've got a surprise for you." Luke's face had a pleased-with-itself look as he took her hands in his. "You know that little gallery we were talking about in Camugnano?"

"The one where Gran used to sell some of her stuff?"

"Yeah, that one. I told them about you and the great work you're turning out. I showed them photos I took on my cellphone."

"You did?" Sarah had thought about talking to them at some point but had intended to do it after she had worked up a bit more confidence, just in case they rejected her.

"They were really excited."

"They were?"

"Of course. They sold a lot Katherine's work, you know, and they'd be really pleased to see what her granddaughter is up to."

"I guess that makes sense."

"Sure it does, especially since your work is great. I told them we'd bring the paintings around this afternoon or tomorrow."

"You what?" The pleasure Sarah had been feeling about the gallery's interest was instantly wiped out by the pressure of having to put something on public display right away, before she'd had a chance to get used to the idea. "How could you do that without asking me first?"

Luke looked baffled. "Aren't you happy that they want your paintings?"

"Yes, but—"

"And you've got enough to show them now."

"But I wanted to get to it in my own time."

Sarah started to pull her hands away from his, but he held on. "Sarah, don't run away. I was just trying to help you get off the ground, like you want to."

"I would have got there on my own."

"I know, but what's wrong with a little encouragement? We'd already talked about that gallery. I just moved the ball forward a bit."

It was true that they had talked about the gallery and how it would be a good place for her to get her work back into circulation again. And it was true she would have procrastinated for ages without his help. Maybe the only important thing was that the gallery was interested. Did it matter how they had got that way?

"How many do they want to hang?" Sarah finally said, and Luke gave her a loud, triumphant kiss on the check. She wiped away the small wet spot with the back of her hand.

"We'll bring all of them," he said.

"The last one isn't dry yet."

"Three then, and we can always run the last one over to them when it's ready." He put his arm around her. "I know you're nervous, but I'm telling you, the gallery loves your paintings and so will their customers. I've seen the other stuff that's in there, and yours is streets ahead."

Sarah smiled. He seemed so sure of what he was saying. Some of his optimism filtered through to her as well. "You're biased," she said, although she wanted to feel he could be right.

"It's still true." He pulled her to him and kissed her. His closeness affected her the same as it had all week, making her body leap with excitement like a joyful dog at the prospect of a game of fetch. Luke grazed her ear with his lips. "But maybe while we're waiting for that last one to dry, we could occupy ourselves in some other way."

"It takes a lot longer than that for a painting to dry completely," she said as his lips moved down her neck and she let herself soften into his body.

"Then we'll go slowly" was his answer, and the paintings found their way to the gallery much later in the afternoon.

◊ ◊ ◊

The owner of the gallery took in all of Sarah's work. The prices he set were low, in keeping with his clientele of tourists looking for paintings of familiar landscapes to take home as souvenirs. Nevertheless, Sarah was pleased. It might be an insubstantial gallery but it was a sure beginning. She had painted again and someone in the business had told her he could find a market for her work. If Luke's action had been presumptuous, it had also been the right thing to do in the end. She needed pushing and he'd provided it.

On their way back they stopped in to visit Annalisa, at Sarah's insistence. "I feel as though I've taken you away from her," she told him. "She loved having you stay with her, and now she's all alone again."

"I know she liked my company, but she's thrilled that I'm spending my time with you, believe me. She's been plotting this liaison for ages." He pulled his car into a narrow gap beside the chicken coop and they got out.

Annalisa certainly did look happy to see them together. She was affectionate and welcoming, and obviously delighted by Sarah's good news.

"*Complimenti!*" She gave Sarah a smothering hug. "That must be very satisfying."

"Well they still have to sell, of course, but the possibility of earning even a little money is a welcome change," Sarah agreed. They sat down to iced tea and biscotti in the kitchen.

Annalisa looked from one to the other. "It's nice to see you two getting along so well." Luke shot Sarah a look of smug satisfaction. "It closes a circle much in need of closure."

"You just like to have everyone coupled up," Luke said, smiling. "Has Katherine talked to you about us yet?" he asked his aunt teasingly.

Sarah kept silent. All this observation and expectation didn't seem to bother Luke in the least. He almost seemed to like the interest. But it gave Sarah a feeling of panic, like a claustrophobic who unexpectedly finds herself in much too tight a space.

"She might have mentioned it, I don't remember." Annalisa was unconvincing in her nonchalance, but she wasn't giving in. She turned to Sarah. "Now that you've made some progress with your paintings, what are you going to do? More of the same?"

"I don't know, actually. I started with the landscapes because they're fairly easy for me. I really prefer to do less literal work, but right now I'm just happy that I've started again and that what I did is for sale in a gallery."

"Well, you don't need to rush. You have a place to stay, you don't need much money. Sometimes it's good just to let things unfold," Annalisa suggested.

Sarah thought most things had 'just unfolded' in her life, and she wasn't too pleased with the results. What she wanted now was to gain some power over where it was going. Still, she couldn't expect to simply turn around one day and make that happen. Annalisa was right; rushing would not increase her chances of success.

"I'm sure subjects will suggest themselves to me if I just keep painting," Sarah said. "The muse tends to feed on itself that way."

"I know you consider me biased, but even a layman like me can see that your art has a future," Luke said. "We should have brought them for you to see, Annalisa, before we took them to the gallery. I wasn't thinking."

"I'll go take a look at them next time I'm in Camugnano. It will be very special to see them hanging in a gallery."

"Would you like me to read to you today?" Sarah suggested. "Since I'm here anyway, we could get a few chapters in."

"I'd like that. But what about you, Luca?"

"I'll go back to the house. We bought some Champagne to celebrate Sarah's sale, and it needs to go in the fridge if it's going to be ready for the evening. Anyway, I've got my own reading I wouldn't mind catching up on."

Luke kissed both women goodbye and went on his way, leaving them to settle themselves in their traditional post out front. "Now, where were we?" Sarah asked, leafing through the book to find the turned-down page.

"Chapter eleven. Massimo has been witless enough to leave, just as Gabriella needs him most."

"Ah, yes. And Gabriella has been witless enough not to tell him she needs him in the first place. I can hardly wait to see how they resolve this."

They covered a few more chapters before closing the book again. "They seem to be getting more stupid as they go along," Sarah commented.

"That's often the case. The frustrating thing about this book is that Massimo never really stops being too proud for his own good."

"If it's frustrating, why are we reading it?"

"It still has a happy ending."

"Oh well, then that settles it. I like happy endings."

"Me, too." Annalisa looked carefully at Sarah. "Planning on making one for yourself, this time?"

"Hmm—really—it's a bit early to go that far," Sarah stammered.

"Sometimes one doesn't need to wait too long to see what's right."

"I suppose. Romance wasn't exactly on my agenda, you know. So Luke has taken me a bit by surprise."

"Romance rarely follows an agenda. Enjoy the surprise," Annalisa counselled. The two rose and exchanged parting kisses.

"I've been feeling guilty, taking up all of Luke's time that he used to spend with you. Do you want to come up to the house for dinner later?"

Annalisa shook her head. "You two have your celebration. It gives me a lot of joy to know you're with each other. More than you can imagine."

Day 19—Highfield Residence, England

When I told Annalisa I was falling in love with you, she wasn't shocked; she could see it happening for herself. But she was concerned for us. It was, after all, wrong on every measure. Even if I had been single it would have been awkward for the precious son of the leading family in the community to go off with a foreigner. It just wasn't a community with that open a perspective; a generation later the family still considered it outrageous. Since I was married, it was completely out of the question.

However, true love runs a course of its own, without sympathy for social proprieties. I was young and full of my own heart, and that's how I felt. Our relationship was beyond the ability of anyone to prevent, let alone the two of us. Who can say what power brings two people together with such a force as we felt? Society's conventions are nothing in its shadow.

All of that August our passion was unstoppable. We filled the house and the hills and meadows with it. Under a star-filled sky, and in the shelter of my room with the rain pelting on the roof above us; in the old claw-footed tub, our bodies slipping against each other in the soapy water; in the midst of making dinner, the pasta boiling to mush, ignored. I cannot recall a time in my life when I felt more brilliantly alive. It was impossible to feel shame.

Chapter Seven

FOLLOWING THE SUCCESS of getting the gallery to hang Sarah's paintings, Luke got them both invited to spend the weekend aboard the *Turtledove*. Although Luke had described Richard as a great guy and a great buddy, Sarah was nervous to meet him and his wife, concerned about the obvious social distance between their world and hers. Richard probably had an Etonian accent, and Caroline at least an 'Honourable' in front of her name.

When they welcomed her aboard, Sarah was dismayed to be right about the accent and awed by Caroline's perfect, glossy, tawny hair, blunt-cut at the shoulder and looking as though it got trimmed weekly. It swung with a soft swish each time she moved. Sarah's own wild, dark mop was caught up with a large clip at the top of her head to prevent it from taking on a life of its own.

But in spite of her misgivings, Sarah found she liked them both. They were as Luke had said, easygoing and apparently genuinely interested in meeting her. By the time she was lounging on the forward deck with Caroline, enjoying the sun, a cool sea breeze, and a beer, her reservations had almost vanished. The boat was anchored in a small bay off the island of Palmaria and the water was calm. The two women lay in their swimsuits and sunglasses, side by side on chaise lounges.

"This is a very acceptable way to spend an afternoon," Sarah said with a satisfied sigh.

"Agreed. I get so lazy after I've been on this boat awhile. It completely changes my sense of time."

"I'm finding it hard to remember that somewhere in another part of my life there are things that need doing."

"That's exactly what I like about it. If Richard and I ever get divorced, I'm going for the boat."

"I should hope so."

"But you know I'm not serious."

"Of course; if you were serious, you'd go for the house, too."

Caroline laughed. "A true pragmatist!"

Sarah smiled. She was the least pragmatic person she knew. "How did you meet Richard?"

"Oh, the usual thing in a way. We met at a party full of sodding drunks. The unusual thing was that I happened upon a man out in the garden who had gone out to escape the madding crowd and was himself almost entirely sober. That was Richard, and I was so impressed to find someone at that party who was still dignified I fell instantly in love." She giggled at her own story, but Sarah sensed that underneath the laughter was the heartfelt relief she'd found such a man.

"And what condition were you in?"

"Ah, you see, that's the amazing thing, the great stroke of fate. I was on antibiotics at the time and couldn't drink, so I was sober too, which is why I needed a break. It's such a bore to be with drunks when you aren't drinking. That's why Richard and I ended up alone in the garden. If it hadn't been for the antibiotics, we might never have met."

"I suppose that means you believe in fate."

"Oh yes." Caroline turned to Sarah, suddenly earnest. "Richard jokes about marrying me for my title, and I joke about marrying him for his fortune. Our union is such a pathetic social cliché! But actually I believe we were meant for each other. I felt it right away." She paused. "There's a lot of crap out there. You've probably noticed yourself. Finds like Richard—and Luke, I think—are pretty rare. Don't you think?"

"Yes, there's a lot of crap," Sarah agreed. Luke felt like a rare find, but how could she be certain? Roger had felt pretty rare too, at the beginning. She didn't trust her own judgment anymore.

"Luke told us he met you when you moved into a house near his aunt's. You've been living there for a while?"

"Almost two months."

Caroline raised her sunglasses to look at Sarah more closely. "Really? So how long have you known Luke?"

Sarah calculated. "Twelve days."

Caroline continued to study her for a moment before lying back in her chaise once more. "Amazing. I thought you'd known each other for months and that Luke had just kept quiet about you. You seem way more comfortable with each other than people who have just met."

They lounged that way for a couple of hours, Richard and Luke joining them to chat idly, nibble plates of salumi and olives the cook produced for them, and dive into the sea occasionally to cool off, bobbing like manatees and feeling lazy.

Sitting in the stern and watching Luke emerge from the water, Sarah savoured a moment of studying him while he was preoccupied with negotiating the ladder. Wet and golden, his lean, athletic body and sun-lightened hair looked decidedly west coast American. His Italian blood was evident only in the richness of his tan. Sarah took in his glistening skin and the movement of his muscles as he wiped the salt water off his face. He really was quite gorgeous. Catching her looking at him, he smiled at her, big and easy, like there was no one else he'd rather see more. Her heart fluttered. Rare. Yes, maybe Caroline was right.

Richard broke into her thoughts. "We have to return to London this week, since we're not all leisure and decadence. Although we do get more than our fair share, for which I'm very grateful. But in September the boat will be in Greece. If you're interested, you're welcome to join us."

"I don't think I'll have the time in September," said Luke.

Richard nodded. "Oh that's right. I forgot you don't like Greece."

"It's not that," Luke said defensively. "It just, you know, we get busy come fall."

Sarah turned to him. "You really don't like Greece?"

Luke frowned, sending a reproachful look at his buddy. "Just not my favourite place," he mumbled.

"But it's so beautiful. And isn't it a kind of Mecca for your profession?" Sarah asked.

"I know it seems crazy," Luke admitted with a sigh. "I was there during university, for the usual exploration of ancient sites. I appreciated them, but not Greece as a whole." He paused. "I have no good reason. I just felt kind of jumpy and stressed-out there. Exactly the opposite of what it's supposed to do for you. Maybe I'd just been studying too hard, but it creeped me out to be there."

"Maybe you were a Theban slave in a former life," Caroline offered breezily. "But really, what does it matter? There are plenty of beautiful places in the world." She stood up. "Now, let's enjoy where we are today. Time to get cleaned up, then we'll have a yummy dinner with some even yummier wine. Life is good."

◊ ◊ ◊

Back in Guzzano on Sunday evening, as Luke and Sarah tried to stretch out their last evening before he went back to Florence for work, Lily called.

"Sarah, hi. I'm reporting in from water world. Are you getting any of this rain down there, or is it all ours?"

"All yours. We're basking in sun and warmth."

"We?" Lily's antennae snapped to attention. "Are you speaking for the general population, or is that hunky guy you met with you?"

Damn Lily for always hearing what wasn't said. "Well, hmm," Sarah squirmed as she watched the object of their conversation wash lettuce. She'd confessed to his existence but had avoided an actual encounter between the two of them. Fearing what? She wasn't sure. Jinxing the whole thing, perhaps.

"He is, isn't he? Tell!" Lily commanded.

"Uh-huh."

"Ooh, lah. And is he still luscious, bonking you to bits and being a slave to your every whim?"

Sarah blushed scarlet. "Pretty much." Luke looked over at her with a questioning flip of his head. She looked down at her feet.

"Wonderful!" cried Lily, delighted. "Let me speak to him."

Sarah looked up to find Luke still watching her, waiting for her to reveal the mystery of her monosyllabic conversation. *Maybe,* she thought, *this would be all right. It had to happen sometime.*

She held out the phone to him. "It's my sister," she said. "Probing for the details of my personal life." She had almost said 'love life' but had stopped herself before it came out.

Luke laughed then, relieved, and took the phone from her. He spent the next five minutes humouring his interrogator, then handed the phone back to Sarah with a kiss.

"Really hot voice," Lily pronounced. "Does he look as good as he sounds?"

"Yes, he does look as good as he sounds." Sarah grinned at Luke. "He also looks pretty composed for someone who's just been interrogated. What did you say to him?"

"I told him you'd had enough pricks in your life and that he'd better take good care of you." She paused. "And that if he didn't I'd fly down there and personally castrate him."

"Oh god, Lily, you didn't," Sarah groaned, frowning her apologies for her sister's behaviour towards Luke, who was openly laughing now. "He seems to be taking it well."

"That must mean he intends to do as I suggested. Are you still finding time to paint with lover-boy about?" Lily asked.

"Yes, I am. The gallery that took the first four want more. I'm rolling now, I think." How satisfying it was to be able to say that.

"You sound a bazillion times better than you did a couple of months ago. It's so good to hear."

"And you?"

"Not rolling quite so successfully, I'm afraid. I might have to get a real jour-nalist job soon, instead of pretending to make money as a freelancer. Not that the real jobs are plentiful in this profession, either. I'm giving it until Christmas, then I'll see."

"Things will pick up for you, Lil, I'm sure of it. It takes time to establish yourself, you know that."

"I know it, but I don't have to like it. I'm feeling impatient. Anyway, I'll let you get back to your sweetheart now. Should I still keep it from Mum and Dad, or can I tell?"

"It doesn't matter one way or the other," Sarah answered, and felt a sense of relief that she was finally sufficiently free of their influence that it didn't. She would have been happier if she'd actually wanted to share the news with them, but she'd settle for freedom.

"I'm telling, I'm telling," Lily incanted in a childish taunt. "Keep up the good work, Sis. I'll call you next weekend, if I don't hear from you before."

"I'll call, it's my turn. Hugs." Sarah hung up the phone.

Luke came up and put his arms around her. "Did I pass?"

"Do you doubt it? Sorry if my sister was a bit over-the-top in her defence of me. Sometimes I think she should have been the eldest. She's always trying to take care of me."

"That's not so bad. Your sister is very…energetic," Luke said, searching for the right word. "But not insulting. I liked talking to her."

"Not worried about her threats?" Sarah asked tentatively.

Luke took her face in his hands and looked into her eyes. "I'm not worried. I'm not going to let you down, Sarah." He kissed her with a convincing warmth and Sarah let herself slip into the joyful belief that he did, in fact, intend to do as Lily commanded.

Chapter Eight

THE RESTORATION STUDIO of Maestro Umberto Santini was housed in two ground-floor rooms off a narrow side street in the Santa Croce district of Florence. The front room was tiny, a rudimentary receiving area for clients, rarely tidied and never cleaned. A wood-topped, glass-fronted display cabinet containing nothing but a roll of brown paper and a ball of twine for wrapping paintings served as a storefront counter. A single wooden chair spotted with paint, in which no one ever sat, stood off to one side. Behind this room was a larger space where the work was actually performed. It, too, appeared to be in a state of perpetual disarray but everything more or less had its place, however unofficial, and Sarah soon came to understand its jumbled order.

The job had come through one of Luke's colleagues. A chance mention that made Sarah glad she'd taken restoration studies along with her fine arts training. Wanting the extra money and figuring it would still leave her plenty of time to paint, she'd been working on and off for six weeks now. Umberto called her when the workload demanded it, so sometimes she spent all week there and other times she didn't come at all. If the work was uninspiring so far, simple cleaning jobs on a number of paintings that were of the current century, a trial of her abilities before she was given something more challenging, Sarah didn't mind. There had been more of it than she'd anticipated, so she knew she'd passed the grade. More interesting things would soon come. Meanwhile, the position had its pluses. She stayed with Luke in his apartment, a ten-minute, easy bicycle ride away, when she was in town. The work paid for the basics of life, she liked her maestro, and the lack of a set schedule suited her well, allowing her to return to the house at Guzzano to paint when she was free.

As she sat in Umberto's studio finishing up the cleaning of a small painting, the maestro entered. He was a short, stocky man in his late forties, with a tumble of dark hair mixed with grey sweeping back from his face, and a close-cropped full beard, also flecked with grey. His eyes were very dark, the pupils and irises almost indistinguishable from one another in their blackness, like the shiny, bottomless eyes of vampires in old films. Despite this strange effect the overall impression he gave was jovial, mostly thanks to a deep and hearty laugh that leapt forth frequently from someplace deep in his ample paunch. He came up and inspected the painting Sarah had cleaned, picking it up gently in thick, coarse hands permanently stained with the chemicals and colours of his trade.

"Fine. Good," he pronounced in his low, rumbling voice. "Next week you'll begin a real piece of restoration work, not just cleaning. The painting isn't very important, but it still has to be done properly and it requires some touch-up as well."

Sarah smiled at the controlled compliment of being handed a more challenging task on an unimportant painting. Umberto was sparse with his praise, but it was clear she had made headway. "I look forward to working on it."

"Are you eating with us today?" His wife, Francesca, had offered Sarah a place at their table for midday meals whenever she wanted it, for excellent and plentiful food at a very modest cost to help cover some of the ingredients. Sarah had taken advantage of it sporadically, preferring often to spend the time wandering around Florence or lunching with Luke when it was possible. That week, however, she'd spent every day with the Santinis because Luke had been in Seattle pitching a new project, and wasn't due back for another five days. In his absence Sarah found herself looking forward to the family lunches as much for the company as for the food. "Yes," she answered. She knew she was welcome; Francesca loved having the extra body there for meals now that her two children had homes of their own.

"Good. Come up whenever you're ready." He lumbered off, the sound of his heavy footsteps resounding on the stairs as he made his way to the living rooms up top. Sarah cleaned herself up in the small washroom that adjoined the studio. When she had first arrived it had been revoltingly dirty, a man's toilet, the seat always up, the spills unnoticed. She had donned rubber gloves and filled a bucket to brimming with disinfectant to render it respectable again amidst the knowing smiles of Francesca and the rolling eyes of Umberto, who was feeling the first effects of a woman's penetration into his male domain of the studio. Sarah felt sure he continued to leave the seat up as a kind of territorial marking, but at least the little room felt usable now.

She entered the upper rooms to be greeted by the heavenly aromas of traditional Italian cooking, a lush mix of broth, garlic and rosemary, of stewing meat and vegetables boiled into a thick soup. Francesca greeted her warmly.

"Your man still away?"

It was nice to be understood. "Yes, I'm afraid so."

Umberto voiced his opinion. "What lunacy to leave a woman in love alone. What could Luca be thinking?"

"It's a condition of the modern world," Sarah answered. "Anyway, what's so terrible about it?" She had a good idea what his response would be, but she liked to goad him when he began to sound dogmatic about personal things. In the amiable, social context of their lunches, her relationship with her maestro became much more relaxed than it was when they were working.

"A woman in love," he began with authority, "has feelings that cannot be contained. She will naturally seek an outlet for them if left on her own."

"Listen to the expert," commented Francesca from her position at the stove.

Sarah laughed. "Really, Maestro, he hasn't been away all that long. I think I can manage to contain my emotional burden a little while longer."

"You laugh now, but you wait and see. It's not good. I know these things."

"And how do you know so much about young women in love?" demanded his wife with mock suspicion.

"I am an observant man. Sensitive. Sympathetic to the feelings of women."

Francesca snorted and dissolved the three of them into laughter.

The meal was brought to the big kitchen table and they spent the rest of the midday break being entertained by Umberto's unlikely stories of his misadventures, enlivened by judicious exaggeration and plenty of gestures.

When her working day ended, Sarah bicycled back slowly along the banks of the Arno. Glints of setting sun filtered through gaps between buildings for their end-of-day dance on the water. The air held a hint of cooler weather to come, and a faint fetid water smell that seemed to rise with dusk.

It had been Luke's suggestion that she should stay with him when she was in Florence, instead of in the single small room the Santinis had to offer. She'd given it about two seconds' thought, briefly reminding herself about her intention to be independent, before she banished that concern and agreed. Of course it was wonderful to come home to her man instead of creeping up to a small room in her boss's house. And it wasn't as though she was in Florence all the time, so she rationalized that it was quite legitimate to want to be with him when she was there. Today, however, the contrast between the lively atmosphere of midday and the silence that greeted her once she'd climbed up the narrow flight of stairs, turned the key and swung open the old wooden half-door, deepened a loneliness that had been creeping up on her all week. It was different than opening up her own door to an empty house. In this home, her heart expected Luke.

She dropped her things on the bench by the door and went through to open the shutters that had been closed during the day, letting in the last of the evening light but failing to dispel the gloom of silence. She took in the flat's simple, comfortable furnishings, the sleek sofa and plush Turkish carpet, books stacked everywhere, a single, large and vivid abstract oil painting propped up on the book shelves. A place to feel at home in, if she wanted to.

In sharing his flat, if only occasionally, Sarah had taken on Luke's life there as easily as slipping on a new coat. He had already been living in Florence for several years and had friends, particular restaurants and bars he frequented, familiar stores and bakeries where he bought his food. Sarah found herself absorbed into this existence she'd had no hand in creating, and with it came a certain laziness about discovering anything for herself, or exploring things she might have on her own. She had originally intended to meet new people and make a different kind of city life for herself, but the situation with Luke was just too convenient. It freed her from having to do all the tedious legwork necessary to establish a social life and everything else. She just appeared, and slipped into place.

What Sarah had noticed this week, however, was that when Luke went away, so did his friends. A couple of them had called over the week, not realizing he was abroad. They talked to her briefly but there had been no offers of evenings out to assuage her solitude. She hadn't been around long enough to become a true part of the fabric of their lives; she was still an accessory, and now that the arm on which she normally dangled wasn't there, she was once again facing an evening on her own.

At the house in Guzzano she expected to be alone. She was familiar with the surroundings and had her painting to occupy her and Beppe for company. If Luke was there it was a bonus. But here, in his space, she felt his absence as a huge void. He had telephoned twice, late in the evening her time, but his calls had only served to make the place feel emptier once he'd hung up.

Sarah dropped her coat on a chair and rummaged in the kitchen for a packet of crisps. In the living room she plopped down on the sofa and munched her way through the crisps as she contemplated the next few days. She had that night and the next to go before she returned to Guzzano for the weekend. The novel she had been reading was finished, she had already seen any film she cared to at the local cinemas, and the television was consistently dreadful.

Then she remembered Carlo, the Moretti cousin who was living in Florence. She found his number, scrunched up at the bottom of her purse, and called him. A sense of relief flooded her when she found he was free for dinner the following evening. She turned on the television. One night of crap she could handle, now that she knew she was going out the next.

Day 23—Highfield Residence, England

That puppy you brought me to keep me company was so adorable. A brown mutt with one white paw. I was terrible at training him, far too quick to indulge him when he looked at me with those soft brown eyes. I called him Lupo, although he was the furthest thing from a wolf one could imagine. A complete softie and not destined to ever get bigger than a beagle. It must have been difficult for you to make him into a proper farm dog, when I left and he had to go back to you. After I'd spoiled him so badly.

Chapter Nine

THE NEXT DAY AT CLOSING TIME, Carlo appeared at the door of the studio in Santa Croce to pick her up. Umberto eyed him suspiciously, noting the shiny silver Mercedes convertible parked outside and its owner's cultivated charm. The maestro made Carlo wait, standing, in the front room and went to the studio to fetch Sarah.

"There's a flashy young man asking for you at the front. He says he's supposed to be picking you up tonight." He shook his head as he spoke, looking as though he hoped she would refute the man's claim.

"Oh, good," said Sarah happily. "That's Carlo. He's one of Luca's cousins, once removed, or second, or third or something. I practically grew up with him." She retrieved her coat and handbag from the corner.

"I don't like the look of him," Umberto said in a loud whisper, although the door to the front room was closed. "He's a real show-off."

"Well, that sounds about what I expected. Don't worry, he's just taking me out to dinner."

Umberto grunted and scowled in response.

"I need a night out. He's harmless." She patted him on the shoulder, refusing to acknowledge his disapproval. What right had he to judge her actions, anyway? She walked confidently through to the front room to greet her childhood friend.

Carlo stood looking out the window, and when he turned to face Sarah at the sound of her footsteps, she was startled by just how good he looked. She had last seen him in an awkward and pimply state in his late teens. He had definitely outgrown that and matured into classic Latin features, with dark eyes and a beautifully angular jaw line. He wore clothes that were casual but very finely made, and Sarah guessed that under them was a body that had been developed carefully at a gym. He smiled and opened his arms to greet her.

"*Tesora, bellissima, che meraviglia,*" he enthused, kissing her on both cheeks and giving her a warm hug. Sarah felt herself enfolded by a pleasant mix of cologne and perfectly ironed linen as she returned Carlo's embrace. She made a mental note to call Lily and let her know how he'd turned out. Lily would approve.

Umberto had planted himself in the doorway between the two rooms, his legs set stubbornly and his arms folded across his chest in stern condemnation.

"*Buona sera, Maestro,*" Sarah said, taking Carlo by the arm and leading him away from the glowering gaze. They drove to Luke's flat so Sarah could change from her spattered work clothes.

As she emerged from the bedroom wearing a short black skirt and a sweater the colour of garnets, Carlo gave a low whistle. "You certainly grew into a beautiful woman," he told her, taking one of her hands in both of his. Sarah felt a hot flush bring the red of her sweater up into her face.

"Thank you. You didn't turn out so badly yourself."

"Are you sure you're spoken for by my unworthy cousin?" He squeezed her hand slightly.

"Ah, Carlo, you were always charming, even when you were an awkward youth. But what makes you think Luke is unworthy?"

Carlo shrugged his shoulders and released her hand, taking her elbow to guide her to the front door as he replied. "Just hoping."

They were at the door when Sarah stopped and turned to him. "Carlo, can we be clear? I'm looking for a friend, not a lover." She didn't want there to be any confusion or advances to fend off. She just wanted an evening out with a friend who was her own, not Luke's. "You and I always got on really well when we were kids, and I was hoping the same might still be true now."

Bowing low with a sweep of his hand, Carlo accepted her terms. "I am your humble prince, as always, ready to do your bidding."

"I'm glad to see you haven't lost your touch."

He took her to an expensive and intimate restaurant in the heart of the old city. Old style, with white tablecloths and perfectly starched napkins. She wondered if he registered her quick intake of breath when she saw the menu prices, since it was then he made a point of assuring her it was his treat. She accepted readily, a teeny bit guilty but mostly grateful not to have to spend her own, limited funds.

Once they'd caught up on what was happening in their current lives, they spent the rest of dinner recounting old times. By the time they'd finished the food, the Prosecco before and the bottle of red during, it was as though they'd been together just days before, not years. The last of the food had been cleared away, the crumbs swept from the tablecloth, and the waiter had delivered two glasses of grappa, on the house. The clear, bright liquid warmed Sarah's esophagus all the way down to her stomach.

"Do you remember when we were playing hide and seek in the woods, and we discovered Alberto and Elizabetta going at it behind some bushes?" Carlo asked her.

"How could I forget? But as I recall, it was *you* who discovered them. Then you hauled Lily and me over to have a look. What an eye-opener that was—literally!" Sarah dissolved into giggles. "It took me weeks to get Lily to ask you about the mechanics of an erection."

"It was you behind that question? God, I was embarrassed."

"You never did answer it properly."

"Can you blame me?"

"No, but it was disappointing all the same."

Carlo smiled at her fondly. "It's great to see you again. Why has it been so long since you've come to visit? England's not so far away."

Sarah paused. She'd been happy, chatting about their carefree childhood days. "Oh, well. Hmm. I wasn't in England these past few years. I was much farther afield."

"Someplace interesting?"

"I guess, sort of." Go on, she told herself. Stop acting as though you're hiding a criminal past. "I was in Indonesia."

Carlo raised his eyebrows. "That counts as interesting. What were you doing there?"

I was painting, she thought. *And then I wasn't. I was loved, and then I wasn't.* As she thought about it, she felt a booze-induced desire to let her story out. Maybe she shouldn't have had so much wine. "It was part of a misguided relationship with a man who was definitely not good for me." She smiled weakly and shrugged as though it were of little consequence. "It's a long story. A boring one."

"Love stories are never boring." Carlo smiled indulgently. "And I'm not in a hurry."

Carlo always had liked to hear all the dirt. Sarah loosened up in the glow of his encouragement. "It started back when I was a student at the Royal Academy. I had this professor, Roger, for a sculpture class."

"Is this a classic student-seduction story?"

"Spot on. Pathetic, when I think back on it. He was fifteen years my senior, a respected if not wildly successful sculptor, and I was flattered by his attention."

"Of course."

"Just why do we fall for that? There were loads of girls keen on him."

Carlo sighed. "I sometimes wish I could be a university professor."

"Whose side are you on in this story?"

"Yours. But I can't help feeling a bit of envy."

"That's the only thing to envy about Roger. He was a very patient seducer, I'll give him that. It didn't feel like seduction at all, it felt like a natural evolution. He took me under his wing, introduced me to gallery owners who could help me establish myself, took me out to dinner but not too often, and ended those evenings with a gallantly light kiss on the cheek."

"Maybe it really was just a natural evolution."

Sarah frowned. "You say that only because you don't know Roger."

"It's true, I don't know him. So what happened next?"

Sarah had another sip of grappa. Now that she'd started, she was relishing telling the tale. It felt like lancing a boil, the pressure releasing as the gunk squished out.

"After a couple of months of this treatment," she continued, "I actually found myself trying to persuade him to let me come up to his flat one evening. Which he let me do, of course. And once I was there, he let me do a lot more, with feigned reluctance and appropriately sensitive questions as to whether or not I was really sure."

Carlo nodded. "That was clever of him."

Sarah eyed him. "You're not taking this in for your own education, are you?"

He held up his hands in defence. "No, no. My mother raised me better than that. It's just interesting, that's all, how the final move was your doing but you still consider yourself seduced."

"Hmph. That's how cunningly he constructed the whole situation, and how beautifully I fell right into it."

"How did you get from his bed to Indonesia?"

"Somehow everything became more complicated after we started sleeping together."

At that, Carlo actually laughed. "You know that's often the case, right?"

Sarah waved his truth away. "Very funny. But the thing is, in this case, Roger didn't want just a physical conquest. He's the kind of man who goes for total control. I moved in with him almost right away, at his suggestion. My family all detested him, even Lily, but their disapproval only made me more determined to stay with him. I had the idea that by doing so I was establishing my independence from them."

Carlo nodded. Also often the case, Sarah figured he was thinking to himself.

"Predictably, I fell into an even bigger dependency on him and on his approval. I'd enjoyed some initial success with the galleries he'd introduced me to, but then he started to deliberately undermine my confidence with little suggestions and comments here and there."

"Such as?"

"He'd look at a series of paintings I'd done and say things like they were failing to show progress, or maybe weren't quite up to the impact of some earlier work."

"Was it true?"

The simplicity of Carlo's question stopped Sarah cold. "Well, I don't know," she snapped, piqued. "Maybe, once or twice. But he was my lover—he was supposed to encourage me."

"And instead he acted the professor, accustomed to criticize."

"Yes. It was very unnerving, especially since he knew I wanted his approval so much."

"Is that when you ran off to Indonesia? To escape him?"

"Um, no." Sarah paused. The retelling was not going quite as she'd envisioned it. "Indonesia was his idea. We went together as an adventure. He took an extended sabbatical. It was supposed to be someplace completely different and inspiring, to make us both feel renewed and unstressed."

"Oh. But I'm guessing it didn't go any better there."

"Not for me, no. While we were there he kept up the criticisms until I stopped painting altogether."

Carlo cocked his head, trying to understand. Not saying anything.

Sarah rushed to her own defence. "It's hard to explain, how insidious his approach was. He was a great manipulator who knew me inside out, knew all the right buttons to push. Besides, he did other things once he had me safely in the islands and completely dependent on him, worse things."

"What could be worse than stopping you from doing what you love?"

"Why do you keep asking me such difficult questions?" Sarah demanded. She wanted him to nod his head and reassure her that she was right to feel betrayed, that Roger was a dick, that she'd been badly treated. She hadn't anticipated that he might see it any other way.

"I'm just saying what comes into my head as I listen to you. Should I be quiet?"

Sarah sighed. "No, no, don't be quiet. It's just hard to explain how it really was, to someone who wasn't involved."

"Of course."

"He appeared at our door one day with a very young island girl, a mere teenager, who was seven months pregnant. He told me calmly that the child was his, and that he felt obliged to take responsibility for his actions so she was coming to live with us."

"Ahh," Carlo acknowleged, nodding. "That one's bad. He didn't expect you to accept it, did he?"

"I don't know what he thought."

"He wanted you out, but wanted it to be your idea."

"You think so?"

"It's what a man who dislikes conflict would do."

"Maybe he didn't want to pay my airfare home. In the end I took the little money I had and used it all to get back to England, so I suppose he got what he wanted right to the last."

Carlo sat looking at her as though trying to figure something out. "You know, I never thought of you as being so easily manipulated. You were strong willed when we were children."

Sarah snorted. "Surprise! I always thought I was strong, too. Isn't it amazing what people do for love?"

"Even bad love."

"Especially bad love."

"But that's all in the past now. You're starting fresh here in Italy. You're painting again, you have a job, you have your own place."

"Exactly," Sarah jumped in eagerly. "Especially after having been back in my parents' place again for months after getting back to England. Gran giving me the house is a terrific chance to finally be truly independent."

"I'm glad for you."

Except, a small voice inside Sarah nagged, that you're not being very independent at all. You're living with Luke in Florence and he's living with you in Guzzano, and the only reason you're not with him right now is because he's gone away on business. Isn't that the same kind of pattern you fell into with Roger, leaping in too fast and regretting it as you slowly lost yourself in his world? She shook her head to rid herself of the thought.

Sarah downed the last of her grappa and suggested it was time to go. All that drink and food had overtaken her system. She wanted her bed. Well, Luke's bed as it happened. But sleep.

Carlo drove her back to Luke's flat, pulling up to the curb and getting out to give her a hug.

"Thanks so much for dinner," she said, kissing him on both cheeks. "It was splendid to see you, even if you do ask too many hard questions."

He squeezed her hands. "It was great to catch up. Listen, some friends and I go to a good disco here most Fridays. Do you like to dance? You could join us anytime you like." He smiled. "You can bring my cousin with you if you must."

"I would like, and I will bring Luke, thanks," Sarah said. "I'll call you soon."

Walking up the stairs to the flat, she felt both lighter and heavier. The unburdening of her past had churned up silt into the previously clear stream of her life. As if it had been badly needed. But now she had one friend who was truly hers in this place full of Luke. *I can reclaim my life*, she thought. *One step at a time.*

Day 31—Highfield Residence, England

I'm not dreaming about us anymore. Why is that? Every since I moved to this place, I can't seem to conjure the dreams I had in Italy. Even when they were bad—so bad—at least you were there, as clear as day. Have you left me, darling? Did you stay in Italy when I had to come here?

I miss you terribly.

Chapter Ten

THE SUNDAY MORNING SKY was as clear and blue as the heart of a sapphire. There wasn't a wisp of cloud, just an unimaginably pure infinity. *Only the Big Hand could come up with a colour like that,* thought Sarah. *Mortal painters can only yearn and fail.* She was lying on her rock staring up at the blue jewel above, having brought her breakfast coffee up to the ridge when she saw what a spectacular day it was. The rock's familiar mineral scent wafted around her as the sun began to warm it. She let her mind wander and found that the thoughts that filled it were of Gianluca.

She'd been enjoying a respite from the dreams throughout September, caught up in her relationship with Luke and the initial novelty of her work in Florence. But when she'd returned to the house from Florence this time, with Luke still in America, a vague anxiety had crept its way back in and she'd had the meadow dream again. The bliss, the terror, the waking drenched in sweat. Why couldn't this story from the past just stay in the past and stop consuming her?

She kept thinking about how Katherine had felt here with Gianluca. Had she been at all conflicted or had she abandoned herself to her feelings? Gianluca's letter had said Katherine felt their love was predestined. Inevitable. Sarah tried to imagine the exhilaration of just letting your heart fly. Even with Roger she'd felt more as though her heart had been sucked in rather than set free. And now with Luke, though she wanted to feel swept away, what she felt was caution. How could she possibly trust her heart when it had proven to be such a bad judge of character in the past? Every time she felt a rush of that unadultered, gushing, over-the-top love for Luke—and she felt it often—some part of her caught herself and took a tiny step back. She allowed a small inner voice to find fault with their relationship, so she could rationalize that her caution was justified: the way their union felt as though it had occurred through some devilish conspiracy of fate, history and the desires of strong-willed old ladies; the way it usurped her ability to figure out who she was without the constraints of a lover; the way it took time from her painting.

Sarah rose from the rock. On the other hand, she had to admit, she felt she was being more true to herself than she had been for years. Luke was undoubtedly a good man. Yes, she was allowing herself to be loved by a good man, that was something. And her confidence was much more firmly in place than it had been. And she was successfully pursuing her painting again. Surely this was all great progress.

To help banish her worries, Sarah began to walk along the crest of the ridge. The kinder temperatures and rains of September had promoted a fresh flush of green growth over the previously parched earth, as millions of seedlings germinated. Their new-sprung shades of mint and lime provided an odd contrast to the shrubs and trees that were preparing for autumn, the first nuances of brown and gold tarnishing their tired leaves. It looked as though the earth couldn't decide just what season it was.

For over an hour Sarah walked through the countryside, regaining some serenity through the activity before turning back, her shoes leaden with clinging globs of clay. She retrieved her coffee mug from where she had abandoned it on the rock and started down the hill towards the house, studying the little building as she descended. It was nestled in its spot as it had been for a century or more, looking unquestioningly content to be where and what it was. An enviable position, Sarah felt.

The phone started ringing as she shucked off her shoes at the door and entered the house, almost as if her return had sparked it. She picked it up. "*Pronto?*"

"Sarah, my dear, you need to roll the 'r' a little more for the pronunciation to sound at all right. But I am glad you're finally answering the phone in the proper language."

"Hi, Gran. How are you?" Sarah felt her serenity slipping away.

"Much the same. What have you been up to lately?"

"Oh, the usual. Working at Santini's and painting when I'm not there."

"I don't know why you're wasting your time at that studio when you could be painting."

"I need the money, Gran. It's not interfering, I still paint."

"I could send you money, if that's what it takes to keep your focus."

That was the last thing Sarah wanted; more reasons to be under Katherine's control. "My focus is fine. The painting is coming along very well."

"Will you send me some photos of what you're doing?"

Sarah hesitated. She had started working with the dreams, but she didn't want Katherine to see that. "Sure," she said, hoping her grandmother hadn't caught the pause between question and answer. "I'll have something to show you very soon." There was no way she was sending a painting of those dreams.

"You're not having confidence issues again, are you? You do understand that you have real talent?"

"Yes, Gran."

A pause. Perhaps disbelief. "All right, then. How is Luca?"

"Luke's just fine. He's been away on business, but he's coming back later this afternoon."

"That's good. He stays there with you, when he's in Guzzano?"

"Yes. I feel a bit sorry for Annalisa: she doesn't get to see him as much as she used to, but we visit her a lot."

"It's better that Luca stays with you. It's where he belongs." Katherine exhaled slowly, a long, extended sigh. "I envy you."

"Me?"

"In the house, with him. With the paints. With all of it. I miss it so."

Was that a quavering in her voice that Sarah heard? Katherine never quavered. "Oh, Gran, I'm so sorry you can't be here. Really, the place is in wonderful shape, and everything is just perfect. I'll send you photos, including one of Luke when he gets back. Just, don't worry, I'm taking good care of everything. Thank you for everything."

"Good girl. Yes, I'm sure you are." Her voice sounded so small all of a sudden. "Bye then. Call soon."

"Bye, Gran. Love you."

Sarah hung up the phone, unnerved to have her stern, strong, never-bending grandmother sound shrunken and vulnerable. Of course Katherine must be having a terrible time imagining Sarah here, with everything the dying woman held dear. Sarah had known there was an element of obilgation, a price to pay, for having what her grandmother didn't any more. But now the burden felt much heavier.

With him, Katherine had said. Which 'him' had she meant?

◊ ◊ ◊

Luke arrived back from the States that afternoon, freshly shaved and showered from having stopped at his flat in Florence to pick up his car before travelling on to Guzzano. Despite the clean-up he looked tired from the long journey, with dark smudges under his eyes. He hugged Sarah tightly with something more like relief than vigour.

"You look knackered," she told him, running her hand through his cropped hair.

"I am kind of beat. It's a long trip." He smiled at her. "It sure feels good to see you again, though. I missed you."

Sarah kissed him. "I have a plan for your resuscitation," she said, leading him by the hand up the stairs. In the main bedroom, sunlight poured through the big window, bathing the room in a golden glow. The bed had been freshly laid with soft, white cotton sheets and on the side table was a platter with grapes and oranges piled high. Sarah led him to the edge of the bed and stopped him there, unbuttoning his shirt unhurriedly but determinedly.

"You just relax now. I'm going to pamper you a bit," she told him.

Luke gave himself over to her care. She removed his clothing gently. "Down boy," she murmured when she'd freed him from his underwear. "For now, just get into bed." She took off her own clothes and joined him, Luke sitting up against the pillows with Sarah cross-legged beside him. She brought the platter over to her lap and began peeling an orange.

"So, how was your trip—were you successful?" Sarah divided the orange into segments. It filled the air with its citrus tang.

"I think so. We hear for certain by the end of this week, but the presentation went well. I'd be surprised if we didn't get it, but you never know." He leaned closer to her. "That orange smells good."

Sarah popped a piece into his mouth and placed the platter between them. The project he had gone to Seattle to try to win was just the sort of thing he adored doing. A wealthy entrepreneur and collector of portraits wanted to establish a small gallery to make his collection available to the public and to help attract related exhibitions. He had purchased a dilapidated but interesting old building that he wanted to extensively renovate for the purpose. Sarah and Luke had discussed the project in detail as he was putting together the proposal with his boss.

"I used the colour ideas for the rooms, the way you and I talked about, and he really seemed to like that I was thinking that way," Luke told her. "I know it's not new but I'd like the chance to play with the idea myself."

"It would be a great project for you. When would it start if you get it?"

Luke frowned. "That's the not so good part. He's eager to get underway as soon as possible, so that means, realistically, detailed drawings begin right after Christmas."

"Is that a problem?"

"Only insofar as I have to be in Seattle to do them. The client wants to be highly involved in the development of the ideas."

"Oh. And how long will that part take?"

"At least a month. I need to stay with it until it's contracted and approved. The client's prepared to pay top dollar, so he expects top service."

"Hm." Sarah concentrated on picking minuscule bits of skin off her last orange segment before putting it in her mouth. She shuddered at the idea of such a prolonged absence, but she didn't want Luke to feel that she was the kind of needy girlfriend that stood in the way of a great career opportunity.

"You could come with me," said Luke. "If you could get away from Santini for a bit. There's lots of great stuff to paint there." He stroked her leg.

Sarah leaned over and kissed him without meeting his eyes. She didn't want to discuss this problem, because she could see no agreeable solution. He would have to go, and she would not be taken from the place where her painting had finally begun to blossom again. Anyway, none of it was confirmed yet; she could afford to put off thinking about it seriously until the project became a sure thing. "It's a tempting offer," she lied. "Let's see once it gets closer." She removed the platter to the side table once again and ordered him to lie down on his stomach. "It's time for a massage."

"Are you always going to greet me this way when I've been away?" came the muffled question from somewhere deep in the pillows. "I might go away more just for the pleasure of returning."

"Don't count on it," Sarah laughed. "This is a first-time special." She sat astride him just below his buttocks, her pubic hair grazing the neat muscled mounds as she warmed some oil lightly scented with rosemary into her hands to begin her massage. She started at his neck and shoulders, kneading away the stiffness of a night spent aboard an airplane, then moved down his back with strong hands, finding all the tight places and working them out.

"You're so good at this," his voice filtered out again. "You might make me fall asleep."

"You won't fall asleep, I promise." She worked her way down his entire body, along his legs and on to his feet, admiring the beauty of his body as she moved her hands upon it. When she had gone over every inch, she sat astride him again and began once more, this time touching him softly and alternating her touches with light kisses. She ran a hard nipple down the length of his back, then drew her finger up the inside of his thigh and lightly stroked what she discovered at the apex. A small groan escaped him.

"OK, I'm not falling asleep," he mumbled.

"Told you." She rolled him over again. His eyes were closed, his face soft with drowsiness, but a full erection told a different story. She positioned herself above it, letting it press against her as she massaged either side of his skull. Again she worked over him until, finally, she lowered herself onto him, savouring the feel of him inside her and of her power over their movement, controlling the build until they lay spent and sated.

Within minutes, Luke was fast asleep. Sarah crept out of bed without disturbing him, smiling to herelf.

An hour later, she revived him with a pot of tea and they went out into what was left of the day. They ambled across the meadow, breathing deeply of grassy air and pausing to take in the view as the sun crept towards the horizon. Luke turned to Sarah and folded her in his arms, pressing her head against his chest. In the warmth of his embrace, as she nestled into the rhythm of his heartbeat, Sarah found herself willing him not to explode. The sudden realization that her dream had snuck into reality made her start, pulling her head abruptly away from him.

A tiny "Oh", surprised and uncertain, slipped from her lips.

"Sarah," Luke said. "What's the matter?" He brought her face up with his hand, kissed her softly on the mouth. A reassurance and a question.

She looked into his eyes, which were definitely not Gianluca's. "I," she began, then faltered, trying to find uncrazy words. "I had a little flashback. To a dream. Well, a nightmare actually. It was just, I don't know, sudden. And unexpected."

"What happened in the dream?"

You exploded, she thought. And then realized, *No, not Luke. Gianluca. I was being embraced by my grandmother's former lover and he exploded.* There was no way she was going to say that.

"I don't think I want to go there right now. Let's keeping walking," she said, starting off again.

Luke took her hand, matching his stride to hers. "Was the dream about me?"

"No." Sarah could feel herself retreating inwards. She wasn't sure, actually. Dream and reality hadn't crossed paths before. She wanted to assimilate this new thing before talking about it.

"Sarah, I'm real and I love you. No nightmare here."

She squeezed his hand. "I know."

"Sometimes you're kinda hard to figure out. Gung ho, then cautious. Does it have to do with what your sister was talking to me about? Pricks in your past?"

Sarah nodded.

"I'm not a prick. You know that, right?"

"Yes, I know that." Out of the corner of her eye she could see he was looking at her. She kept her eyes on the ground in front of her as silence hung about them, but the rising tension made her break it. "I feel, sometimes, that we've jumped ahead very quickly. It's taking a little while for me to accept that it's OK. My head has to catch up with my heart."

Luke put his arm around her. She could sense his relief that she was talking about it. *How confused he must be*, she thought. *I greet him with passion, then turn away at the memory of a nightmare.* There was no explaining it in any way that sounded reasonable.

"I guess we have gone fast," Luke said. "I hadn't thought about it, because it felt good to me. And, frankly, somewhat beyond my control. You know, kinda irresistible."

"Mmhm." Irresistible. The same word Katherine had used. That was exactly what was spooking her. She slipped her arm around his waist, solid and warm and real. "I'm sure my head will come around," she said, not at all convinced.

◊ ◊ ◊

On a lake of crystalline blue surrounded by steeply sloping, wooded hills, a small boat floated undirected in its course. Sarah lay in the bottom on velvet cushions and a blanket of softest down, moaning with unrestrained pleasure as Gianluca's mouth pulled and teased at her breasts. Her body was in the grip of an erotic fever, every nerve ending bristling. When her lover moved his mouth to the warm, wet place between her legs she cried out at the intensity of it. Her body felt it would burst and yet the feeling went on, until he entered her with all the force of a waterfall dropping from a great height, liquid and beautiful, bruising and unstoppable.

A wisp of awareness threaded its way in: she was dreaming. But the pleasure was so great she let herself slip back into it. Gianluca's thrusting rocked the little boat, sending waves along the water to match the waves that coursed through her body. After, they lay still in each other's arms, the only sound the gentle lapping of water at the sides of the boat. The sun's rays heated Sarah's exposed arm and breast with a pleasant warmth and she was aware of a slight scent of rosemary and olive oil rising from Gianluca's dark hair as it rested against her cheek.

Gently, the craft bumped up against a pebbly shore. They floated from their places; Sarah's bare feet touched the shore's cool, slippery stones. She turned and saw Gianluca now sitting, oars in hand and dressed in a military uniform, waving goodbye to her. The sun disappeared before a swirling fog that enveloped the boat and pulled it away, so that in moments she could no longer see it at all. Lost and alone on a barren shore, she called out to him and heard nothing but the start of a wind, a sound she recognized and had come to dread. A familiar panic seized her and she called louder, knowing it was fruitless but feeling compelled to scream his name into the rising gale.

Hands grasped her shoulders and she awoke in mid-cry to find Luke shaking her gently to pull her from her nightmare. She fell against him, sobbing as he held her in his arms and comforted her. She buried her face in his chest, clinging to the flesh and blood of a real man. Her man. Not the ephemeral and cruelly vanishing touch of a nocturnal phantom who refused to be forgotten.

As Luke slumbered on in some jet-lagged time zone of his own the next morning, Sarah rose with the sun and slipped out of bed. Let in the cat, feed the cat, put the coffee on, make Nutella toast. Her morning routines helped her feel rooted back in the here and now.

She sat curled up in the big chair, stroking Beppe absent-mindedly on her lap, and thought about what had happened in the night. A new dream. Gianluca invading again. And she had been so glad to see him, to feel him. Until the fog had swallowed him up.

What had Luke heard? Had she been moaning with pleasure? Had he only awoken to her screams? Had Gianluca's name been audible, or had her screams been the muffled moans of the tortured sleeper? She wanted to know just how much she was going to have to explain when he got up. He'd asked nothing of her in the night. He'd held her and stroked her hair, comforting her as though she were a small child, until his hand had slowed and he'd fallen back into his own leaden sleep. It had taken her a while longer.

She heard his feet thumping down the hallway upstairs and got up to make him a coffee. It seemed the least she could do after making him wake up to a hysteric in the middle of the night. A hysteric who'd just made incredible love with someone else. Even if it was only a dream, an aura of guilt clung to the memory.

"Morning," he mumbled, still groggy, and kissed her lightly. He had the rumpled look of somebody moving several hours ahead of his body clock, wandering around the kitchen on autopilot to get his cereal. Sarah waited until he'd settled himself at the table, brought him his coffee, and sat opposite him. She was glad he didn't seem too sharp.

"That was a helluva night," he said.

"Yeah. Sorry. Was I actually screaming?"

Luke sipped his coffee and nodded. "Oh yeah. Clear as a bell. Gianluca."

"Oh."

"You going to tell me what it was about?"

Sarah studied him. He looked so dependable, so non-judgmental. As well as groggy. Maybe she should try. "It's pretty weird."

"Dreams are always weird. Who's Gianluca?"

"Your great-uncle."

"*That* Gianluca?" Luke looked more awake now. "Why were you dreaming about him?"

"I've been wondering that myself. It's been happening ever since I first moved here. I didn't know who he was, at first."

"You're right. It's weird."

"Mhmm—well—that's not all. Apparently he was Gran's adulterous lover, here in this house, before the war."

Luke closed his eyes for a moment, mulling over the news before opening them again. "Well, that's an interesting bit of family history I never knew. When did Katherine tell you?"

Sarah studied the grain of the kitchen table, wondering how to explain everything without sounding crazy. "She didn't. That's what's so strange about it. I started having the dreams when I first moved in, before I even knew there was a Gianluca, let alone an affair. Then I saw his photograph at Annalisa's and realized that's who I'd been dreaming about."

"You'd seen the photo before, obviously, but just didn't remember," he suggested. "But how did you find out about their affair?"

"I discovered some love letters from him to her, hidden at the back of the pantry drawer. The drawer fell out, and there they were. As though they were begging to be found."

"I don't think letters are able to do that. But, anyway. Wow."

"It was a really big deal, their romance. Not just some summer bonking but a major love affair that only ended because of the war."

"No wonder Katherine was so crazy about this place."

"Yes, exactly," Sarah said, relieved to be sharing at last. "It's as though their love was so strong it left an atmosphere in the house that's pervasive. Not like a ghost, but maybe like a force, a sentiment that's floating around waiting for my mind to grab a hold of it from time to time. And so images come to me in my sleep. From him."

"You really believe that?" The skepticism in his face was clear. Sarah felt her relief fade. He wouldn't understand. Who would?

"Well, I know it's not exactly an everyday occurrence, but I think it might be possible, you know, by telepathy or something."

"He's dead," Luke pointed out. "How can he be telepathic?"

Sarah shrugged. "Maybe thoughts hang around for a while."

"Fifty years?"

"All right, so it's not a perfect theory, but I can't think of any other explanation," she snapped, her irritation rising at his inability to imagine something she had come to think of as plausible. She forgot he'd had no time at all to get used to the idea.

Luke looked at her, chewing his cereal. Thinking. "What happens in the dreams?" he asked.

Of course it would get to this; she'd known it would, and yet now that he'd asked, all she could do was flush beet red and stammer. She was sure she was giving herself away completely. "Well," she began, searching for a neutral tone, "they start off romantic. A nice feeling." She looked away, anywhere but Luke's eyes. Did he sense how much she was hiding? Better get to the part he actually heard last night. "Then there's a sudden shift, it happens fast. He explodes, or he disappears, and I'm helpless to do anything."

"That's when you start screaming."

"Yes. It's not just his disappearance. The emotion of it is so strong, it's like a deep, deep keening. I've never felt anything as terrible in real life."

"Maybe he represents something."

Sarah sighed. He was really not going to get it, she could see that now. No one was going to get it. "It doesn't feel like that at all. He isn't of my psyche. He invades my psyche."

"Well, you know, they're your dreams, so you must have made him up, really. Don't you think?"

"No, I don't. But I can't explain it in any way that would be believable."

Luke reached across the table and put his hand over hers, squeezing. "Hey, Sarah, I'm trying to understand. But from outside your head, it seems that if you've dreamt about him, it's probably because you saw his photo at some earlier time and it appealed to you enough to stick in your mind. You said yourself it was a very compelling picture. Then, when you moved to this house, your subconscious remembered his face and put him into your dreams."

Luke's calm tenacity, the way he hung onto his rational view, was frustrating Sarah more than she wanted to let it.

"Mhmm," she mumbled without even trying for conviction.

"Maybe now that we've talked about the dreams it'll help them go away."

"Maybe." She didn't believe that for a second. And she realized—a horrid thought—that in a way she didn't actually want them to go away. Despite the terror, the sweetness and passion of their beginnings was addictive. In her dreams, she felt with an intensity she'd never allowed in her waking life.

She squashed the thought. "Anyway," she said with forced lightness, "something good may come of them. I've started to paint the dreams and they make really good material. I've got a couple of canvases going, but with the layering and veiling they take a long time to complete. They're more complex than my landscape studies."

"Seems like a tough way to get your inspiration, but I guess it beats cutting off your ear or something."

"Fortunately I haven't gone completely mad, yet."

"Can I see the ones you've started?"

"Seems the least I can do if I'm going to wake you in the night with my inspiration," she said as she got up from the table. They went into the studio where the two paintings were bathed in the soft, cool light of an autumn morning. The first painting, which was further along, showed two abstract but still discernable naked, pale figures from directly above, clutching each other in a swirl of darkness that started black nearest their bodies and became a lighter bluey-purple at the edges of the maelstrom, sky and ground merging. There were places where the bright points of shining stars showed through vaguely as an underpainting, but in other places they had been obliterated by darkness. If Luke was surprised to see that by 'romantic' Sarah had skirted around the obvious sexualy intimacy of the dreams, he didn't let on.

The second canvas was barely started, with a sketch of what looked like a woman prone and rigid on the ground, viewed from the level of the grass so that she dominated the foreground. Something encased her and a tiny figure could be seen in the distance. Some of the undercolours had been laid down, including the sky. Sarah explained what it was to be.

"You see here, this woman, she's partially encased by a plaster cast, like a statue, that is pinning her to the ground. And this figure here disappears into the woods. The whole tone will be darker, more like the other one, by the time I get all the layers down."

"You use the same sky colour as Katherine used in all her paintings upstairs, and the one in the kitchen," he observed.

"Yeah, I noticed that right away, it's part of the weirdness. I mixed that colour myself, using Gran's pigments, the first week I was here and before seeing her work. At first it creeped me out to realize it was the same and then I thought maybe she'd showed me, when I was young, how to create it because the sky does look like that occasionally in these parts."

"It's a beautiful colour."

"Yes. Although it's rare in real life, in the dreams the sky always looks like that." Sarah stopped abruptly, suddenly aware of something so obvious she wondered how she could have missed it up until now.

She rushed from the room to the kitchen and looked at the painting there. A meadow, filled with flowers. But not just a meadow; it was the very beginning of that dream, before it turned ugly. Sarah had been focused on the scary parts so intently, she hadn't even noticed that this scene reflected the very beginning of the dream. The same picnic elements were there, the same blanket. How could she not have seen that? She ran upstairs, with Luke following her at a calmer pace, and pulled the other paintings out of the cupboard, lining them up hurriedly against the wall. These she hadn't seen since the day in the summer she had first taken them out but, as she looked at them afresh, she was astounded. There were the two other dreams she'd had. One showed lovers on the terrace at the start of their embrace, but from a normal human angle rather than above, with part of the house apparent. The other had them together in the little boat. In all three of her representations of the dreams, Katherine had rendered moments that came early on. The sweet parts. And Sarah, in her obsession with the darker side, hadn't even recognized them.

Sarah stared at the paintings dumbly as Luke put his arm around her shoulders. "What is it you're seeing here?" he asked her.

"They're the same dreams." Her voice was thin. "These are my Gran's paintings of them. They're scenes that come earlier on than the ones I've been painting, but they're absolutely part of the same dreams."

"Come on, Sarah. How could that be possible?"

"I don't know, but I'm sure of it. I thought I was only borrowing Gran's leading man, but it's the whole dream. All of them. Maybe she's sending them to me somehow, or maybe they're here in the house, just, I don't know, hanging around or something, and now that she's gone I'm receiving them instead."

Luke was silent for a moment, then he spoke quietly, as though calming a nervous animal. "Let's consider another possible explanation. You saw the work your grandmother did and the images from her paintings suggested themselves to you in your sleep, the same way the photo of Gianluca made you think of him as the subject. So parts of what you dream are what you've seen in these paintings, and the rest your own head makes up." He put his arm around her and drew her tight, kissing the top of her head.

Sarah remained looking at the paintings. "You're probably right," she said dully after a while. Now she knew for sure he would never understand.

She felt as though her mind had been taken hostage. It had been scary enough when she had believed she was connecting with passing emotions as they floated through the atmosphere of the place. Now that she thought entire dreams were being fed into her brain, it was far more frightening. How could she fight against it? What did Gianluca want? Where would it stop? And yet, while these thoughts roared around her head, another wound through them: the knowledge that she wanted Gianluca to keep visiting her. She'd somehow shifted from total dread to a disquieting yearning for his presence and what he made her feel.

She picked the paintings up in silence, putting them back into the depths of the cupboard as though she might be able to lock the dreams themselves in with them, then she shut the door emphatically and turned towards the bathroom.

"We'd better start getting ready if we're going to get into Florence this morning," she said to Luke. For the first time since she'd moved in, she felt in a hurry to leave.

Day 32—Highfield Residence, England

The sun is shining here this morning and it's reminding me of our bicycle rides together. You oiled up the old bicycle in the shed of my house, and fixed the tires, so we could pedal around together. How slowly you had to go for me! I wasn't conditioned for those hills the way you were, riding everywhere on that old black thing you magically kept functioning with wire and string. You were very clever about keeping things working with little but your wits. Repairing bicycles and tractors, that loose shutter, the banging pipe for the kitchen faucet.

I loved watching you do those things. Your hands were big and strong but worked delicately, as though the motor or whatever were some tender living thing that required a careful touch. I didn't watch anyone work with their hands in England. When things broke my father called someone to fix it, and James did the same. It wasn't something one watched, it just got done.

Chapter Eleven

IN SANTINI'S STUDIO, the new piece Sarah had been given to restore provided a welcome distraction from fretting about the dreams. In front of her was a late-nineteenth-century painting of modest size and sentimental style that mimicked earlier masters while adding some then-popular twists of its own. It was called 'Coming Home' and it showed a huntsman, dead rabbits slung over his shoulder, returning at sunset to his little cottage and the greetings of his stout wife and three small children: the kind of bucolic pastoral scene that romanticized country life and ignored the realities of subsistence living. Although it wasn't valuable, having been painted by a long-forgotten, second-tier artist, Sarah was drawn to its unapologetic sentiment of love and belonging. Nobody was questioning their emotions in this painting or working themselves up over the past. The tender expressions of the subjects revealed themselves more fully as Sarah cleaned them.

They looked far happier to be reunited than her family had ever been at the end of a day. Perhaps it was the thought of rabbit stew, more than the sight of Papa. Still, they were smiling. What Sarah remembered most about her own homecoming as she was growing up was a faint tension. The family always took the evening meal together, where Sarah and Lily would submit to a ritual interrogation about their days. She supposed her parents had meant it as a way of keeping in touch with their growing daughters, but judgment always hung in the air like a dim electric thrum, making the conversation something to be endured rather than enjoyed. It occurred to her now that when she had moved in with Roger things hadn't changed much. It wasn't until near the end of their time together that Sarah had begun to notice the same tone in his voice, an expectation of disappointment, when he asked her what she had been doing for the day. Had it always been like that? She couldn't remember whether she had seamlessly gone from anticipating unfavourable judgment from her father to her lover, or if she had managed a period of self-esteem in between.

As she thought about it, Sarah's mind began to stray back into the dangerous territory of her long-sought independence. She had given herself very little opportunity to come home only to herself and to her own judgments of her day. She had intended to do so indefinitely when she'd moved to Guzzano, then Luke had appeared and she'd found herself once again encountering someone else many evenings. Not that Luke was judgmental. Maybe he was a bit obstinate in his own opinions about things, but who wasn't? His refusal to accept her theories about the dreams was as close as they had come to a real disagreement.

Still, she knew his presence resulted in myriad tiny shifts in her behaviour each day. They were minor adjustments in favour of increased compatibility: an inclination to dredge up a bigger smile than she might have felt, to subdue an irritation, to engage in conversation when she might have preferred silence. She had abandoned these minuscule particles of herself without thinking, discarded them as easily as the flakes of dead skin she scrubbed off in the shower each morning and sent swirling down the drain to oblivion. But now, as she contemplated her interrupted autonomy, she began to see in each small compromise the loss of something more important. Perhaps, after all, it wasn't possible to be independent and still be involved with someone. Perhaps those two desires actually were mutually exclusive, and she had been deluding herself in thinking she was setting her own course, free of restrictions. God knows, she had deluded herself before.

Then there was the house. Sarah looked at the one in the painting, a benign little cottage with nothing odd or foreboding about it. Hers was supposed to have been the same: a haven, a settling place. But now she felt less at home there than ever, the way the strange forces within it kept intruding into her thoughts.

She felt as though in accepting the house, she had unwittingly agreed to take on a burden of the past that wouldn't leave it. It was still very much Katherine and Gianluca's place, not hers. She couldn't even have her own dreams there, for god's sake.

Somehow Luke, the house, the dreams, and Katherine and Gianluca's love were all linked. Morettis bound to the women who lived in the house, each in their generation, and the women bound in return. In coming to this place, to what she'd thought was a clean canvas on which she could paint her own, true story, she had stumbled into a scene already set, with obligations, expectations and historical baggage that crowded and threatened her barely renascent sense of self. Maybe she had been wrong to come here.

No. Stop.

Coming to Guzzano was, at least, something about which she could be certain. If she hadn't come to Italy she would still be in her parents' home and feeling lower than ever. Sarah struggled to get herself back to a more positive frame of mind. So she'd had a few dreams that seemed to be linked to some that Katherine had years ago. She supposed that was possible; she'd heard of shared consciousness before, and she and her grandmother did have a strong bond. And so what if her lover was another Moretti? With both Luke and her having backgrounds that involved Guzzano, it was natural enough for them to have met, by coincidence. He was a good man, she could see that. It wasn't his fault she was feeling obsessed with the need to seize control of a life that always seemed to be wandering off the course she tried to set for it.

Perhaps all this doubt was only due to not having been active enough in constructing her own new life here in Italy. It was her style to let things happen to her, and she knew she was better off when she took more action.

Racking her brain for just what kind of action she could take, she only managed to come up with the idea of calling Carlo and inviting herself to the disco that Friday. She'd bring Luke, of course, because she'd want to dance with him. Yes, that could work. It was about time she took the lead and organized a night out with her friends instead of his.

"Do you remember me telling you I'd gone out to dinner when you were away, with one of your innumerable distant cousins?" Sarah asked Luke at dinner that evening, back in his apartment.

"Yeah, with Carlo. I think I know which one he is. The one time I met him he was kind of gangly and pimply."

"He's not at all that way any more. In fact, he's rather handsome."

"Well, it's always better to go to dinner with someone good-looking. So much more appetizing."

Sarah could see he was holding back a smirk. She ignored his failure to rise to her feeble attempt to make him jealous. "He mentioned that he goes with some friends of his to a dance club here in Florence most Fridays, and I thought it would be fun to join them."

"Sure, that'd be great. Which one?"

"Il Shock, I think he said."

"Oh, it's good, that one. I used to go all the time last year, until it got too hot to think about anything that energetic. I don't know why it's never occurred to me to suggest it myself, before this."

It was oddly dissatifying to find that, although it had been her idea to go, it was already 'his' club. Sarah knew it was silly and petty to want to retain ownership of a suggestion, but it irked her all the same. Could she not lead in this relationship just once? And who had he gone with 'all the time' last year? They never discussed his previous girlfriends. Would they run into one of them there?

"Great," she said, although she wasn't feeling nearly as great about it as she'd expected to.

◊ ◊ ◊

When Friday came, Sarah and Luke walked to the disco. It wasn't far and the evening was fine. Down their narrow, cobbled street they strolled arm in arm, past rows of motorini and cars parked fender to fender in their precious spots, the cafés and shops shut, their shutters pulled down and locked for the night. In the narrow slit of sky overhead between the buildings, stars twinkled. A scooter roared past, its tinny sound ricocheting in the narrow space before quiet settled on them again.

From this relative peace, they opened a thick wooden door and entered the throbbing atmosphere of the dance club. Coloured neon lights pierced the gloom and Sarah could see that the dance floor, which was huge, was jammed with people moving to the beat of techno music pounding loudly enough to make her rib cage shake. She looked to her right and saw Carlo standing up at a table next to the dance floor, beckoning them to join.

The two men shook hands and clasped each other's shoulders. With Carlo was another stylishly dressed man and two young women, one peroxided blonde and the other brunette. They were squeezed into body-conscious dresses so tight that the curve of their ample breasts popped above the low necklines like apples bobbing to the surface in a water-filled barrel, and every subtle shift of their butt muscles could be detected even in the dim light. Sarah had thought her own sheath dress was revealing but she felt dowdy by comparison. Introductions were made all around—Tomaso was the other guy, Stella the blonde and Gabriella the dark-haired girl—then conversation more or less died against the volume of the music. It was dancing people came here for, not chatting.

Sarah ordered vodka and tonic. The other women had drinks the colour of tropical sunsets and adorned with small paper umbrellas. After a few fortifying gulps of her own, pure, colourless drink she got up to dance with Luke. She knew he was a great dancer just from the bit he'd twirled her around at home when he'd put something he loved on the stereo. In the club he showed he could dance to anything, his movement fluid and looking the way his voice sounded, sexy and hot. Sometimes he would dance in his own space, then he'd take her hand and move her around with him, effortlessly incorporating her into his rhythm even in the cramped space, lending her his gracefulness for a suspended moment. When the music slowed, he took her in his arms, holding her close but separate, their bodies brushing against one another tantalizingly. In those moments she felt as though they existed in a bubble, apart from the crowd, filled with their own music and moving like a single being.

The others were also up on the dance floor. They danced alternately with one another and on their own, returning to the table frequently for refreshments. Before long, Carlo took an opportunity to break in on Luke and dance with Sarah, leaving Luke to join up with Stella. The music slowed again and Carlo held Sarah discreetly, complimenting her on her dress in his most charming Italian way.

"Those girls you have with you tonight," Sarah began carefully, "are they your regular dates?"

"Regular enough, but nothing you'd take seriously. They just like a good time," Carlo said. "They're fun to dance with and generous later."

It was so straightforward. Sarah couldn't remember a time when she had ever been that casual. She might fall fast, but she didn't fall easily. She glanced over at Luke and was astonished to see Stella's hands groping his buttocks, thrusting her pelvis towards him and trying to establish contact as she gyrated to the beat. Luke had his hands on her hips and was holding hold her off while laughing unselfconsciously at her efforts. Although he was not responding to her in kind, neither did he appear at all to mind. Quite the opposite. He was having a great time being accosted.

Carlo followed Sarah's eyes. "I told you they were good-time girls," he said, smiling. "She's a bit drunk, and pretty forward to begin with. But harmless."

"Uh-huh," Sarah said doubtfully. Latin versus Anglo-Saxon—there really was a difference. Suddenly in need of a drink, she told Carlo she wanted to take a break and returned to the table.

When Luke came soon after to sit beside her again, Stella sat across from them and rolled her eyes at Sarah. "Such a sexy man you have," she said, her breast jiggling as she giggled. Sarah tried to smile and took another sip of her drink, uncertain whether she wanted to down the whole thing at once or throw it at Stella's amazing cleavage. She knew she was being peevish. Luke was kissing her ear and obviously not interested in Stella. So why did this bouncy girl make her feel so insecure?

As the evening progressed, the dancing became looser and the girls even more tipsy. Sarah herself was beyond her limit but not quite teetering as she went to the ladies' room, only to find herself side by side at the sink with Stella.

"Where did you find him?" asked the girl. "He's so gorgeous and such a smooth dancer."

Sarah looked at her in the mirror. In the light of the bathroom, Stella's makeup was more evident, the skin beneath it uneven, her eyes more tired. "He found me," Sarah answered. "My house in the country is close to his great-aunt's." She washed her hands quickly, not wanting to linger.

"Lucky you. Is he as good in bed as he is on the dance floor?"

"Uh. Hm. Not your business," she stuttered.

The girl shrugged. "Then I guess you wouldn't consider a trade for tonight."

Sarah snorted in surprise. "Certainly not!"

Raising an eyebrow, Stella set her eyes on Sarah with an appraising look. "He must be good, then." She laughed and turned on her heel.

When Sarah returned to the table, Stella had started the process of winding Carlo up for the evening's finale, her hand stroking his chest, her head moving in close. Clearly, the evening was coming to a close. Sarah said hasty goodbyes, not wanting to watch this part, and hustled Luke out into the street.

"Wow," he said, "you're in a big hurry all of a sudden. Should I be pleased about that?"

Sarah punched him half mockingly and half seriously on the arm. "Didn't you get enough with that blonde tart humping your thigh on the dance floor?"

"Stella, yeah, she'd had a bit too much to drink. Not quite my type, but she tries hard."

"She asked me in the ladies' room if I'd consider a trade for the night," Sarah said, still miffed. "She wanted to know if you were good in bed."

At this, Luke laughed out loud. "A trade? That's a helluva thought. Her charms fell a bit short, I think." He put on a sober face. "I gather, since you're here with me and all, you turned down her proposal."

"Brilliant deduction."

"But how did you answer her other question?" he persisted.

"What other question?"

"You know—did you tell her I'm good?" By now he was grinning broadly.

"Luke Moretti, that is such a stupid male thing to say!" she rebuked him, not nearly as harshly as she'd meant to. He danced in front of her, caught her by the waist and pulled her to him, kissing her until her legs began to melt.

"OK, so you are," she admitted when he finally gave her a moment to breathe.

He nuzzled her neck. "Ha," he murmured into her ear. "I knew it. Let's go home and make sure you're right."

◇ ◇ ◇

Sarah stood looking up at the imposing cliff before them and wondered how they were going to get up its sheer, ragged face. She looked behind her to cool, pine-scented woods. She remembered, dimly, a clearing, and mossy ground, and lovemaking. Now, on their way home, this cliff had appeared.

He stood behind her, his arms wrapped around her, his breath warm on her neck as he whispered in her ear. "I must go," he said, and Sarah gasped in surprise at the sound not of Gianluca's rolling Italian murmurs but of Luke's low voice. She whirled to look at him but he scrambled up the cliff as fast as a phantom, his image wispy and indistinct so she couldn't know which one it was.

A small, brown dog of indeterminate breed, who had until now been sitting patiently at her feet, started to bark wildly. Sarah left him to run in circles as she started up the rock in pursuit, of whom she wasn't sure but she knew she had to reach him. Her strength was extraordinary as she hauled herself up, her nails broken and bleeding from each tenuous handhold, her skin stinging with scratches from thorny shrubs she encountered as she climbed. As she neared the top the sky turned a foreboding shade of deep purple-blue and the unmistakable low howling of the wind made the hair on the back of her neck stand on end. She clambered over the top and stood up. Katherine's flowered dress had materialized on her body and it swirled around her as she searched the encroaching darkness for signs of Gianluca or Luke. Behind her was the daunting cliff she'd just scaled. Before her was a dense wood of dark conifers and the matted undergrowth of brambles: how could she penetrate that? There was no indication that anyone else had forged a way in; there was no indication that anyone but she had been up there at all. Far below, the frantic barking of the dog continued.

The urge to scream began to well up in her as it always did at this point in the dreams, a visceral response to the sense of abandonment and loss. It started as a hard knot in the pit of her stomach and swelled to encompass her entire body in an inconsolable ache. But screams were futile, she knew by now. She collapsed in a heap and began instead to weep, the pain seeping out of her in a river of tears until she finally awoke, a still, fetal ball of sadness.

She awoke without moving. She was back in Guzzano, had been back for days now, with Luke in Florence, alone in her bed in the house that wouldn't forget. For a long time she continued to lie there, curled up and still, her tears drying on her face. The passage from dream to reality had brought with it little relief. She waited, defeated, for exhaustion to pull her back into a sleep she hoped was black and dreamless.

Chapter Twelve

ᴸILY, FINALLY FLUSH ENOUGH to go halves with Sarah on a cheap flight to Italy, breezed in the front door as soon as Sarah had retrieved her from the airport, dumped her bag in the hallway, and went straight to the studio.

"Wow, Sarah, very impressive," she enthused. "I don't think I've ever seen you in better form. These paintings really pull you in to study them, they're so intriguing." Three finished canvases of Sarah's dreams were lined up against the far wall. A fourth painting, lacking only some final veiling, sat on an easel. "A bit menacing, that's the feeling I get from them. Is it what you meant to convey? You could call the series 'The Scary Side of Passion'."

"They are meant to be a bit menacing, like being on the verge of going from light to darkness." Sarah ran a hand lightly across the sky of the fourth painting. "They're those dreams I've been having. The ones I told you about on the phone." Sarah had told her sister the basics but she hadn't yet divulged her theories about them, nor Katherine's story. "I'm still waiting to have the fifth one. There should be five altogether."

"Why five?" Lily asked.

"That's how many dreams there are."

"Come again?"

"I've been wanting to tell you, but it's so much better in person. There's something strange about them. They aren't just normal dreams I'm coming up with on my own, they're something more."

Lily sat down on a wooden stool. "Such as?"

"Well, you know how when I told you about them, I didn't know who the guy was?"

Lily nodded.

"I do now." Sarah kept glancing over at the paintings as she spoke, as though they might reveal something further.

"He's someone real?"

"Real, but dead. His name is Gianluca and he's Annalisa's brother. Or was. He died in World War II. Luke's great-uncle."

Lily raised an eyebrow. "Creepy but intriguing. Did you see his photo and go off on a wild dream fantasy with him or something?"

"Weirder. I started dreaming about him before I saw his photo at Annalisa's. She's the one who told me who he was."

"I guess we might have seen the photo already, though."

"When we were kids? Yeah, that's what Luke says. And I guess that could be true. But here's the kicker: Gianluca and Gran had a major affair in this house before the war, the first summer she came here."

"Gran? Wow, imagine! I can't believe you kept this from me."

"It's kinda big. I didn't want to tell you by phone."

Lily waved the offence away with her hand. "How old was she? Was she already married? What happened? And how did you find out?"

For a moment Sarah regretted telling her about Katherine's past. Had she betrayed a trust, telling first Luke, and now Lily? Sarah and Lily had never had secrets between them. Still, Sarah proceeded cautiously. "I found out because I discovered some letters he'd written to her and his photograph was with them, a photo I recognized because Annalisa has one like it at her house."

"Love letters to Gran? Holy crap, this is so exciting! Where are they?"

"I suppose, I mean—" Sarah stopped short. "I don't know Lil, it's all rather strange. I shouldn't have read them myself in the first place, should I? So I feel badly showing them to you now."

"Gran doesn't have to know. I'll get them from you later. Just tell me what happened."

"Well, she was married, she was twenty, and she'd come here alone for the summer to paint. She met Annalisa and through her met Gianluca, and they fell madly in love. I think they would have eloped, but the war prevented them, then it killed him."

"Ooh, that's a serious affair, when someone's ready to leave their husband." Lily rubbed her hands together with the deliciousness of the scandal. "You mean Grandpa wasn't her big love? They hung in there pretty well, considering."

"I suppose they did. But Gran continued to carry the torch for Gianluca, even after he died. That's why she kept this place, and why Grandpa never came here with her."

"He knew? Damn. They seemed to have a decent relationship."

"Too decent, maybe."

"It's true, when you think about it now, that they seemed more civil than passionate."

"Who expects anything more in their grandparents?"

Lily suddenly looked aghast. "Sarah, with the timing of this—is Mum..."

"Grandpa's daughter, not Gianluca's."

"I guess I'm relieved. But do you suppose Gran was happy about that?"

"It would explain why she and Mum never got along too well."

"Wow. This is a lot to take in. Gran had a lover, Grandpa was just a legal appendage, Mum was unwanted. I had no idea we had such an interesting family."

"You make it sound as though it's a fun thing, all this mess."

"At least it's more exciting than the standard middle-class past I thought we had."

"Well I'll tell you, when it rises to haunt you every night it gets way less attractive."

"Ah, right, the dreams. I'd forgotten. So you think it's Gran's lover you're shagging in them?"

"Do you have to put it that way?"

"You told me that's what happens."

"Yes, but the thing is, they're not just about sex. The power of them comes from the joy I feel when I'm with him. There's none of the emotional inhibitions of a normal relationship. It's just incredible. Then he disappears and the whole thing gets awful."

"Sarah, he's a dead guy. Gran's dead guy. And he's only a dream. Don't you think it's a bit twisted to feel that way about him? You talk as though he were real."

"He feels real, in the night. And he feels like he's mine."

"This is giving me the creeps."

"You? Imagine actually having these dreams."

"I can't, honestly. Why did you say before that there are supposed to be five of them? You can't predict your own dreams."

"That's the strangest part," Sarah said, leaning towards Lily, her voice serious. "They're not my dreams. I believe they're Gran's and I'm having them myself somehow, now that I'm living here."

Lily took her hand between hers. "Sarah, darling, do you have any idea how mad you sound?"

"I know, I know." Sarah looked at her paintings and quietly removed her hand from Lily's protective grasp. "But you see, Gran painted the dreams too, many years ago. Her versions of them are up in the hall closet, plus that painting that I hung in the kitchen. They look different from mine because she painted the early parts of each dream, but I recognize the scenes. That's how I know how many dreams there are. She did five paintings."

"How do you know you're not just having your dreams because you saw Gran's paintings, and found the love letters, and were inspired by them? Isn't that a more plausible explanation?"

It was disappointing to have Lily, of all people, searching for a rational explanation instead of just believing her. Sarah started to feel very much alone. Was no one going to understand what was going on?

"I wish the rational explanation was valid, I really do," Sarah said. "But I had the first dream before I saw Gran's paintings. They were hidden at the back of the hall closet upstairs."

"The hall closet? We used to play hide and seek in there. You probably did see the paintings when you were younger, you just don't remember."

"I don't think so, Lil, I really don't. The timing of the dreams, the photo, the letters, the paintings, it doesn't work. There's something bigger at work here."

Lily got up and spoke soothingly. "Let's have some tea, I'm dying of thirst. And you can tell me more."

They went into the kitchen, made their tea and resettled themselves at the kitchen table. Sarah knew her sister was buying time, probably trying to figure out how she could convince Sarah that it was all just her imagination. Maybe even hoping she could be distracted from talking about it anymore at all. But Sarah needed to have her understand. She started up where they'd left off.

"I don't think it's possible to explain, for certain, why anything this peculiar is happening," Sarah began. "But I think that Gran might be doing some kind of telepathic thing with me. Or maybe there's some kind of force in the air here, unspent emotions or something, that I tap into somehow."

"Maybe."

Sarah could see her sister was struggling to be the earnest listener despite her reservations, but it was falling short of the support she had hoped for. "You don't believe my theories at all, do you?"

"Well, I suppose anything is possible. It's just a bit, you know, hard to digest when it comes at you for the first time." She gave an apologetic shrug. "Have you talked to Gran about them?"

"No. Our phone conversations are more about performance: my painting, my sales, how well I'm taking care of the house. I'm going to ask her about all this when I'm there at Christmas, though."

"Look, Sarah, you need to know that Gran's not at all well. I mean, she'll probably still be around at Christmas, but she's weakening. The cancer's spreading. She doesn't have more than a few months."

Sarah swallowed hard and looked down at the ground. "I thought that was probably the case. I want it to take longer. That's terribly selfish, isn't it? Gran probably wants it to be done with as soon as possible."

The sound of tires on the gravel drive filtered through the window. Sarah looked up. "That'll be Luke," Sarah said.

Lily stood immediately, looking relieved at the interruption.

They heard the front door open. Luke came into the kitchen, kissed Sarah, and hugged Lily before the two of them stood back from one another for more serious scrutiny.

Luke spoke first. "Is this where I say I've heard so much about you? I'm sure it's mutual, but I don't really want to know the details."

"There's a clever lad," agreed Lily.

"Your timing's good for coming here; I guess Sarah told you I'll be away for a week in Madrid, so you won't have me prowling around, getting in the way of your conversations."

"Very thoughtful of you."

"Have you seen your sister's latest work?"

"It was the first thing I did."

"Pretty great stuff, isn't it?"

"It is indeed. Sarah, you know that newish gallery in Soho, The Mallet? They're having a special showing of up-and-coming artists over the Christmas period. I happen to know this because I wrote an article on them for a London arts rag. Why don't you let me send them some pics of your work? If they still have available wall space, maybe they'll take all four. Or five, if it comes to that," she corrected herself. "They're the coolest gallery."

Sarah quelled an instinct to panic at the thought of her work being back in sophisticated London again. She'd fantasized about the possibility herself but balked at the scrutiny of educated buyers. It was a totally different thing from selling paintings to tourists as mementoes of their trip. "I'm more 'down-but-reviving' than 'up-and-coming'," she said. "Do you really think they'd like them?"

"They'll love them!" Luke interjected.

"You always say that," Sarah responded. She new his optimism was heartfelt, but there were times when she wanted to trade that unrelentingly positive attitude for something more critical. She continued to look at Lily.

"I believe they will," agreed Lily. "Your latest canvases are just the kind of thing they love to promote. And don't even think about the 'down' thing when you talk about your art. It deserves better than that."

Sarah took a deep breath. "I suppose I have to try to break out of the local market sometime. So go ahead and send them shots. But don't tell me if they crap on them. Let me down gently."

"They won't crap on them," Lily assured her.

Day 35–Highfield Residence, England

At some point I had to face the fact that I had a marriage back in London and the path to a future with you was riddled with obstacles. It would have been impossible for me to simply stay in Italy and never return to England. That's what we agreed. I'm trying to remember why. Was it the social shame of living openly together? The condemnation of the Church, that central pillar of Italian community? We fantasized about running away to a new place where we were unknown, then fretted over the reality: we would have had no means of support, no families left to love us, no history. That was a high price to pay. We believed it would have unravelled our love, put a pressure on it that couldn't be borne. I wonder if that would have really been true.

I wonder about a lot of things we believed at the time. But it was clear that I had to return to London, at the very least to sort out my marriage or dissolve it. You can't just disappear from your whole life that easily. I needed to finish the one thing before I could even think about a new life with you, if that was to be. It was with a miserable heart that I left you to return to London and determine my future.

Chapter Thirteen

ONCE SHE HAD AGREED, Sarah found that taking the step towards getting her work back into respectable circulation felt good. She attacked the completion of the fourth painting with vigour, finishing it by the next day as Luke and Lily kept each other amused singing bawdy songs at the piano and visiting with Annalisa. Then Luke went off to Madrid, leaving the sisters to their own devices.

One of the first things the two of them did was to trot back down to Annalisa's house. The pretext was tea, but really Lily was keen to get more information on The Great Scandal, as she had taken to calling it.

That sat in the parlour. The tea had barely been poured when Lily went over to the shelf and picked up the photo of Gianluca.

"He was very handsome, this older brother of yours," she said, studying the photo intently.

Annalisa, lounging on the sofa with her tea, nodded. "He was. Every girl for miles around wanted him, but no one got him, in the end. The soil of Greece was his eventual bride."

"Well, of course our grandmother did get him for a bit," Lily corrected her quietly. "In practice if not in law."

There was a moment of suspended, anticipatory silence. Sarah was shocked; Lily was so direct. She had no sense of restraint.

"For a bit," Annalisa allowed, finally. She reminded Sarah of an enormous clam, closed and implacable.

"You might not know this, since Sarah is more discreet than I am, but Sarah already knows most of the their story."

At this, Annalisa softened a little and allowed a grunt of acknowledgement to escape her clam lips. Sarah stirred the sugar in her tea with unnecessary focus.

"Of course, when we were younger she never let on, but now Grandpa's dead and we're adults, and anyway it's a modern world, isn't it? Not like back then, I guess," Lily went on. "I think their story is quite tragic."

"So did Katherine," said Annalisa. Three words of comment. Lily was making progress. She loved to get at the heart of a story; she couldn't stand to be in the dark about anything.

"It's hard for Sarah and me to imagine it, sitting where we are today, but I guess the war changed everything for quite a few people, didn't it? A lot of hearts must have been broken."

"Broken hearts were the least of the war's tragedies," Annalisa said, "but often they're all that's left to those who stay behind."

"It was a very long war," interjected Sarah. She had been holding her breath previously, for fear her sister's inquiries would offend or sadden the old lady. Since Annalisa seemed to be softening, she felt emboldened. "Do you think Gran and Gianluca would have actually got together once it was over, if he'd survived?"

Annalisa shrugged. "They would have tried. Katherine is very pig-headed, as you know, and she was powerfully in love. She wouldn't have let her husband or her baby stand in the way of being with Gianluca, if she'd thought there was a chance for a decent life together."

"Was that a big 'if'?" asked Lily.

"I think so, yes. Both of them were very romantic, but that wears off after a while, doesn't it? Can you imagine Katherine as a farm wife?"

Both sisters shook their heads. "Not too easily," answered Sarah.

"Exactly. I think in part it was the fact she was different—inappropriate, in fact, but never mind—that had Gianluca so in love with her. She was far beyond anything he was going to find here. She was a breath of fresh air, for all of us."

"And why do you think Gran fell so hard for your brother?" Lily asked.

"She fell in love with him when he played the piano for her."

Sarah had a sudden vision of herself on the piano bench with Luke. Is that what it had been like? Had they gone up to bed after that, or had they made love on the kitchen table? She shook her head. What a thing to be thinking about. It was *Gran*, for god's sake.

"How romantic," Lily said. "With a start like that, I think they might have had a chance to withstand the test of time."

Annalisa shrugged. "That's what Katherine chose to believe. If an ardent woman is married to someone she doesn't feel passionate about, memories of a dead man might look pretty attractive."

Sarah thought about the highly charged eroticism of the dreams. If they could have that much impact on her when she already had Luke, imagine how they must have felt for the lonely Katherine.

"Do you have any photographs of them together?" Lily asked.

Annalisa looked as though she was weighing the wisdom of making the affair that much more real with a photo. She sighed. "I have one, yes. There was a boy in the valley who'd managed to acquire a camera, which was a rare item here then, and he took pictures for a small price." She heaved herself off the sofa and rummaged around in the first drawer below the photograph shelves. "If Katherine knew I had this photo she'd never forgive me; I told her Gianluca died with it on him, because I didn't want her to have it. I didn't want to feed her sorrow or her fantasy." Under piles of paper was a worn, cardboard-covered diary. Annalisa opened it and thumbed through a few photos that were stuffed inside until she found the one she wanted. "Here we are," she said, picking it from the pile and handing it first to Sarah.

Sarah stared at the photograph. There he was, her dream lover, with his arm around her grandmother's shoulders in a gesture of casual affection. She couldn't reconcile this man, who appeared exactly as she knew him, with this woman, whom she knew more than sixty years on.

Lily hunkered down beside her sister, peering at the evidence. "Incredible," she exclaimed. "That picture looks just like you and Luke. I've seen him do that half a dozen times, put his arm around you that way. And the stance, that sexy slump he has—it's just the same," she pointed out.

The recognition made Sarah's gut lurch. "He doesn't look like Luke at all," she argued. "They aren't even the same colouring."

"Details. If you look at the gist of him, especially beside Gran, the effect is very similar."

It was eerie to look at the photo and know exactly what that arm felt like around her own shoulders. Was it only because Luke did the same thing, or was it from the dreams that she knew it? The lines between the two experiences blurred in her memory.

Annalisa stepped in, taking the photograph gently but firmly away from them and closing it back up in her book, sliding it back into the drawer under the other things. "Of course, genetics," she said. "You're going to see some similarities aren't you? People always do. Enough talk about the dead. Tell me more about what you've been up to. I like to focus on the living."

◊ ◊ ◊

Several days in Florence followed. Sarah let Lily loose to salivate over unafford-able clothes in the shops while she finished up some work for Maestro Santini, then they toured every current exhibition, and throughout it all they talked a great deal. Following her hunch, Sarah set up a dinner with Carlo early in the week and lost her sister for two more nights after that, but they agreed she'd come back to Guzzano for the weekend, with or without him. It had fascinated Sarah to see how easily the two of them played at the game of seduction over the course of that initial dinner. Within minutes of meeting him again after so many years away, it was clear Lily had decided that the boy who had taught her how to French kiss when they were both twelve might have some other interesting things to show her now that they were both consenting adults. A consummate player, however, she dragged out their flirtation over the course of the evening, leaving just enough room for doubt about the outcome that it never became a forgone conclusion.

On the last day of Lily's visit, she and Sarah climbed to the top of the ridge to sit side by side atop the rock and enjoy a final opportunity for a chat.

The November air held a chill breeze that cut through the remaining warmth of the afternoon sun. Sarah pulled her jacket tighter around her. "Good holiday?"

"Great holiday," said Lily. "Thanks for helping me with the plane ticket, Sarah. I really needed the break."

"It didn't cost much. Anyway, it was entirely selfish on my part. I needed your company, and lord knows it's a lot more fun having you come here than having me go back home to see you."

"Fun is right. A juicy scandal about Gran, shopping in Florence, even if it was only window shopping, and some hot sex with our old friend. I got everything a girl could ask for."

"What did you think of Carlo, anyway? Now that you've had more than one night of sex and a shared dinner." Sarah sat with her face turned up to catch the sun and her eyes shut against its brightness.

"Precisely three nights of sex and numerous shared meals later, I'm not sure I think much differently about him than I did on day one." Lily sprawled on her back on the rock as she spoke. "He's charming, pleasant, and certainly good-looking. Very attentive in bed, no question there. Puts most of his English counterparts to shame."

"I would have thought so. It'd be a point of honour with him." Sarah waited a moment but nothing more was forthcoming. "But?" she asked. "There's a reservation there."

"Hmm, yes. I'm trying to figure out what it is. Have you noticed, he listens well when you talk to him, asks you the right questions, responds to what you say, all the things that you'd want, but somehow he just doesn't *engage*. I think that's what it is. He never talks about what drives him or makes him happy or sad. Maybe it's because he's a salesman and can't get out of the habit when he's off-duty, but I find it off-putting," she concluded. "Even in a fling I want more connection than that."

Sarah thought about her own interactions with Carlo. He had become some-what indispensable to her as a solid friendship that was separate from her relationship with Luke. "I hadn't really noticed that about him, but I've been using him as my sounding board, so he could be a rock and I would probably just keep blathering to him without seeing if he was actually engaging or not."

"I suppose. I enjoyed his company and he's a sweet and generous guy. But there were moments when his distance was particularly annoying. For instance, when he's at his moment of glory," she said, her face grimacing in imitation, "you just know he's somewhere else."

Sarah started to laugh. "You always did like to get right down to the details."

"Well it's the world's most interesting subject, so why not? Does Luke ever seem like he's somewhere else at that moment?"

"No," Sarah answered. "No, he's always right there with me, I can feel it. He doesn't go anyplace else."

Lily sat up to look at her sister. Her voice was uncharacteristically quiet when she spoke again. "He's a keeper, Sis. Loyal and true and over the moon about you."

"I know."

"*I know*? That's all? You should be gushing with romantic joy to have bagged someone like him."

"I'm not much of a gusher."

"Oh, please. Try for some unadulterated happiness, then."

"I am happy. But no one's perfect."

"What's wrong with him?"

Sarah screwed up her face, knowing she was sounding shrewish and difficult. "He's, well…sometimes, somehow…a bit too positive."

Lily threw up her hands in exasperation. "But you wanted that. Someone positive and supportive, who wasn't going to undermine your confidence."

"All that is true. And I do love him."

"So why am I hearing this big '*it's just that…*'? Even if you aren't actually saying it, I can still hear it."

They sat in silence while Sarah tried to make sense of it herself. Birds sang in the nearby trees and the sun shone warm on her body as she surveyed all that lay before her. She lived in a charming home in a breathtaking landscape. She got to paint. She had a wonderful man who loved her. So what was the problem?

"I really wish I knew," she answered slowly. "I don't really think it has to do with Luke's flaws. They just become a kind of excuse for doubting." Sarah caressed the rock absent-mindedly. "I came here to get my life back in order. To try and establish some control over it—and on the surface that appears to be happening. But there's this feeling, an irrational doubt that any of it's really mine. The house still feels like Gran's, and I fell into this whole thing with Luke as though it was already set up and all I had to do was step in and play my role. The painting is mine, I'll grant you that, but the content—even that—is somebody else's dreams."

"So you believe."

"So I believe. And I can't shake the thought. It's idiotic, I know, to be doubting any of this. I tell myself not to. But there's something weird about the whole thing that I just can't seem to put my finger on." She couldn't hope to explain adequately why those dreams were so disturbing. How their unpredictable presence and their sense of borrowed experience contaminated everything else. And how much Gianluca's touch had started to mean to her. She had begun to feel as though she were cheating on Luke in the night. But she didn't want to stop.

She glanced at her watch. "We need to get going shortly, if you're going to catch your plane," she said abruptly. "Let's go back down."

Lily put her hand on Sarah's arm. "You have a frightening capacity for self-destruction. What does it matter how you come by the good things in your life? Does it matter whether they've clicked easily into place or whether you've had to struggle endlessly for them? Think about what your friend Caroline said when you were on her boat, how unapologetic she was about being lucky. That girl's got her head screwed on straight. *You're* a lucky girl too, Sis. And maybe, just maybe, you deserve to be."

Chapter Fourteen

DECEMBER ARRIVED, its crisp silver mornings shrouded in hoarfrost and glinting softly in the oblique touch of a late-rising, colourless sun. Sarah tried to capture the sense of it in study after study, using scraps of wood as her test boards, but was dissatisfied with the results and never graduated the idea to canvas. She had one of her better attempts on the wood framed as a Christmas present to her parents. The others became kindling.

Her dreams continued to be the only subject matter that yielded success. Variations of those emerged from her brushes as though they were already set inside the bristles and needed only the touch of canvas to pull them out. Sometimes she let herself paint them but mostly she resisted, feeling that putting them on canvas somehow fed the dreams themselves. She had begun to dream in vignettes, fleeting extracts from a summer of love, and was occasionally revisited by one of the original four. Their ability to exhaust her had not diminished with familiarity.

As the days shortened, Sarah felt an increasing need to hibernate. With a book in her hand and Beppe generating warmth in her lap, she nestled in the big chair by the fire and shut out the rest of the world along with the wind and cold. Then Luke would come and pull her from her lethargy. They never discussed the dreams unless she woke him with her screaming or crying, and even then he glossed over them as though talking about them might give her wild theories credence. Instead, he forced stimuli upon her in an unspoken attempt to blot them out, taking her to films, galleries and exhibitions back in Florence, and refusing to let her slip into an easy nothingness. She supposed she was happy to have him force-feed her in this way. It was important to stay in form because The Mallet had, much to her astonishment, agreed to include all four of her Dream Series paintings in their Christmas show. They had, in fact, been excited enough about the paintings to set a much higher price on them than Sarah was expecting, which would have been a good thing if it hadn't made her even more panicky about rejection. She reluctantly accepted their judgment in the end, deciding that she'd been out of the London market too long to have a good idea of what a painting could bring these days.

The show was opening December 18 and Sarah and Luke were going to London for the launch-night drinks party. Against her true desires but knowing it would be impossible to avoid, they were staying until Boxing Day in order to have Christmas with her family. Already there had been an altercation with her parents. Her mother and father had insisted on putting Luke in the spare room, in some kind of puritanical refusal to accept that they were sleeping together. Equally obstinate, Sarah had announced that they would stay in a hotel instead, although she couldn't afford it. Battle lines had therefore been drawn before anyone had so much as said 'how do you do'. It was not an auspicious start.

Luke just let the furor wash over him, emphasizing how enjoyable it would be to be in London with all its galleries and theatre to see. He had sprung for airplane tickets instead of facing the tedious prospect of driving all the way there and back, and had booked a decent hotel with his credit card, packaging it all up with a bow and presenting it as an early Christmas gift. It was his gesture of understanding that this wasn't an easy trip for Sarah. Between her nervousness regarding how her art would be received, her troubled relationship with her parents, and her intention to talk to Katherine about Gianluca and the dreams, there was a lot on her plate.

By the time they boarded the airplane, Sarah had managed to chew and pick the skin around her fingernails into a reddened mess and had resorted to wearing gloves on her hands to ensure they recovered in time for the opening of the art show. Luke kept up his steady optimism regarding her undoubted success and

Sarah, begrudgingly, had to admit that without all his exhausting positivity she would probably fall apart completely. But even with his comforting presence there beside her, she felt, as she stared fixedly out the airplane window, that if Christmas got as far as being merry she would be amazed.

◊ ◊ ◊

"Do I look all right?" Sarah asked Luke nervously, between tense little sips of white wine from a glass she was holding so tightly she was in danger of crushing it. The Mallet was thrumming with suppressed energy. An eclectic but all-modern collection of paintings and sculpture popped against soft white walls and a pale wood floor. It was just before the start of the opening-night party and the artists drifted about, drinks in hand, trying not to show their nervousness. The gallery owners moved among them with the serenity of priests bestowing blessings, calming them and making sure everything was in order.

Spending money she didn't have, Sarah had bought herself a chic, charcoal grey dress cut long in the arms and high in the hem. She had teamed it with high-heeled shoes of a startling, deep red, matching lipstick, and nothing else.

"You look stunning. You'll easily be admired as much as your paintings. Now," Luke advised her, "drain that glass to calm yourself, then switch to water before you go too far and blow your poise."

"What poise?" Sarah asked with a short laugh, then obligingly drained her glass as she'd been told. She took a deep breath and exhaled slowly. "That feels better."

A pleasant-looking young man in a white silk T-shirt, baggy black trousers and canvas running shoes approached them, smiling. "Sarah, delighted to meet you." He thrust out his hand. "James Coleridge. We're thrilled to have your work here. It'll be snapped up, you wait and see." He turned to Luke and they shook hands in turn.

Sarah introduced them. "Luke, James is one of the gallery owners, along with his brother Geoff."

"Interesting concept you have for your gallery," Luke said as he looked around. "Only up-and-coming artists?"

"That's right. The whole idea was to give unestablished but promising artists a start. Our aim is to take them from obscure to in demand."

"What happens when they get established?"

James laughed. "That's the trouble! Now that we've been at this a few years, we'll have to open another gallery for our high earners so we can continue to benefit from all the success we've managed to create for them."

"You certainly have the 'obscure' part with me," Sarah said.

"Don't be so sure about that. We'd heard of you before, when you were just starting out. You had some really cool paintings in the Academy show. But then you dropped off the map."

Sarah was startled by this news. "I was doing a little soul-searching," she mumbled by way of excuse.

"Never mind, you're back in form now," James told her, putting his hand reassuringly on her arm. "And those paintings of yours will have you back in the limelight, believe me. Now, if you'll excuse me, I have to make the rounds. If Geoff or I don't manage it, you may have to introduce yourself to the press," he reminded her. "They're all wearing yellow name tags." He disappeared into the crowd.

Shrinking back into herself after being briefly buoyed by James' words of praise, Sarah turned to Luke. "The press," she said in horror. "What in god's name am I going to say to them if they ask me where I've been?"

"Italy?" Luke offered. "Indonesia?"

"It can be so damning for an artist to confess that they suffer long spells of being dried up," she said, starting to pick at her thumb before abruptly stopping herself. "Especially right at the beginning of their careers when they're supposed to be prolific."

"It didn't seem to bother James," Luke pointed out.

"That's because he's pleasant and sympathetic. The press won't be so kind."

"So tell them you were in the Far East and your work was selling there. They're not going to check your story or anything. You're not on trial. And anyway, it's true."

"If you consider the truth to be somewhat elastic."

"Courage," Luke told her, taking her arm in his as the first of the clientele started coming in the door.

Hip, chic and studiously restrained, the patrons murmured to one another, careful not to show too much excitement for one thing or another, while the artists answered questions and tried to look equally unconcerned about whether or not a sale was made, although they were all desperate to do so.

Sarah loosened up after the first four people she met went so far as to nod and say they thought her work was very good. She found that the press were not, actually, viciously focused on what she'd done before, but were more interested in what she might do in the future. Lily showed up, effervescent as usual.

"Rave dress, Sis," she said, then gave Luke a kiss on the cheek before turning her attention to the display of her sister's paintings. "Your work looks great. If I ever manage to get a flat of my own, will you paint me something as a birthday present?"

"Gladly." Sarah could see Lily eyeing James Coleridge as he talked to another of the artists. "You can run along and talk to the true object of your affections here if you like. I won't be mortally wounded."

Lily gave her a mischievous smile. "There's just something about him that's quite yum."

"So I see. Go get him, then."

Later, Richard and Caroline appeared. "Ooh," said Caroline. "I feel so trendy knowing one of the artists here." She looked at Sarah's paintings. "And the most talented one, at that. I see two of yours have sold already. Can I buy one of the others?"

Sarah blushed. "Well, of course. But you don't have to feel obliged to buy my work."

"'Obliged' isn't in Caroline's repertoire," said Richard.

"Not a chance," Caroline agreed. "I just love your paintings." Sarah pointed Geoff out to her and she went off to do her deal, returning triumphantly with a small red dot sticker in hand, which she stuck with great flourish on the painting that depicted the boat dream. "I wanted to put it on the painting myself," she declared, "like pinning the winning horse."

"Just one more to go," said Luke.

Caroline turned to Sarah. "That won't be for long. Listen, with all the money you're going to get from this, would you like to come looking for some naughty underwear to spend it on tomorrow? I need to do a little tour of the competition; I know all the best places for the most fabulous stuff." As a designer for an upscale lingerie manufacturer, Caroline had more enthusiasm than most for underwear shopping.

"That sounds like the perfect way to detox after lunch at my parents' place," Sarah said. "Afternoon OK?"

"Absolutely."

"Can we come?" asked Luke.

Caroline looked him up and down. "No. This is a girlie outing. Sarah will surprise you later." She and Richard wandered off to see the rest of the show, after first agreeing to meet up for dinner after it was over.

Someone else who had managed to fix a dinner date for that evening was Lily, who came back to Sarah looking flushed and pleased with herself after having bagged her booty. Shortly after she reappeared, their parents arrived. Sarah introduced Luke to them.

"Good of you to come all this way with Sarah," said her father, Charles.

"I wouldn't have missed it for the world," said Luke.

Victoria looked around the gallery. "Is there anything more, um, traditional here?"

"No," said Sarah, "it's a modern gallery."

"Oh. Well, your work looks lovely, dear," she said reassuringly.

"All those red dots," said Charles, "do they mean your paintings have sold, or that they haven't?"

"They've sold," said Sarah.

Her mother squinted closely at the cards to check the price; she didn't like to wear her glasses out. "Heavens! People pay a lot for art these days."

"Well, well," Charles beamed. "That's one daughter off the payroll." He looked pointedly at Lily, who looked the other way as though she hadn't heard at all.

A strained silence ensued until Lily came to their collective rescue. "This is the gallery I wrote the article about," Lily told her parents. "Let me show you around." She led them off with a backwards glance and a wink at Sarah.

"Thank god for Lily," Sarah said to Luke. "This isn't a good night for me to deal with them."

"They tried to be encouraging," Luke offered.

Sarah frowned. "Encouraging is not one of their better skills."

The fourth painting sold that night as well. "Next time, we'll up the price," James told her excitedly when the sale went through. "Your buyers tonight feel they got a very attractive deal."

By the time she and Luke left the party at nine for their dinner out and a bottle of victory Champagne, Sarah was euphoric. Dinner was a high-spirited, noisy affair, with the four of them vying to tell the worst jokes and recite the silliest limericks.

When they returned to their hotel room at the end of the evening Sarah, giddy on Champagne and success, dropped her small bag on the floor the moment they entered the door, backing Luke up against the wall with her mouth resolutely on his while she wrestled her arms out of her winter coat, letting it fall alongside her bag. She began undoing the buttons of his coat as she kicked off her shoes.

"Hotel rooms make me very hot," she said, opening his coat and letting her hands explore within. She was pleased to see that her sudden attack had produced a gratifying response.

"I can see that," Luke said, enjoying her confident pursuit and letting himself be dragged into a marathon session of loud, celebratory sex that must have left their next-door neighbour in a state of irritation, tinged with envy, far into the night.

Day 36—Highfield Residence, England

I was so despondent in London. I had arranged for you to send me letters through a trusted friend so we could correspond in secret but oh, my darling, every letter I got from you just opened the wound afresh. James was quietly saddened by the emotional wall I'd brought back with me. I would sense him staring at me, trying to figure out what was in my heart, but I wouldn't give him a thing. And although he never asked me outright, my reluctance in bed made things pretty plain. We had a few encounters when I first returned. It was his prerogative, and I thought I might be able to hide the truth by letting him have this. But it was so much harder than I expected to accept him making love to me when I wanted it to be you. I soon started to rebuff him. As with everything else, we didn't speak of it. We just silently agreed this would be the way of things.

James probably deserved better. But I couldn't give it to him.

Room service delivered their breakfast the following morning. *How much better this was than staying with her parents,* Sarah thought as she lifted the linen napkin off a batch of warm croissants. *Wild sex and a better breakfast.* Luke emerged from the bathroom clad only in a white towel wrapped low around his hips.

"This hotel idea was a good one," Sarah said to him as she broke the end off a croissant and popped it into her mouth, savouring its buttery crispness. He leaned over her from behind and slipped his hand inside the front of her bathrobe, bringing a receptive nipple to life.

"It has its benefits."

Sarah gently removed his hand. "Don't get me started. We're supposed to be seeing my grandmother at ten and I can hardly tell her we're late because we couldn't stop having sex."

Luke laughed. "She'd probably approve, anyway. But I'll contain myself." He sat down opposite her and poured himself a coffee. "If you like hotels, why don't you come with me to Seattle in January? I'll be in a very nice one there; you can stay for as long as you want." His firm had won the project they'd bid on there, and he would be going a week after they got back to Italy. Up until now, he hadn't pressed her again on the idea of going with him. Sarah had responded to his initial suggestion by refusing to think about the whole thing at all.

She stopped in mid-croissant and looked at him steadily. "You know how much I hate to see you go," she began.

"I feel a 'but' coming on."

Sarah smiled. "But," she said slowly, "I need to get on with my painting now that I've had this initial success. I can't let a second chance pass me by." She wasn't actually certain why she didn't want to go away but she didn't, not even for a week. The house, the cat, her painting, Gianluca; she was beginning to resent being parted from it even for the few days she spent in Florence working at Santini's. And here in London, despite her success, she was already feeling the pull to go back, although she still had many more days to get through before she could.

"You could paint in Seattle. It's beautiful. We could find you a studio."

You see, a wheedling little voice in Sarah's head told her, *how he's trying to get you to do what he wants, instead of what you need?*

"It's not that easy," she said. "I can't just go anywhere, bring my brushes along and expect the art to flow. I have to be in my own space if I'm going to maintain the momentum started in the dream series."

"I get it." Luke stared into his coffee cup. His miffed tone didn't match the words.

"I don't know how to explain it so you'll understand, but I need you to accept it. You want to make that gallery, and you can only do that by going to Seattle. I want to make another series of paintings as good as the last, and I can only do that by staying in Guzzano."

Luke looked up and searched her eyes as though gauging whether there was anything she wasn't saying. "Point taken," he said at last, apparently satisfied. He got up and went over to his suitcase, dropping his towel as he rummaged around for something to wear.

Sarah sipped her coffee and watched him. Just enough muscle and that lovely tight bum. She was going to miss him badly when he went to Seattle. She wished she wanted to go with him. She *did* want to go with him. She just didn't want to leave the house.

Chapter Fifteen

*H*IGHFIELD RESIDENCE LOOKED, from the outside, just as it did in the web site photographs. Although it was only a ten-minute walk from the Tube station, a winding drive through lawns dotted with old oaks made it feel as though it were deep in the countryside. A low sun was trying in vain to dispel the chill of winter with a feeble glow. So different from the crisp light of Italy. Sparrows chattered in the bare branches. The large stone residence loomed, stately and imposing, at the end of the drive. It had once been someone's grand mansion and it had kept much of its elegance intact in its redevelopment as a nursing home.

"Beautiful place," offered Luke. He held her hand tightly in support as they walked down the drive.

"Gran hates it here."

"Yeah, well, that would probably be true no matter what."

They walked under a large, pillared portico to the front door. "Nice sidelights," said Luke, admiring the architectural details.

"Don't care," said Sarah.

Luke put his arm around her. "I know, you're nervous. I'll just shut up now."

What Luke didn't really know was why. It wasn't just the thought of seeing her diminished, dying grandmother for the first time in months and possibly the last time ever. As if that weren't enough. But Sarah had determined to speak with her about the dreams, and Gianluca, and the paintings. She had no idea how to broach the subject, and with every step she took towards Katherine she wondered if she shouldn't just forget the whole subject and pretend nothing strange was going on. She felt her heart flutter in panic as Luke opened the thick, wooden door.

They entered a lobby lush with dark panelling and the hushed tones of a private club. A receptionist, attentive as a high-end concierge, gave them directions to Katherine's room. As they left the lobby and started down the corridor, however, the sense of luxurious club faded quickly. Wood floors and Persian carpets gave way to the practicalities of laminate hallways with metal hand rails running the length of each wall. The artificial cheerfulness of pastel colours and exuberant floral prints superimposed itself over an eerie hush, as though everyone in the place were in a state of suspended animation. Which, Sarah supposed, they were. This place was a prelude to the nothingness of death. She tried to quell her revulsion as they made their way towards Katherine's room.

"Is anyone alive in here?" she whispered to Luke, afraid to raise her voice. "This place gives me the creeps."

"It is kinda quiet," Luke agreed. "Maybe it's nap time?" He stopped before Sarah could reply. "Here it is, room one-twelve." He squeezed her hand before letting it go so she could enter.

Sarah took a deep breath. Opening the door a crack, she made a tentative move to enter. "Gran?" she called softly.

"Yes, you have the right cell," she heard her grandmother answer in a thin but bright voice. "Come in, Sarah."

Sarah had assumed the old woman would be prone in bed, tubes sticking out of her and looking emptied of vitality, but that was not the case. Katherine was sitting up in a soft, chintz-covered chair by the window, in a room that was unexpectedly livable, the intravenous stand that showed her true condition tucked discreetly into a corner. The relief that Sarah felt was sapped, however, when she noticed that her grandmother couldn't rise to greet her, and that she had been clearly emaciated by her disease. It was a subtle illusion, a tableau of well-being. Sarah forced her best smile and leaned over to kiss Katherine as though this was the way they had always visited. "Super to see you, Gran."

"You too, my dear." Katherine spoke reedily but resolutely, the sound of invincibility rising from a body that was battered but not yet beaten. She raised her cheek to be kissed by Luke in turn. "And you, Luca, are an added treat. How lovely to be able to see both of you together like this." She waved her hand to indicate they should seat themselves on the small sofa opposite.

"I'm just here for a minute today," said Luke. "You and Sarah will have some catching up to do without me, I'm sure. I only wanted to say hello."

"So let's start with you. Are you still playing my piano?"

My piano. The words hung in the air briefly, an unheedful expression of territory.

"Yes, Sarah is serenaded whether she wants to be or not."

"Mostly I want to be." Sarah said.

"Well, who wouldn't?" asked Katherine. "When the playing is good. And do you still get over to see Annalisa often, or do you spend all your time holed up in the house with my granddaughter now?" She had lost none of her bluntness with age. Sarah blushed but Luke remained unfazed.

"A good Italian boy never neglects his relatives."

"Quite so. How is she?"

"Hale and hearty, despite coming up on ninety. I hope I have some of those genes. Sarah visits her more often than I, actually. She's in Guzzano more."

"Ananalisa has the constitution of an ox," Katherine conceded. "Not like mine, I'm afraid." An awkward silence greeted her comment. "So, Luca. Are you building that gallery in Seattle Sarah told me about?"

"Yes, I will be. It's a great project, I'm really looking forward to it."

"When does it start?"

"A couple of weeks."

"You'll be gone a long time."

"A month. Possibly more." His voice took on a slight edge of avoidance.

"Not so nice for you," Katherine directed at Sarah.

"I could go, but I want to stay in Italy and paint. I'm just getting back into form; it would be a shame to pause now." Sarah avoided looking at Luke as she spoke.

"Absolutely right. Your sister tells me you've some good paintings on display here in London."

"Only four. But all of them sold on opening night. I brought photos of them to show you, like I promised." Despite being terrified of showing her the subject matter, a part of Sarah was eager to show her work again to the woman who had been her initial inspiration in the art world.

"Splendid! Let's see."

Luke interrupted. "Excuse me ladies, but I'm on my way. Lunch at your parents' house at twelve, Sarah?"

"I'm afraid so. I'll meet you there. You still have the address?"

"Yup. Katherine, it was a pleasure to see you. I'll be by again before we leave London." He stooped to kiss her on the cheek, then Sarah on the lips, before departing.

Katherine watched him leave. "Luca reminds me so much of him," she said wistfully.

Sarah was stunned. Had she heard right? "You mean...Gianluca?"

"Yes, of course, dear. So many of the same facial expressions, the way he holds his body. That look in his eyes."

"Their eyes aren't even the same colour," Sarah snapped, then wondered why she felt so hostile. Did Gran even know what she was saying? It was the first time they'd ever spoken of Gianluca.

"There's more to eyes than colour," said Katherine evenly. "So, you do see him. I thought you would."

Sarah should have known that the choice to talk about Gianluca wouldn't be dictated by her. Katherine was accustomed to being in control and, while she might have lost a lot, she hadn't lost that.

Katherine studied her intently. "You were about to show me your paintings."

"Yes." Sarah had been unconsciously clutching the photographs to her chest as they spoke. She laid them out on the table now, all four in a row.

Katherine studied them slowly, moving her eyes from one to the next, smiling and nodding at each one as though she were recognizing the photographs of loved ones she hadn't seen in some time. The only sounds in the room were the muffled noises of the rest of the nursing home: shuffling feet, a medicine trolley rolling down the hall, the low hum of someone's television set.

"How wonderful," she said softly, without taking her eyes from them.

"You know what they're about?" Sarah asked warily, afraid of the answer.

"Oh yes, they're the dreams."

The hair on the back of Sarah's neck stood on end at her grandmother's reaction. Katherine was not surprised. In fact, she looked very pleased.

"Your dreams," Sarah clarified.

"Yes, yes. My dreams. But now they're yours, too."

"I've seen your paintings of them," Sarah almost whispered. "Upstairs. The meadow, the lake—you painted the pleasant bits, the scenes from the beginning, before—"

"Before he disappears and they turn into nightmares." Katherine had a distant look on her face. "The lovemaking. That's what I painted. It was great lovemaking, so intense. It was in real life, too. Do you know, the first time we did it, there was the biggest storm raging outside. That's when I knew it was going to be something extra special—the heavens were in an uproar."

Sarah was speechless.

"Is it Gianluca who loves you in the dreams? Or does your mind substitute your own Luca?" Katherine asked.

Remembering the last dream she'd had, in which she hadn't been sure exactly which one it was, Sarah hesitated. "It's all rather confused," she began, then stopped. What kind of a question was that to be answering? "Don't you find this conversation at all embarrassing?"

"Actually, I'm finding it a pleasure to be able to talk about it after so many years of having to keep it to myself. In any case, if we've both had the same experience, dreaming the same intimate dreams, then it's not as though I can hide the details from you, is it?"

"But this is not even close to normal, having the same dreams. Especially dreams that are so—"

"Erotic?" Katherine finished for her. "No, I suppose it's not. But then, my whole experience with Gianluca was not normal. I was struck by lightning in the first place, more smitten than I ever imagined being, and then, once I'd lost him, I was haunted for the rest of my life. Not in a ghostly way, but more powerfully. I've had many years to accustom myself to accepting the presence of a force that surpasses understanding."

"I wish I could say the same. I find them so disturbing, Gran. Why is Gianluca coming to me? He wasn't *my* lover."

"Do you like it when he comes to you?"

This was the thought that had been plaguing Sarah for some time, the degree to which she gave herself over to Gianluca's touch willingly, anticipating the exquisite heights to which he would bring her. It was only when the dreams turned dark that she longed to be free of them.

Katherine saw the wordless answer. "So perhaps that's why."

"It's not exactly me he comes to, at least it wasn't at first. It was you and me, both. I would kind of watch you, but feel everything at the same time. Now, though, its pretty much only me, and that's unnerving as well." Would Katherine be jealous? They were only dreams, but they were such real dreams.

Katherine simply nodded and stared out the window into the distance, seeing something in her own mind to which Sarah was not going to be privy.

"It feels perverted, Gran. To be sharing dreams with you about somebody you had as a lover years ago. How could such a peculiar thing be happening?"

"You're receptive."

"What is that supposed to mean? Receptive to what? I don't understand where the dreams are coming from."

"I always wondered that, myself. It's a mystery. Some things in life simply are."

Sarah felt deflated. She'd wanted answers, and had ended up with more distress. "I don't want the dreams. They're far too depressing," she said. "Even the loving parts aren't worth the pain."

Katherine turned suddenly and focused her old eyes on her granddaughter with the intensity of a snake charmer forcing a reluctant pupil back into position. "Do you really believe that? That the wonder of their love isn't worth the pain?"

Smitten dumb by the severity of her grandmother's look, Sarah merely nodded.

"Then you have a lot to learn about love," Katherine said, letting her eyes slip back to the window and relieving Sarah of their palpable weight.

Sarah began to breathe again, aware only then that she'd stopped. She shifted in her chair. "What's the fifth dream?" she asked.

"I never had a fifth dream, only four, over and over," replied Katherine, her eyes softened now.

"But there are five paintings upstairs, all in the same style."

The crinkled old face smiled. "Oh, that one wasn't a dream. It was what I thought about during the days. A vision of us together, without restrictions. Without the terror or the loss." Katherine looked at the photographs again. "Your paintings are quite different from mine. They're not as happy."

"I paint the moment when the lightness turns to dark."

"Not the most beautiful part."

"The most powerful, though."

"For you, perhaps. When you have the dreams, is the sky in them always purple-blue?"

"Yes."

"And does the wind howl and whine when he leaves?"

"Yes."

"But the lovemaking is perfect."

Silence.

"It's rather sweet, really, you having the dreams."

"How is that?"

"When I die, you'll keep our love alive. Immortality, even if it's just my emotions that linger, is a very attractive concept when one is a few short steps away from death."

The double dread of Katherine's death and never being free of the dreams turned Sarah's blood cold. "You think I'll have them forever?"

"Oh, well, I can't know that. Perhaps having Luca will be enough."

Something inside Sarah instinctively resisted her grandmother's assumption. "Luke and I are just starting out, Gran. We're not absolutely permanent quite yet."

"Nonsense. You two are a perfect couple. It's like seeing myself again with Gianluca, only without the problems that kept us apart."

Sarah was silent. I don't want to be your reprise, she wanted to shout, but a glance at her shrivelled grandmother made her stop. Surely the old lady deserved some peace at the end of her life, and if Sarah's relationship with Luke offered that, what did it matter?

"But you are still utterly in love?" Katherine said, with a hint of alarm.

"Bewilderingly in love is maybe closer to the truth. I hadn't planned on the intrusion, but I don't think I want it to go away."

"You have no idea how lucky you are."

"I do know," Sarah insisted. "But it's hard to reconcile the demands of romance with the independence I've been seeking."

"Independence is a lot easier to come by than true love. Be careful you don't misplace your priorities."

"But you were independent, Gran. Always."

Katherine shook her head. "I was never independent of Gianluca. I never wanted to be, and I never have been."

"Emotionally, that is. But...I'm not sure how to say this. It's just that, you know, if someone is there, physically, there are different kinds of compromises one has to make, all the time. And I'm struggling with them a bit as I try to sort myself out."

"Foolish girl!" Katherine barked, and Sarah jumped as though slapped. Katherine carried on vehemently. "My whole life was a compromise, because I had no choice. But for you, it's all possible. You have the Moretti you're meant to have. You have the love, the house, the art—and you dare to speak to me of the compromises involved."

Katherine's words confirmed with a horrible certainty the reason for Sarah's nagging sense of linkage between Luke, the house and the dreams. It was as though Katherine were willing the bonds that had been torn apart years ago to live again in Sarah and Luke. "All those things are what *you* wanted, Gran. I'm still trying to work out what I want. They might not be the same things," Sarah said quietly.

"That would be a terrible waste."

"For whom?" Sarah asked. "Really, for whom?"

Katherine shook her head, irritated. "For everyone. You will realize that some day. I just hope you're not so pigheaded that you realize it too late." She sighed and slumped in her chair as though whatever air had been holding her up had suddenly escaped.

"Go, now," she said. "I need to rest. Tell the nurse on your way out to come put me to bed."

Chastised and feeling guilty that she'd driven her grandmother to exhaustion, Sarah started to fuss. "I'm sorry, Gran. I should have—you're right, of course. What can I do? Do you need something?"

Katherine waved one hand weakly. "Just go, child. I'll see you tomorrow."

Sarah kissed her cheek. "All right then. Tomorrow. I love you, Gran."

"Yes, dear. That's a good girl."

And out Sarah went again, walking like a somnambulist back towards the Tube, thinking to herself, *What the hell just happened in there?* And knowing there was no one who would understand.

Chapter Sixteen

"WHITE OR DARK MEAT?" Charles asked his eldest daughter as he prepared to slice the Christmas turkey.

"A bit of both, please." Dishes clattered, wine gurgled into glasses and cutlery clinked as the festive lunch got underway. They were gathered at the round dining room table in their usual order except that Sarah, as the eldest, now occupied Katherine's traditional spot to the right of Charles. Luke had been properly placed as guest of honour to Victoria's right. Sarah had wanted him to sit beside her but her mother insisted that it would be insulting not to give him the place that etiquette demanded.

The table was set with the white damask cloth that came out for every formal occasion. Red napkins with a green trim, a little faded now, had been stuffed into ceramic holders with painted holly motifs on top. In the centre of the table a faux wreath that had decorated their Christmas table for as long as Sarah could remember sported four red candles. Familiar smells rose from the bowls littering the table: the turkey, chestnut stuffing, brussel sprouts, buttery mashed potatoes, thick gravy, caramelized onions, green peas. Victoria dished out neat dollops of everything to everyone, whether they wanted them or not. Sarah stared at the hated brussel sprouts on her plate and wondered how she could get away without eating them. She could have been eight years old again, or ten, or fifteen. The rituals of seating, cooking, eating, and conversation were timeless.

Victoria served herself last, and sat down with the small martyred sigh of someone who feels they've just done a great deal of work they're certain won't be properly appreciated. "Another year gone by," she announced as though the others might not have noticed. It was her standard opening to the Christmas meal, the way other people offered a toast of good cheer. Sarah and Lily glanced at each other with suppressed smiles.

"And what has each of us accomplished?" Lily asked, beating her father to the traditional next line.

"Don't be stroppy," said Victoria.

"It's a serious question." Charles's sober voice retrieved the conversation from potential chaos. "And from you, especially, the answer deserves some thought at least once a year. Christmas isn't just a time for presents and eating; it's an opportunity for reflection as well." Sarah glanced surreptitiously at Luke. She'd warned him about the family script. She worried he might start to laugh at how precise her prediction had been, but he seemed to be giving it the seriousness her father expected.

"Well, we can dispense with my year pretty quickly," Lily volunteered. "I've had limited success as a freelancer, am therefore still living at home, have not settled into a serious relationship with any man, and have no discernible savings in the bank." She counted each failure on her fingers as she went along, unrepentant.

"Not the most impressive year you've ever chalked up," noted her father.

"I'll make some New Year's resolutions to rectify the situation."

"I should think so," said Charles.

Victoria made a show of relishing a brussel sprout in the face of their general rejection by the rest of the family. "Mm, these really are delicious. Did anyone notice the roasted almonds I added this year? I think they add a perfect bit of crunch."

"And you, Dad?" Lily asked, ignoring her mother and pressing her luck. "How was your year?"

Charles sat up straight and daubed at his lips with his napkin before speaking. "I've had a good year, I have to say. Apart from a small failure to get my remaining daughter off her bottom and out successfully on her own." He glanced pointedly at Lily for that but otherwise addressed the whole table with an air of gracious and unassailable authority. Sarah marvelled at the way he could appear to look directly at each person in turn without ever really making eye contact. She wondered if he'd learned the trick at a sales course. "I've landed the position of second-in-command at the company, managed to find those rare Irish stamps I'd been looking for to add to my collection, took an excellent holiday with your mother to Portugal, and finally replaced that dreadful tool shed in the garden," she heard him say as she tried to figure out just how he did that thing with his eyes.

Sarah thought about the rotting, vine-covered shed with nostalgia. Mouldy and leaky as it had been, it had posessed a romantic charm. The new, vinyl-clad version was all brisk efficiency, built to last a hundred years. And it could be hosed down any time dirt or moss tried to impose themselves on its perfect surface.

"You have had a good year," piped Victoria. "Bravo, darling." The daughters nodded dutifully.

"How about you, Mum?" Lily had commandeered the role of Master of Ceremonies with just enough credibility that her father was unable to claim it back without getting into an unseemly wrestling match over the position, but he couldn't quite let it go completely.

"Yes, let's hear from you now, my dear," he agreed.

"My year reflects your father's year, of course," Victoria said. "But on my own account, I dare say the church enjoyed a stellar year for fundraising, and our choir had very favourable reviews in the local paper for our Christmas concert."

"Oh, well done," said Sarah. She'd meant it to come out with enthusiasm but was guiltily aware that she hadn't quite hit the mark. She saw Luke defeat a rising smile by taking a large mouthful of mashed potaoes.

"Eat your sprouts, dear," said her mother.

Lily beat her to it, tucking into a large one and then exclaiming, her mouth still full, "You're right, these are delicious!" Sarah shook her head at her sister's brattiness, half admiringly. Of course she knew their mother wouldn't be able to reprimand her for speaking with her mouth full when she was complimenting the food.

Swallowing, Lily turned to Sarah, barely preventing herself from laughing aloud. "And my big sister. I think you're going to get this year's prize for most advancements. Go on, then."

Sarah shot her a murderous look, even though her turn would have come eventually. She concentrated on serving herself cranberry sauce as she answered as briefly as possible. "Escaped Roger, got a house, got a job, got a new boyfriend, sold some paintings." Actually, it *was* a pretty good year. Why didn't she feel more victorious?

Charles nodded his head slowly. "I'd call that good progress."

Sarah kicked herself for feeling a surge of pleasure at winning approval, an old habit dying hard. Surely she was beyond this?

"It's only unfortunate that the house is my mother's dilapidated old place out in the middle of nowhere, in a foreign country," commented Victoria.

A small fire rose in Sarah. "A place is only foreign when you don't live there. And the house is in good condition, actually. You haven't been there for almost twenty years—how would you know anything of what it's like?"

"Don't argue with your mother, Sarah," said Charles. "She understandably wonders why you can't live in your own country, here in England. In a place that's a bit more civilized."

"Italy is pretty civilized," Luke offered. "At least, a lot of people seem to think so."

Utter silence greeted his comment as everyone stopped eating and turned to stare at him, a forgotten guest attending an event so ritualized it left little room for him. Sarah noticed that in his previous silence he had had a good opportunity to work through his dinner, generally considered to be good behaviour in the Powell household. She couldn't help thinking he should get some extra points from her mother for having eaten at least a few of his sprouts. Even if he was speaking out of line.

"Of course," Charles said. His knife was poised in mid-air, as though even a gesture as simple as cutting his meat had become uncertain now that the family's previously steady progress had been interrupted. "But the house itself, it's somewhat remote from what people would think of as the civilized parts, wouldn't you agree?"

Luke shrugged. "Near enough. Sarah's in Florence half the time. If she had a charming little cottage in the country in Sussex and commuted into London part-time the same way, no one would think of it as living in the middle of nowhere."

Sarah wanted to rush around to the other side of table and hug Luke with all her might. No one ever contradicted their father. This was a welcome break from the usual. Despite her inner joy, she kept her face discreetly neutral.

Charles was studying his adversary silently. It was bad manners to argue with a guest. "You may have a point," he said finally, with forced joviality. "But mothers always want their children where they can visit easily, eh? So, in that sense, of course, the house is in the middle of nowhere," he concluded, neatly pinning the problem on his wife's shoulders while maintaining his stake on being right. Luke said nothing. Charles continued. "So, young man, we haven't heard about your year yet."

What on earth was her father doing, requiring a guest to expose their year to judgment, Sarah wondered? Luke must have really irked him. She looked around the table and saw that even her mother seemed to be a little surprised. But Luke appeared quite prepared for the question, as though it were only natural that he should be included.

"I try to look at my life as a progression rather than as an annual tally, but as it stands right now, I'm good with it. I live in a place that fascinates me, work in a field I'm passionate about, and have an opportunity to see other parts of the world. I have confidence in my future, and my heart is happy because I love your wonderful daughter." He raised his wine glass to Sarah. "So, really, pretty much all good."

Lily started to laugh before anyone else had a chance to recover. "Sorry, Sarah, but you do not get the prize, after all. I think our charming guest deserves it, don't you?"

"Stop being so silly, Lily," snapped Victoria. "We're not awarding prizes here. We're just sharing the events of our lives, as we always do."

"Oh, sorry. I guess I was mistaken."

"Don't be stroppy," her mother said again. She held up the bowl of brussel sprouts. "More, anyone?" she asked, smiling graciously.

After dinner, Sarah, Lily and Luke sequestered themselves in the kitchen for the washing up. The Formica countertops were scored from years of use and the wood-veneer cabinets were a mock-country style particularly popular a couple of decades prior. Victoria wasn't the sort of woman who would spend money frivolously remaking a kitchen that worked just fine.

"Whew!" whispered Lily once they'd shut the door behind them. "I swear they get worse every year."

"It frightens them to lose control over us," said Sarah, her voice equally hushed. "That's what makes them so overbearing. Especially Mum." She pulled on a pair of rubber gloves and ran hot water and dishwashing liquid into the sink.

"Why are we whispering?" asked Luke. "Are they listening?"

Lily pulled two tea towels from a drawer. "Probably not, but keep it down anyway. You get mega extra points in my book, Luke."

"For what?" He was watching the two sisters go into action over the dishes, a dance they had performed so many times together in this room there was no question about who did what, or how, or when. He accepted one of the towels from Lily.

"For enlivening our normally stilted, predictable Christmas lunch."

"I was just trying to be part of the conversation."

"But Florence *is* civilized," mimicked Sarah.

"I view life as a progression, not as a pointless annual tally," said Lily, and the two women dissolved into laughter. "Oh thank you, thank you, thank you, for not being one of us."

"Honestly, it's my pleasure," Luke said, drying the first of the wine glasses.

Lily turned to her sister. "You've had a decent stay though, despite the obviously less pleasant bits?"

"London's always interesting."

"Stroke of genius to stay in a hotel," continued Lily.

"A sanity-saver."

"How have you been feeling about Gran?" she asked gingerly.

Sarah paused in her scrubbing of a large platter. Large lumps of suds dripped slowly off her rubber gloves into the sink as she gazed out the window. "Peculiar," she said. "In all kinds of ways."

"Such as?"

"First of all her appearance, of course. It's been nearly five months since I've seen her, and she's just wasted away in that time. You go expecting to see somebody looking the way you remember them, and it pulls you up short to see how different they actually are."

"We've watched her go downhill bit by bit," said Lily. "And it's still shocking every time I see her."

"She's so…small. It doesn't feel like her at all. Then there was the whole, creepy business of the place she's in. It all seems so un-Gran-like, despite having her chintz furniture in there."

"It's hard to hide the fact that it's a nursing home."

"Unfortunately."

"Did you talk to her about, you know, the dreams?"

Sarah began to scrub again, more vigorously, concentrating on the dirt. "Yes. I'm having dreams she had herself. She described them to me. They're the same."

"You didn't tell me that," Luke said, surprised.

"I needed time to come to terms with it, myself." It was a poor answer to give someone who loves you, she knew. She glanced at Luke just long enough to catch his furrowed brow and thoughtful frown before turning back to her task. It had become difficult to share her feelings about the dreams with him; his skepticism mixed badly with her feelings of guilt over Gianluca. She put the gleaming platter in the drying area and went on to the next one.

"You mean Gran actually said they were the same?" asked Lily.

"Yes."

"How is that even possible?" asked Luke.

"Did Gran have any explanation, like telepathy or something?" added Lily.

"She was vague. She said I was receptive, whatever that means."

"Weird. And what did she think of it?" Lily wanted to know. "Was she freaked out?"

"She thought it was sweet."

"*Sweet?*"

"That's the word she used. She was expecting it. She wants me to be having them."

"But why?" Luke put his arm around her shoulders and she flinched unexpectedly at his touch. Gianluca's gesture. Then she put her head briefly on his shoulder, to try and make up for it.

"It's all mixed up." Sarah sighed heavily. "For a start, she seems to think that if I continue to have the dreams, it's a way of keeping Gianluca and her alive in a sense. Like a form of immortality."

"Doesn't she see how much they upset you?" asked Luke.

"She thinks I'm being short-sighted not to see how lucky I am to be having them."

"Gran was always like that, making everybody who didn't think her way feel as though they were in the wrong," Lily said.

Sarah had never thought of her that way before, but now that her sister said it, a hundred examples rushed into her head all at once. "You know, I always thought of Gran as being really generous. Tough, but generous. She has been, to me. But this visit she was just as you say. She kept getting angry at me for not seeing things her way."

"Gran's never taken contradiction well, in my opinion. But you generally agreed with her in the past, so you probably never really noticed."

"Maybe she feels she's running out of time, that she has to convince me quickly, so she's being more forceful."

"Convince you of what?" Luke asked.

"To be what she wants me to be."

"I thought you already were," Lily said. "An artist."

"There's more to it than that. She has this idea that Luke and I are some kind of a reprise of Gianluca and her. She didn't get a happy ending the first time around, so she's living the whole thing again through us and hoping for a better result. She goes on and on about how much Luke reminds her of Gianluca—same gestures, same look in the eyes, same piano talent, same body movements—as though Luke's a reincarnation or something."

"Is that why she was so happy to see me in Guzzano? I always wondered about that."

"Yes, I'd say so. Not that you aren't charming in your own right. But you stepped right into the dream."

"That's kinda gross when you think about it."

Lily was nodding her head. "But you know, I get what she sees there," she said.

"Like what I saw when Annalisa showed us that photo of Gran and Gianluca," Lily reminded her. "And it looked just like the two of you."

Sarah turned back to the washing, away from Luke's protective arm. She'd been refusing to acknowledge things that others had remarked from the start. Gran, Lily, even Annalisa, she realized, noticed the similarities that she hadn't wanted to see but which were becoming difficult to discount. Sarah was feeling more and more convinced that her life was just a colour study of her grand-mother's. Same theme, same setting, all the elements in the same positions, including the man. With a rosier hue, just the way Katherine wanted it.

But Sarah didn't want somebody else's life. The whole point of moving to Italy had been to build her own. Instead, she found herself falling neatly into the role Katherine wanted for her. She was being readily manipulated once again, as she swore she never would be. The weight of Katherine's expectations, and the force with which she promoted them, felt like a suffocating mass of earth on the lid of a coffin.

"I don't feel like someone who's been reincarnated," she heard Luke saying in a tone that suggested it was all a bit far-fetched.

"How would you know, actually?" asked Lily. She was speaking in that excited way she had when she was on the track of a juicy story she wasn't going to let go of.

"I always thought people who were reincarnated had flashbacks and stuff. I've never had anything like that."

"No repetitive dreams, no unaccountable phobias?" persisted Lily thoughtfully. Sarah stopped her washing.

"I don't think so," said Luke.

"Didn't you tell me he was afraid to go to Greece?" Lily asked Sarah.

Damn her for remembering every word of every conversation. Don't go down this road, Sarah thought to herself. Her hands had a stranglehold on a half-washed ceramic serving dish.

"I wouldn't say *afraid*," said Luke. "Just not comfortable there."

"But isn't that where Gianluca got blown to smithereens in the war?" Lily continued. "So if you were reincarnated, that'd make sense, right?"

The serving dish fell back into the sink with a splash, sending soapy water flying. "Will you stop this ridiculous conversation?" Sarah shouted, the words leaping out with a force even she found surprising.

"Whoa! Sorry," said Luke, holding up his hands in surrender. "I'm not really reincarnated. Your sister was just making stuff up."

"Well don't. It's not fun. Not for me. And I wish somebody would finally understand that." Sarah looked at the silent faces before her and wished they could all just be having a nice, normal merry Christmas like people were supposed to have. That they were not talking about this weird thing that was gnawing at her like her grandmother's cancer, insinuating itself into every facet of her life.

"I just don't want to hear that Gianluca is channelling inside my boyfriend's body, all right?" Sarah said. "I get enough of his presence during the night."

Please, she added to herself, *let something in my life be just mine.*

Day 40—Highfield Residence, England

I was so desperate for another chance to see you, I secretly arranged a second trip to Italy for November, but the idiot Agency ended up telling James when they were arranging the bill, and he cancelled it. This time he wasn't going to give in. He told me it was far too dangerous to travel to the continent at that time. That might have been true; Britain was officially at war with Germany by then, though not much was happening yet. I think it was his revenge. There is nothing like a trip arranged in secrecy to let a husband know the true situation with his wife.

I suppose I could have escaped and gone anyway, but I knew that if I went then, I would no longer have the option of returning to the relative safety of my home in London. Was I too much a coward? You said you agreed with him, that it was safer to stay.

I thought the situation might just be temporary. I was scheming and knew how to get my way. All I needed was patience. I thought so many things that weren't true, in the end.

Chapter Seventeen

IN THE LIFELESS GREY CHILL of a mizzling Boxing Day morning, Sarah made her way to The Mallet to pick up her cheque before she and Luke returned to Italy that afternoon. Walking the last few blocks from the Tube station, she was happy for the chance to clear her head from the dark thoughts that had settled in it. She was overwhelmed by Katherine's desires and confused about her own. Luke was a great guy who loved her despite her increasingly strange behaviour, and yet she couldn't embrace him fully. Why not? Because she was weirdly drawn to a phantom in her dreams, and in her waking life Luke was too much like the dream for her to accept? Even she had never imagined she could be that screwed up.

A talk with Luke the night before hadn't helped. He maintained the simple philosophy that if it felt right between them, as it always had, the expectations of others made no difference. As for the dreams, if they really were some kind of telepathic projection, she should be able to block them. Maybe there were books on the subject that she could read to learn how. And he was definitely not reincarnated. He didn't, of course, know how drawn she was to Gianluca; there was no way she could tell him about that.

After that, Sarah had been plagued all night with visions of her grandmother forcing Gianluca towards her. The two of them had followed her around everywhere she went in her dreams, spectral parasites impossible to dislodge. She awoke the next morning feeling irredeemably irritable. Thank god she at least got to pick up a cheque today.

"Can we perhaps go for a coffee?" he asked.

Sarah turned to Geoff, nonplussed and not wanting to answer. She shook his hand in both of hers to reassure him that he was not part of the problem. "Thanks for everything, Geoff. I've spoken to James about future possibilities. I'll be in touch."

Then, throwing her head towards Roger but not willing to look at him, she said "Let's go outside." Once on the street, she faced him again. "What do you want?"

Roger gave her his most charming and reassuring smile. "Just as I said. I saw you'd had a successful showing and was pleased, and I wanted to congratulate you in person."

"I don't need your congratulations."

Roger looked at her quizzically. "So much animosity. Aren't you the least bit interested in stopping for a coffee, for old times' sake?"

"I can't think of anything in our old times that I'd like to resurrect."

"Oh, come now. We had plenty of highlights."

"I'm afraid you pretty much negated those with your later moves. Where's the mother of your bastard?"

"Tika returned to her parents' house, with the baby. I felt it was time to return to England but she didn't want to live here. I send them something each month."

"Very civil of you."

"I heard you're living in Italy now."

"Yes." She had no wish to fill him in, and she was getting cold, just standing there in the chill. But she was damned if she was going to give in to coffee, regardless of how much she actually wanted one right then.

"Did you get your grandmother's old place?"

"None of your business. Look, is there a real reason for this chat? Because I have better things to do."

Roger appeared genuinely perplexed. "Don't you have even the slightest curiosity about me, after all the years we were together? I'm curious about you."

"You wasted five years of my life and murdered my creativity with your incessant, negative comments," Sarah hissed at him. "I was a wreck by the time you were done with me. Why should I care what you're up to now?"

"I wasn't 'done with you'. As you may recall, you're the one who left," he answered.

"A detail. You used me up and spat me out. You can count yourself lucky that I had the wits to leave you in peace with your new prey."

Roger's eyes narrowed. "You're very accusatory. I wasted your life, I used you up, I killed your creativity, et cetera, et cetera. When are you going to understand that you're the one responsible for how your life unfolds? You've always had trouble accepting that."

Enraged, Sarah was about to start shouting at him when the terrible thought entered her mind that his words held a grain of truth. *Had she let him treat her badly? Had there been a choice in the matter, one she had ignored for ages?* They hadn't even had the encumbrance of marriage to keep her under his thumb, only her own inclination to go along with whatever he wanted.

In her silence, Roger continued. "You think I took your creativity from you, but you're the one who stopped painting. Did I ever suggest you stop? I did not. My criticisms were meant to improve your work. It was you who chose the easy route of giving up, rather than facing the difficulties and self-doubts involved in becoming very good."

No, no, no, it was not like that, she thought frantically. *It's his old, manipulative way of talking to me; I can't let him get to me again.*

"Stop talking to me!" she shouted then, turning on her heel and marching down the street, hugging her coat tightly to her. She was shivering but wasn't sure if it was from anger or the cold.

Roger trotted after her. "What a coincidence, we're going the same way." Sarah ignored him, trying to walk faster without actually breaking into a run.

"You haven't even let me tell you the reason I wanted to see you. I brought the paintings you did manage to complete in Indonesia back with me. What do you want me to do with them?"

Her early work. Sarah felt deflated and defiant all at once. She wanted to see them, to search for traces of a talent in which she still didn't quite believe. But they were from a time she wanted erased from her life altogether, their very existence a testimony to years she was better off without. "Keep them, sell them, burn them. I don't care what you do with them," she said.

Out of the corner of her eye, she saw Roger shake his head. "Don't be foolish, Sarah. They could be worth something now that you're on the rise."

"I said I don't care."

"Mmhm. Well, you should. And to show how much I understand that you're not acting in your own best interest right now, I'm going to turn around and go back to The Mallet to arrange their safekeeping with Geoff and James."

"Whatever you like." She was, actually, relieved. Not that his action made up for any of the rest of it.

"Sarah, stop for just a moment so we can say goodbye."

She stopped. Roger held out his hand to shake. Sarah looked at it, then at his face. A slight, patronizing smile said *Here I am, taking care of you again.* She turned and walked away.

"Be well, Sarah!" he shouted after her as she hurried off, her brain buzzing with the awful, untenable possibility that everything he'd said had been right.

Chapter Eighteen

WHEN SARAH RETURNED TO GUZZANO, snow clung to the ground and the cold had seeped deep into the thick walls of the house. Despite the fires she'd kept going in the big fireplace and the wood stove in the studio for the past day and a half, she could still feel it and had reluctantly turned the expensive electrical heaters on to their lowest level. As she got ready for bed that evening, she put a few more logs on and scooped red hot coals into a small tin pan. The pan had a looped wire handle, like a pail, which she held gingerly with an over mitt.

"Come on, Beppe," she said to the cat, who had become a permanent fixture on the fireside chair. "You can earn your keep by keeping me warm." He looked at her briefly before going back to sleep.

"Selfish beast." Sarah turned off the light and went upstairs. The coals were for warming her bed; in her room was an ancient and ingenious wooden hoop from which she hung the pail, placing the whole apparatus under the covers. By the time she'd finished brushing her teeth the bed would be toasty, without having caught on fire. She carefully tucked her cozy, flannel pyjamas under the covers, too.

In the bathroom, she splashed water on her face and looked at herself in the mirror. Still haggard. That wasn't good. She turned her back on the mirror to brush her teeth, then headed back into the bedroom and changed as quickly as possible. Removing the heater, she slipped into the warm embrace of her bed and lay there, cocooned but wide awake.

Bewildered by all that had transpired over the Christmas trip, Sarah needed this small respite from everyone and everything. Luke was staying in Florence for a couple of days to organize himself for his upcoming assignment. She'd postponed seeing Annalisa until tomorrow and had deliberately put off returning to her paints until then too, wanting the time to think things through in solitude and without obligations.

Roger's accusation that she always let life happen to her, instead of taking charge, was still irking her. And she was doing it again, with Katherine. Her subsequent visits to the nursing home to visit her had been odd. Katherine would be her old self, talking about painting techniques and her favourite artists the way she always had with Sarah. Then something would send her off into a reminiscence about Gianluca and she would get fierce again, making Sarah promise to keep the memory of him alive, to stay with Luke, to keep painting, to take care of the house. Their final visit had been an emotionally wrought rollercoaster of generosity and demands.

Five months ago, Sarah had felt that for the first time she was free, striking out on her own and setting a fresh, new course for herself. The house was supposed to have been her big chance. What had happened?

Now she felt she was far from free, in the grip of a force she felt certain existed even though she couldn't explain it. It was more than just Katherine's will at work. Last night Sarah had dreamt again, as she knew she would. It was as though the unresolved past entered her thoughts while she lay sleeping and clamoured for recognition in her actions when she awoke, creating a din over which it was impossible to hear the thin starting notes of her own life. How on earth could she figure out what she wanted with all that going on?

Welcome back, she thought resignedly. She considered leaving the house and retreating to Florence, but was so full of ideas for painting that she wanted to stay and at least start getting them onto canvas. She couldn't remember ever being so fired up about her work.

At least the dreams were good for that. Luke was right: it was one hell of a way to get her inspiration. Cutting off her ear might start to look good, soon.

In the warmth of Annalisa's kitchen, Sarah cupped her hands around a steaming cup of tea.

"Remember how you were complaining of the heat in the summer?" asked Annalisa, sitting opposite at the table. She pushed a plate of biscotti in Sarah's direction.

"I know, you warned me and you were right. I miss the feel of sweat."

"Still, at least we haven't had a metre of snow. It happens, sometimes."

"Ugh."

"How was the art show? That's the first thing I want to know."

"A great success. I sold all my paintings, and the gallery wants more."

"What wonderful news! How did the rest of your holiday match up?"

"You'd rather not know. I survived, at any rate. How was yours?"

"Excellent. I stayed at Eduardo and Costanza's house in Bologna, and everybody was there for the feast, the way Christmas should be."

"How many in total?"

"Eighteen, if you count the new baby."

"That makes two great-grandchildren, right?" Sarah guessed.

"That's right."

"Heavens. Our dinner seems badly underattended by comparison."

"Well, your family isn't exactly made of breeders, is it?" For Annalisa, a large family was the only kind of family to have. A lack of children was almost a blasphemy, as though people had a profound responsibility to continue their line. "Was Katherine there?"

"No. She's always hated the event, you know. I guess I understand why a bit better than I used to. And now she has her illness to excuse her."

"How was she?"

Sarah sighed. "Greatly diminished in frame but her spirit is still powerful. It was really strange to see her at the nursing home that way. Even now, having been there, it's hard to imagine her there. Or worse," Sarah swallowed, "gone entirely."

"Who knows what happens when someone dies. I still believe in heaven. Or I hope for it. It's very comforting."

"I wish I had the same faith. Something that does seem conceivable, to me, is that some psychic energy remains after death. You know what I mean? Especially, for example, if someone had unresolved emotions. Do you suppose that's possible?"

Annalisa eyes plumbed the depths of Sarah's strained face. "You've been dreaming again," she said matter-of-factly. "Like Katherine did. Is it Gianluca?"

"How did you know?"

"With respect to Katherine, I know everything. For some reason she loved to confide in me, whether I wanted to hear things or not." She paused. "As for you, it was just a hunch, from things you've said."

"I believe my grandmother gave me these dreams," Sarah confessed in a great rush. Was this finally someone who could understand what was going on? "The ones I have are exactly the same as hers; I talked to her about them, and she wasn't at all surprised I was having them. She was pleased, in fact. She's been trying to get me to dream them, using telepathy or something like that, in order that she and Gianluca can live on through me."

"That sounds like something that would appeal to Katherine. Sharing her emotions always seemed to give them more substance for her. Regardless of whether the person on the receiving end wanted them, I'm afraid."

"I do not," Sarah claimed, trying to convince herself it was true. "The dreams are disturbing, and confusing. I get all mixed up as to whether it's Gianluca in them, or Luke. And the dreams are changing now, as though Gran gave me the original material but now they're mine and I can't get rid of them. They're stuck to me like gum on the sole of a shoe."

Annalisa nodded slowly. "The living should never be confused with the dead. But my brother and Luca are quite alike, aren't they?"

"I never actually *knew* your brother, remember? I only dream about him."

"I expect that's not much different, given what Katherine said about the dreams."

Sarah blushed scarlet at the thought of how much Annalisa might know. "Don't you think it's pretty strange, all this?"

"Yes, it's strange, all right. But if you live long enough, nothing seems impossible."

"People say that history likes to repeat itself."

"Do you believe it?"

"I don't know. It feels like it. The more Luke gets mixed up with the man my grandmother failed to keep, the more confused I get as to just whose life I'm living here. And as long as I feel myself to be a player in Gran's grand design instead of my own, I'll want to free myself."

"Whether it's good for you or not."

Sarah paused. "Well, that's the tricky part, isn't it? Knowing what's good for you."

"Indeed," Annalisa said. "For that you need to listen only to your own heart. Not somebody else's."

"I don't seem to be very good at that."

"I didn't say it was easy. But you're old enough now to start giving it a try."

Sarah smiled. "Overdue, I think. I'm working on it."

"All right, then." She pushed a paperback book across the table. "Let's read a story about some other girl's crazy romance. It will be a nice escape for you. This one's about a business woman who falls in love with her arch-competitor, and how they try to ruin each other before they figure it all out."

Sarah laughed. "That will be a good escape. I'm hopeless at business; maybe I'll learn something."

◊ ◊ ◊

The morning of her third day back, Sarah was awakened by the sound of Beppe's persistent purring in her ear. She opened one eye to find him curled up on the pillow beside her, taking advantage of its emptiness. Since it had become cold outside, the cat stayed indoors as much as he was able, abandoning his cushion in the potting shed for central heating and human company. Sarah stretched and lay in bed for a few minutes more, scratching Beppe's head lazily. Outside the bedroom window she could see that the sky was grey and cold, the branches of the trees tinged with frost. Not a compelling sight for embracing the start of day.

As she lay there, the dream she'd had the night before came floating back into her head. The boat again, and Gianluca. Lovemaking and then—had it been Luke there, instead? She tried harder to remember but found the two of them jumbled in her memories of the dream. When he rowed away, though, she thought it had been Luke, dressed in his business clothes. She had watched him go in silence, felt the familiar, aching void as he disappeared from sight, woke up drained before falling back into an exhausted sleep. Yes, it had been Luke. His impending departure must be bothering her more than she'd thought.

The desire for a coffee dragged her from the bed. It was perfectly still outside, as though the hard frost had petrified not just the landscape but everything in it. No dogs barked or roosters crowed. Any creature of intelligence was still tucked into whatever warm spot it had found for the night. Unless, of course, that creature craved caffeine.

As she made her way down into the kitchen Sarah realized how completely the silence enveloped the house as well as the outside. The only sounds were the creak of the stair's wooden boards under her feet and the padding of Beppe's paws as he hurried into the kitchen for his breakfast. It would stay this way for at least a month when Luke went to Seattle. He'd be far enough away that he couldn't pop back for a weekend, and she was sure he'd be working flat out in any case. She hadn't recognized until then the degree to which she enjoyed the solitude of the place only because she knew that Luke would arrive before long to break it. Now there would be no piano, no laughter, no conversation, no sounds of lovemaking. Not while awake, anyway. Just the same emptiness that had been waiting for Katherine when she'd returned to the place after Gianluca's death.

You wanted independence, Sarah thought to herself, *now see how well you handle it*. Defying the urge to preserve the hushed atmosphere by tiptoeing about, Sarah banged the coffee maker onto the stove with a satisfying crash and jiggled the grill of the oven noisily in preparation for making her toast. The sounds echoed around the room, the clatter of everyday existence confirming that the living were still in residence.

In the afternoon, the crunch of Luke's car in the gravel of the drive interrupted Sarah from her painting. For a moment she felt the unadulterated happiness that his arrival had always brought her, before her gremlins leapt in to remind her of the conflict and confusion he now brought with him. She watched him approach the window, saw how he took a deep breath, closing his eyes for a moment. Was that because he loved the air of this place, or because he was worried about how she'd be with him after she'd been so grumpy in London? But he looked up when he got close and, seeing her through the window, smiled his beautiful, large smile and waved.

Sarah rose to meet him as he entered the studio, his arms outstretched. "Hi," he said, wrapping her in a hug and kissing her as warmly as he always did. No hesitation. "Has it put you to rights to be back home after the pleasures of London?" He kept his arms around her waist as he leaned back to study her.

"Was I so obviously out of sorts there?" She made a small move to leave his embrace, a minor stiffening. "Watch you don't get paint on yourself."

"You were fine until you saw Katherine, then you kinda went downhill." He let her slide out of his arms slowly. "I'm not sure it's worn off completely."

Sarah shrugged. "It's good to be back to work."

Luke turned to the painting she'd been working on. If he was frustrated with her, he was being careful not to show it. "The Coleridge boys ought to like this," he said.

"I hope so."

"Is this the start of a second series, then?"

"If I can keep it up. James says there's a good market for the light/dark thing he liked in the first series. He thought it conveyed a kind of sexual tension."

Luke raised an eyebrow. "Hmm. If it's sexual tension he wants, maybe we could research some different aspects of it." He put one hand at her waist, feeling his way, checking her real distance from him.

Sarah allowed herself a small smile. "Maybe," she said, catching his eye for a moment with a vestige of her old self.

Taking her into his arms again, Luke's movements were wary but determined as she let him hold her this time. "Oh yes, I can sense that this makes good subject matter," he whispered into her ear, then kissed her neck, trying to penetrate her resistance. "You're tense, but sexy." He ran his hand over her breast and she softened against him. "And if you're worried about getting me covered in paint, we can always take those things off." Despite her tension, or perhaps because of it, Sarah felt her body respond to the familiar, promising touch of his fingertips. A quickening of her breath was all the answer she gave him, but it was enough for his mouth to find hers and for the rest of him to lay successful siege to her remaining defences.

◊ ◊ ◊

For New Year's Eve, they had declined Carlo's invitation to what would undoubtedly be a wild party at his house. Sarah didn't want to give Carlo's blonde friend a fresh opportunity to rub up against Luke. They had also said no to other, quieter get-togethers with Luke's friends in favour of an evening alone at the house at Guzzano, since Luke would be leaving for Seattle in two days. They'd dressed up as though they were going out and had Champagne with dinner. Now, as Sarah lay stretched out on the parlour sofa, her high heels long since exchanged for house socks, staring at cracks in the ceiling while listening to Luke play the 'Moonlight Sonata', she wondered if staying in tonight hadn't been a mistake. With no one there to distract them, the entire evening had been tinged with melancholy as the two of them faced a new year that would begin with an extended parting.

"I'll miss you," Sarah said.

The notes paused in mid-phrase. "You could still come," Luke said without looking at her.

"You could still stay." It was impossible, she knew. A petulant, childish response.

"I meant just for a visit." The playing resumed, filling in her silence. She could, of course. He'd cover the expense, just as he had at Christmas, the ease with which he took care of such things an unintentional reminder of how little financial stability she'd managed to accrue for herself to date.

"I might," she finally answered after a pause so long that he might have forgotten the conversational thread to which she was responding. He hadn't.

"You won't." Luke stopped playing, the echo of the unfinished line of music suspended uneasily in the air like an unanswered question. He came and lifted her legs to sit on the sofa, replacing them again across his lap once he was settled. "Are you going to tell me what's eating you? It's more than just me going away." He stroked her fuzzy socks as though her feet were small pets.

"I don't fully know." Sarah shifted a pillow behind her so she could look at him better. "Do you ever have doubts?"

"About what?"

"About anything. I mean, I seem to have doubts often and about many things. I know my confidence has taken a beating in the past, but I don't think I'm all that abnormal. You, however, never seem to have doubts."

"You think I'm abnormally doubtless?"

"Maybe you just don't let me see them."

Luke remained silent for a long while before answering. "I have doubts. I try not to indulge them, because I think if I dwell on them, they could turn into self-fulfilling prophecies."

"Like what?"

"Hm. Well, baldness. I worry sometimes that I might go bald, because my father has a receding hairline."

Sarah frowned. "I don't think I've ever heard of a case where someone has made baldness a self-fulfilling prophecy. Come on, Luke, I'm serious."

"Sorry. I'm not used to talking about this. I sometimes doubt my talent as an architect. When I have trouble with an idea, that creeps in."

"You have doubts like that?"

"Of course I do."

"But you always seem so…positive."

"You make that sound like a bad thing."

"No, of course it's not ."

"But…"

"It's just that, for me, sometimes it gets tiring, trying to be up with you. I feel as though I'm supposed to meet some level of expected happiness and productivity, when maybe what I really want to do is wallow in self-doubt and despondent sloth."

"You manage to anyway."

Sarah paused. "Occasionally."

"Then I try to get you going again."

"Why can't I do that in my own time?"

Luke was silent.

"Do you think I wouldn't?"

"No, I think you would. But you'd take longer than you need to. Look, Sarah, being helpful isn't usually seen as malicious. Why are you making it sound as though I've been behaving badly?"

"I'm not."

"You are. So here's my biggest doubt: I doubt you'll still be here for me when I get back from Seattle."

Sarah froze. Yes, she had entertained doubts about them and harboured excuses to find fault. But she'd never actively contemplated what the future might be like without him.

She couldn't speak, so Luke continued. "You've been very preoccupied since you spoke to your grandmother in England, and you haven't talked to me much about why. I know you're having trouble with the Gianluca dreams, that they bog you down. I know you're struggling to gain some independence for yourself. But why do you lump me in with those problems when all I try to do is help you be what you want to be?"

His hands were still on her feet, but barely touching. She stared long at him, searching for her answer in her own head.

"Somehow," she began hesitantly, "you're not separate from those problems. I wish you were. But you're lumped."

"I don't see how."

"You're part of all the compositions. Picture one is Gran's: the house, the art, the love of a Moretti man. Then he gets blown up and is only left in her dreams. Picture two is mine: the house, the art, the love of a Moretti man. I get the dreams, too, so I'll know how to create a perfect colour study of the original, but with happy hues instead of tragic ones. The way Gran painted the scenes, rather than the way it worked out for her."

"But if the picture looks good, what's wrong with living it?"

"It's Gran's creation. I don't want to be just a realization of what she couldn't have herself. I want to be my own creation."

Luke loosed an exasperated sigh. "It's only history. It's part of who we are, but that doesn't mean it's all that we are."

"It's not 'only history' for me. It lives again every night in my head. The dreams drain me, Luke. And confuse me. I have more and more trouble keeping the present separate from the past. It's scary."

Luke leaned across the back of the sofa to touch her face softly, tracing his fingers across her cheek. "I'm sorry you're going through this. I wish I knew how to help you. But it seems so simple to me. We have something great between us, that's my belief. I love you. I don't need to understand why; it's just my belief. And I find it very frustrating that you could stop loving me in return, just because I'm too much like something Katherine wanted."

"It's not my intention to stop loving you," she said slowly.

"It's not the kind of thing a person does intentionally, is it? But it's possible to let it happen, when you're distracted by other things." Luke took her hand. "I'm about to go away for at least a month. It would be really nice to know how you feel before I go. And even better to know that how you feel is that we're really solid."

The interrupted notes of Beethoven that Luke had left hanging in the air earlier returned to Sarah now, playing their unanswered question over again in her head. The melancholy notes lingered in the silent room like ghosts, longing to be reunited with the remainder of the sonata.

"I just don't know," was all she could answer.

Chapter Nineteen

"IT'S A PLEASANT ENOUGH PAINTING" said Umberto. "It idealizes reality too much for my taste, but it's pleasant."

"I could use a little idealization of reality," Sarah replied. They were looking at the 'Coming Home' painting. Its owners had suffered a financial crisis, leaving Umberto to sell the work now that it was cleaned, in order to get his bill paid.

"Why don't you buy it then? I'll give you twenty percent off the asking price because you did such a good job of cleaning it."

Sarah laughed. "That only tells me you were asking more than it was really worth in the first place. So my counter-offer is an additional twenty percent off, for the fine cleaning."

"But I've already paid you for the cleaning!" he cried, changing his tack with a total lack of logic. "I would be paying you twice."

"Really, Maestro, don't be so penny-pinching. It's all I can afford, and it frees you from the task of finding another buyer."

Umberto sighed dramatically and raised his hands in divine supplication. "*Madonna*, I am being robbed. But you may have it."

"Thank you," Sarah said crisply, trying not to smile too much. She couldn't afford it really, even at its reduced price, but she felt the need to have something hanging in the house that illustrated so many of the things she felt were lacking in her own life. She would hang it in the front hall where it would greet her each time she came in. "Can you just take it out of my pay over the next couple of months?"

He stared at her. "You've talked me down and you don't have the cash?"

Sarah nodded.

"*Porca miseria*, at least bring me half. This is a business I'm trying to run."

"All right. Half, in cash. Does it have provenance papers?"

Umberto waved his hand around distractedly. "Somewhere."

"You know it's worth nothing without them."

"And you know it's an original because you just cleaned over a century of grime off it. Why do you need the papers? You aren't going to sell it on now that you've stolen it from me, are you?"

"Heavens, Maestro, have some trust. I'm going to keep it. But if I ever did want to sell it, I'd need the papers. So if I'm going to buy it, I need the papers. Do you want me to look through the files? I don't mind."

"No, no, don't go through the files. I think I have the papers for that one upstairs. I will find them."

Sarah smiled. "Wonderful. I'll take it home with me tonight if that's fine with you, and bring you the cash when I come in next week."

◊ ◊ ◊

In the first of four days she had off over that weekend, Sarah hung 'Coming Home' over the fireplace in the kitchen as a kind of hopeful talisman, put her book into a drawer where she couldn't hear its plea to be read, and turned the volume down on the answering machine so she couldn't hear whomever might be calling. Since she was on her own, she wanted to make really solid progress on the next series of dream paintings and was determined not to let anything interrupt her. It turned out her precautions were unneccesary. Her need to paint the dreams was overpowering; nothing could have interrupted it.

Ideas for canvases flew into her head so quickly that she decided to do small sketches for them as they occurred to her, which she could later use as references as she began the real work on each one. By the end of the four days she was astonished to see that not only had she begun two new paintings in earnest, alternating between them as paint layers dried in turn, she had also accumulated more than a dozen sketches. She took them into the kitchen and laid them out on the table to sort through them for the best ideas.

She'd rendered each sketch quickly and without much mental editing, allowing the images to leap out of her head and onto the paper directly as they came to her, in order to best capture the essence of the thoughts. What surprised her as she looked through them now was the degree to which she had started concentrating on the sweet, intoxicating elements as opposed to the darker side that had occupied her first series of paintings. There was a heightened sense of intimacy in these sketches, of romance and of sensuality. In more than half the sketches there was some explicit detail of physical contact, and the sight of all the drawings together on the table brought a hot flush to Sarah's face. One particularly riveting sketch showed lips grazing an erect nipple, and as she looked at it she recalled the sensation she had felt while dreaming the image, Gianluca's lips pulling at her breasts in that delicious way he had. *How would Luke feel if he saw the sketches?* Sarah wondered. The man was clearly not him.

Sarah went back into the studio to look at the canvases that were underway. The first one still verged on the dark side. An experience of loss. But the second one was an abstraction of intense eroticism. James Coleridge was going to get the sexual tension he sought, in spades.

As Sarah contemplated where a third painting might take her, Annalisa rumbled past the studio window. Sarah hurried to the front door to greet her. "Hello, please come in. This is a nice surprise. Did you walk all the way up the hill?"

The old lady was barely out of breath, considering the climb. "Exercise, it's good for me." She removed her head scarf and the enormous winter coat that made her look even larger than normal.

"Would you like some tea?"

"I would, yes." Sarah led the way into the kitchen, still wondering why Annalisa had come, when her thoughts were answered. "Luca asked me to look in on you. He was worried because you haven't been answering your phone for a few days."

Sarah immediately felt guilty. She'd heard the phone ring a few times, always while she was in the midst of either painting or sketching. Afterwards, listening to the sound of his voice in the recording, she'd told herself she'd answer next time. That she'd take a break and go into Camugnano to email him. But she did neither, afraid of breaking the spell of her intense creativity.

"I had the sound off. I was trying not to let myself get interrupted," she said. Even to her own ears it sounded lame.

As they entered the kitchen, Sarah realized the explicit sketches were still laid out across the table. She started to collect them up as casually as she could, embarrassed to have her lurid ideas exposed. But she was too slow for Annalisa, who put a gentle hand on her arm to stop the collection once she saw what they were about.

"I can see why you haven't had time to answer the phone," she commented. "Have you done all these just recently?"

"Yes, and started two canvases." Sarah laid the sheaf of the sketches she'd gathered up back down on the table and busied herself with putting the kettle on to boil, so she wouldn't have to watch Annalisa's expression as she looked at the sketches.

She could hear the old woman shuffling the drawings around. Inspecting them all. "You capture my brother very well," said Annalisa.

"I guess you know they're the dreams." Sarah turned to the cupboard now for cups and tea bags.

"Yes. They're very evocative. Will you make them all into full canvases?"

"No. I was sifting through them to see which ones would become paintings, or parts of paintings, just before you arrived," Sarah answered. Waiting for the kettle to boil, she was forced to turn around. Annalisa was looking at her steadily.

"Do you think you can exorcise the dreams by painting them?"

"I don't know whether I'll exorcise them or encourage them. But I don't think I have a choice in the matter. They just pour out of me."

"I think, perhaps, you need to be a little careful about spending too much time alone here."

"I'll be going back to Florence tomorrow morning. Maestro Santini has a new painting for me to work on." Sarah poured the tea and brought the cups to the table, sitting down opposite Annalisa. With the sketches strewn before her, Sarah looked up to the spot above the fireplace where 'Coming Home' hung in stark contrast to the turmoil on the table. She wondered if the people in that scene were really as happy as they appeared. Were they actually starving most of the time? Did he beat his wife when he'd had too much to drink? Were the children illiterates, doomed to a life of drudgery? You never knew what lay behind the thin veneer of a single glimpse like that.

"Still staying at Luca's apartment?" asked Annalisa, bringing her out of her revery.

"Of course. Why wouldn't I?"

The old lady shrugged. "I just thought perhaps you'd had a falling out, since you hadn't answered his calls all weekend."

What could she say? Any normal woman who claimed to be in love would leap to the phone if her lover called. Instead, she'd kept him shut out along with the rest of the world. "No falling out. I don't have a good excuse. I just wanted some time to myself," was all she could offer in explanation.

Annalisa looked long and hard at her, and Sarah sensed she was managing to fill in all the blanks of what had not been spoken. "Will you call him today, so he doesn't worry any more? I know you're trying to avoid a long distance bill, but just one short call to let him know you're still here. In all respects. It would be kind."

Sarah stared at her tea. What kind of a person was she becoming? In the blur of painting, Luke had seemed like someone living on another planet, in some other life. Not like her lover, simply abroad for a bit. "You're absolutely right. I don't know what came over me. I'll call him as soon as we're done tea."

Draining her cup, Annalisa got up to leave, her mission accomplished. "That would be soon, then. I'll being going now, while there's still light."

"That was quick." Sarah stood uncomfortably, feeling that something more needed to be said. "I should come read for you again soon. We barely got started on that new book, and then I kind of holed up by myself."

"You do need a reason to get away from all this once in a while. Call me when you get back from Florence."

"I'll do that," Sarah promised. "Do you want a lift?"

"No, thanks. Going back down is the easy part."

She left the house and Sarah watched from the front window as her figure retreated down the road at the slow, deliberate pace of an ancient tortoise. She'd been walking that road all her life; with Katherine, with her brothers, with her husband and her generations of offspring. She had no questions about her sense of place, or what was home, or who she was. Those deliberations were left for Sarah, who stood watching her until she disappeared from sight, watching and wondering how it was that a person got to be so sure of everything.

Sarah glanced at her watch. Almost five o'clock; Luke might still be in his hotel room. She went to the phone and dialed.

As she waited for a moment in the black telephone void, she wondered what she was going to say to him when he came on the line. Then his smoky voice filled the receiver.

"Hello?"

"Hi, it's me."

"Sarah, am I glad to hear from you! I was worried something might have happened to you."

"Well I'm fine. I've just been painting a lot and ignoring the answering machine."

A brief silence greeted her inadequate excuse before Luke continued. "It's going well, then, your painting?"

"Yes, very well. The work is pretty much leaping off the brush."

"That's good. That's great. Still painting the dreams?"

"Yes."

"So you've been having more of them."

"Every night."

"Oh. Sarah—are you all right, really?"

"Yes, fine, absolutely," she answered too quickly. "How's your project going?"

"Slowly. There are some structural glitches we're trying to solve because the building's old, and the way he wants the paintings grouped doesn't really fit with the size and flow of the rooms that would result from the simplest structural approach, so we have to get into something more complicated now."

"Are you still enjoying it?"

"Yeah, it's good. It's living up to my expectations."

"That's good." The phone line hissed softly in the silence.

"Have you seen Annalisa?" asked Luke.

"Yes. She just left. She told me you were worried about me."

"Is that why you called, then? Because she said to?" There was disappointment in his voice. Sarah knew their stilted conversation was doing nothing to alleviate his concerns.

"No, no. It was just a reminder. I was about to call you anyway," she lied.

"Of course."

"Look, Luke—this is awkward, this long-distance telephone conversation thing. I'm not good at it."

"Yeah, that's kind of coming through."

"But I'll call you again."

"Use the phone in my apartment when you're there. Then you don't have to worry about the phone bill." As though that were the only barrier.

"All right."

"Sarah—I love you. And I miss you."

"I love you too," she said. "Good luck with the project. I'll call you from Florence."

She wanted to tell him she missed him. But the truth was, she was far too busy with Gianluca.

Day 42–Highfield Residence, England

As a result of those sad unions with James I was pregnant, which may serve to explain, if not exactly forgive, my shortcomings in truly caring for Victoria when she was born or anytime after. She didn't feel like the child I should have had. A child with Gianluca.

It wasn't James's intention I'm sure, but getting me pregnant was the best possible method for keeping me at home. I was fierce with denial and continued to write to you, still planning for our eventual reunion god knew when. I never told you I was pregnant. I understood that if you knew, you would call it all off. To oust a man from his wife was bad enough, but to take her away from her child would be unforgivable.

From your perspective.

I would have made that trade in a heartbeat.

Chapter Twenty

SARAH DROVE INTO FLORENCE the next morning with mixed feelings about leaving her painting for the cleaning work. The new project Umberto had for her was at least an interesting piece: an eighteenth-century nude of some real value that had been neglected in an inheritance dispute. Left for too long in a closed house that was too cold and dry in winter and too hot and damp in summer, it was up to Sarah to bring back to life the plump figure with the come-hither look. It was that expression Sarah was most looking forward to restoring. A languorous smile played on soft, red lips, slightly slack and fully relaxed. Sarah wondered if the model had just made love to the artist before he painted this part of her, her expression was so convincingly sensual and satisfied. Or was she remembering some other encounter?

Sarah parked at Luke's apartment where it was cheaper and rode her bike to the studio. As she neared the front door, however, she noticed two *Carabinieri* standing in front of it and a couple of *Guardia di Finanzia* patrol cars parked at the curb. Fraud police. Wary, she dismounted from her bike and approached the Carabinieri officers.

"*Buon giorno, Signori,*" she greeted them respectfully. "May I ask what's happening here?"

They looked her up and down before one of them answered. "Do you know Signor Santini?"

Instinct told her what to answer. "No, I've never met him. I was just coming to inquire about getting some restoration work done on a painting."

The officer laughed. "Better find yourself somebody else! No more work is ever going to go through this studio, I can tell you that."

"Thank you for letting me know," Sarah answered. She got on her bike and rode off at what she hoped was a neutral pace, willing herself not to look up at the apartment windows above. Was the Maestro in there right now, with the police, or had they taken him to the station already? And what had happened to Francesca? The Guardia di Finanzia meant serious business. A small amount of fraud—cash deals and the like—was normal. If they seized your company like this, though, it had to be something much bigger.

Once she'd turned the corner, she pedaled straight back to the apartment, hurried up the stairs, and locked the doors as though she were being pursued. What on earth had Umberto done? She thought about the provenance papers for 'Coming Home'. Could it be he didn't have them because they didn't exist, or the piece was stolen and he had to forge them before he could give them to her? Had the whole studio been a front? Anything was possible.

The idea of a stolen painting gracing her kitchen made her stomach turn. She thought about whether or not she could be associated with anything that had gone on. Paid in cash, no papers signed. Unless Umberto gave her up for some reason during questioning, no one would be able to link her. Luke's friend could be relied on to keep quiet. Most people, in fact, would rather not come forward to the Guardia di Finanzia, for their own reasons.

She paced the living room. There was no way she could call her Maestro to find out what was going on, and she hoped all the numbers in his phone weren't being catalogued right now for follow up by the police. In fact, as she thought about it, she realized that beyond the first call she'd made to contact him about the job, they had never actually spoken by phone. They'd always made their arrangements, week by week, in person. Had he been protecting her? The police would never bother following up on a single call in. They'd be after the regular numbers.

If he had been protecting her, it would be because he'd been at this fraud for years and understood the dangers. Sarah wondered if Francesa knew, or if she was innocent and caught unawares. Imagine, discovering your husband was a criminal of enough stature to warrant being seized by the Guardia.

Amidst the churning of all these questions in her head came the realization that this was the end of her job and her steady cash infusion. She was owed her pay from the last two weeks, but she wouldn't see it now. At least she hadn't yet paid him for the 'Coming Home' painting. That cash was sitting in her purse, which was a good thing given the painting was now economically worse than worthless, without provenance and probably stolen.

So, she had the proceeds from her London sales left to live on, then she'd have to sell some more and earn her living as a bona fide artist without a safety net. She sighed. Wasn't that what she'd wanted, anyway? The victory felt hollow. Her arrival at this point hadn't been on her own terms, or in her own time. Although she'd arrived at where she had intended to be, she realized that once again she wasn't in control of events, that life was a torrent in which she bobbed, pulled along like mad Ophelia floating upon the waters. At least she hadn't gone under yet, although she had smashed into more than her share of rocks along the way.

Roger would claim it was her own fault, that she let herself be carried along in this way, unresisting as life rolled over her. She worried that he might be right.

Sarah put the kettle on to boil. When her tea was ready, she put soothing music on and curled up on the sofa with her mug. She stared at the phone. She needed to speak with someone who could console her in this crisis.

"Hello?" came her sister's voice after the third ring, accompanied by background noise of traffic and the car radio.

"Lily, hi. It's me."

A horn sounded. "Shithead!" Lily yelled, then after a moment's silence continued. "I don't mean you, of course. I'm battling the Hammersmith roundabout. Bugger off!" she added to whomever was making her progress difficult.

"Road rage?" asked Sarah.

A chuckle at the other end. "Whew. I guess. Anyway, I've pulled over now that I've managed to get to Fulham Road, so I can talk without putting life and limb at risk. What's up?"

"How do you know something's up?"

"Because you never call me when the phone rates are high in the middle of the day like this, not even from Luke's phone. So, is something up?"

"Yes. I went to work at Santini's today and the place had been seized by the Guardia di Finanzia. Carabinieri were guarding the door, so I didn't even go in."

"Shite. Did they question you? Are you in trouble?"

"They didn't question me. I pretended to be a potential customer. I don't think I can be linked, given that it was all cash, no papers and such."

"Thank god for that. What did he do?"

"I have no idea, but it has to be big. It's not as though I can phone him and ask or they'd be onto me instantly. I have to keep completely away from the whole scene."

"Man, that's something. You just never know about people, do you? First we find out Gran was having a torrid affair, and now your maestro is selling stolen paintings or something."

"Thanks, that's a comforting observation."

"Sorry."

"You know this means I have no job left."

"Oh yeah. Ouch. But your work is selling well now."

"Sold well," Sarah corrected her. "Once. Now I have to pull that off consistently, and I haven't prepared myself for that mentally. I really didn't anticipate being in this position."

"Well if my opinion is worth anything, I don't think it's going to be a problem turning out saleable work. You're back on track now."

"I hope so."

"Maybe you should look at this as a kind of fortunate kick in the pants."

"I'm feeling more terrifed than fortunate at the moment, but I'll work on that."

"Have you told Luke?"

"No, it's the middle of the night. You were the first person I called. I'd wake him up if I called him now."

"You are going to call him about it, aren't you?"

"Yes, at some point."

"He'd want to know."

"But what difference would it make? I'd just be interrupting his project with a problem he can't do anything about."

"You'd call him for the same reason you're calling me, daft one. For comfort. If you had your head on straight."

"Let's not go there."

"Honestly." Lily sighed. "So what are you going to do now? Since you don't have your job, I mean. Go back to Guzzano and paint in seclusion?"

"I guess so. I'll have to make excuses to come in to Florence so I don't go crazy, I think. See some people, go out. But I find once I get to the house, it's often hard to rouse myself enough to leave again."

"Better make sure you have some social engagements arranged before you go, then."

"Mhm. Actually, I'm supposed to go to a big, modern art fair with Carlo next weekend, so that's a good one to get me out."

"How is our handsome friend?"

"Same as always. Is that a hint of nostalgia I hear?"

"Not from me, no. I'm a reformed girl."

"What?" Sarah thought for a moment as to what this could mean. "James?"

"Quite so."

"Monogamy?"

"Absolutely."

Sarah let out a low whistle. "How shocking."

"Four weeks' worth of shocking, so far. I've renounced all others. They don't even get to take me out anymore."

"Lucky James. I like him. He's very scrummy in a low-key way."

"I agree. I haven't missed the others—not yet anyway. We'll see how it goes."

"I hope it goes swimmingly for both of you. Next time you see him, could you tell him I'll be shipping him a few pieces soon? Same theme as the last series, only more so. He'll know what I mean. That way I'll be under the gun to get them done."

"Consider it done. See what I said? Already you have something more to sell. You'll be fine."

"Thanks, Lil. I guess I'd better go now. Midday rates and all. And you're probably late now for whatever it was you were driving to."

"Lunch, with James. Don't worry about it. I was glad to be here for you. Always."

Day 55–Highfield Residence, England

All my scheming, my dreaming, my refusal to accept the reality of my married motherhood, it was all pointless in the end. You were gone so soon in the disaster that was Italy's war on Greece. You remain a part of the soil of that country. That was one year later, in the autumn of 1940. When Annalisa's letter finally got through to let me know, I had an infant child, a shell of a marriage and the feeling that every ounce of passion I would ever possess had just been blown to oblivion in Greece. I was twenty-two years old.

How can something so powerful not persist? It was inconceivable that you and our love would simply disappear from my life altogether. What would I have left if that happened? Not enough to live on. I was certain of that.

Chapter Twenty-One

WHEN SARAH PULLED UP AT THE HOUSE a few hours later, all was still and quiet under a gloomy sky. The weak light of day was already fading into early twilight, or what passed for twilight on these dull days. Instead of the visual richness that hour often brought, with its clarity of jutting hills glowing with the sun's last rays against a blue-black sky, the day simply smudged its way limply into a thick night. As she came up to the front door, Beppe sprinted around the corner from his other home in the side shed, the one he was relegated to when she went away. He pressed his face to the door opening, making sure he wouldn't be left out in the cold.

"A bit eager, are we Beppe? All right, we'll light a fire as soon as we get in, and you can have the chair while I make dinner." He darted through the door the moment she opened it. Sarah struggled through with the five plastic grocery bags she'd filled with the clothes she'd had at the apartment, transporting them back to the house now that she was no longer going to be in Florence as regularly as before. She dumped them in the front hall to be dealt with later. As she entered the kitchen, 'Coming Home' failed to comfort her in the hollow silence that was her own return. Beppe's plaintive meow for his dinner seemed a poor substitute for the heartfelt greetings of loved ones.

She went through her own rituals of homecoming: turning on the boiler to ramp up the heat in the cold house; lighting the fire she had left prepared in the big kitchen hearth; giving Beppe his much-craved dinner. She poured herself a glass of wine and brought it in to the studio. Three canvases were lined up, two on easels and a third, just begun, lying at the base of one of them. What she saw pleased her; they were complex but not complicated, strong work, suggestive. Taped to the wall to one side were the sketches she'd selected as the references for the next pieces. They would keep her busy for a while. As she looked over the sketches, a sudden gust of wind rustled the fallen leaves outside the studio window, lifting them to hit against the glass like lost souls demanding entry. Sarah looked up at the sound. The old nursery rhyme played in her head.

> *O wind, that sings so loud a song!*
> *I saw the different things you did,*
> *But always you yourself you hid.*

The gust died as quickly as it had begun, leaving the house in stillness as darkness settled on the landscape outside and the night arrived in earnest.

Sleep was elusive, arriving in fits and starts too brief to be truly restful. And yet, despite waking up each morning with dark splotches under her eyes, she had energy to paint. That she did prolifically, trying to dispel the residual sadness that clung to her from the dreams by depicting the pleasurable parts, just as Katherine had sought to do. Sarah felt an inexorable pull downwards all the same.

Initially, the weather became fine for a few days and she found she could keep her thoughts bouyant with a daily hike along the ridge to keep her blood moving. She was careful not to give in to drinking endless coffees, limiting herself to three a day and ensuring she was eating a somewhat balanced diet. It was a conscious effort to keep herself steady and disciplined in the face of no need at all to keep regular hours or take care of herself. Who was there to see her, after all? Annalisa might drop by and admonish her, but that was it. Instead of arranging a precautionary social schedule as she had first planned, Sarah had opted to give herself a first week of solitude, to get the business of painting well underway.

When Luke called mid-week she was still adhering to her routine reasonably well, telling herself that the extra coffee she'd allowed herself that day was understandable. She heard his voice come over the machine and answered it this time, not wanting another worried trip from Annalisa. Telling him about Umberto's seizure by the Polizia, she tried to downplay it, maintaining that it actually was a great opportunity for her. A 'kick in the pants' as Lily had suggested. She offered her excuses as to why she hadn't told him something so momentous right away: not calling while she was in Florence because of the time difference, not bothering to run in to town and email him because —well because why, exactly? Because she was shutting out the rest of the world and Luke along with it. She didn't have to say so for it to come through, and their conversation faltered and shrank on that realization. Eventually he rang off. It was exhausting. She made herself another coffee.

After that, the collapse of Sarah's carefully concocted routine felt like the predictable sinking of a poor swimmer beneath the waves. With it came the peculiar relief experienced when the inevitable, however undesirable, comes to pass. That fifth coffee on the day Luke called was the start of her decline. A skipped dinner followed, for which she substituted a couple of pieces of salami and a glass of wine late in the evening. She did force herself to call Annalisa and tell her she was unexpectedly back, permanently, promising to visit on Friday, even though privately she had no desire for it. Although all she really wanted was to hibernate, she had a sense that Annalisa was a lifeline she needed to keep. A thread to find her way back to the world.

On Thursday, dawn broke to a ceaseless, perishing rain mixed with fat globs of wet snow, preventing her from taking her hike. She ran out of fresh food but couldn't bring herself to drive through the downpour to get some more, making do instead with dried pastas, bottled sauces and soup from packets. And more wine, of which there was still a plentiful supply in the small root cellar.

By Friday evening, having been sent home from Annalisa's with a small supply of good food, she went to bed early and found that, having doubled her original coffee quota, she was unable to sleep although she could barely keep her eyes open. A small dog barked intermittently somewhere outside but when Sarah went to the window to look, she could see nothing. As she lay there trying to relax, she regretted that she hadn't taken Lily's advice. She should have made more specific social engagements, knowing how easy it was for her to slip into a destructive solitude.

It was only her painting that was profiting from her time alone. Physically, she was undernourished, under-rested and overstimulated. She felt, aware of the irony, that she could use some of Luke's irritating positivity but couldn't seem to make their connection work on the phone. Maybe he had been right in thinking she wasn't so good at keeping herself pulled together. Still, if she was churning out such great work, how could she complain?

Tomorrow she had a chance for escape, meeting up with Carlo for the international art fair in Florence. Apart from seeing what other artists were producing, it would give her a chance to check out which dealers might be most interested in her own work. In the evening, they'd have dinner out, and she'd stay at Luke's apartment. She might actually be able to count on a good night's rest: the dreams never followed her there.

Finally, contemplating this longed-for escape from the shambles of her collapsed routine at Guzzano, she drifted into what passed for sleep at home.

◊ ◊ ◊

The night sky was shifting unhurriedly to the silvered light of dawn when Sarah rolled over in bed and came up against the firm, muscled body beside her. His back was to her and she put her face to his dark hair, breathing in the sweet, familiar scent of rosemary it always held, before folding herself into his sleeping form, her lips against the back of his neck, her arm lightly embracing him. It felt peaceful and serene in their warm, feathered world. Nothing stirred outside.

The steady rhythm of his breathing shifted subtly, a slight awakening. She kissed the back of his neck, the short hairs there soft against her lips. His hand came up lazily to stroke the fingers of the hand she'd draped over him, then pressed her hand against his chest until she began to move it in exploration, his skin smooth beneath her fingertips. His hand came up again, this time to move hers downwards. She smiled and rolled him over towards her, their bodies entwining, their kisses soft in the sleepiness of early morning as they made love with exquisite slowness.

In a half-doze later, Sarah felt him leave the bed and she opened one eye slightly to watch as he walked across the room towards the door. A gust of wind sprang up, banging the shutters against the outside wall, and his figure vanished.

Sarah's eyes popped open, fully awake with dizzying immediacy, her heart in the frantic grip of an adrenaline panic. He had been here. Gianluca. It had felt so real, and, even more worrying, so natural and right. In terror, she whipped back the covers to look for signs of their lovemaking. Nothing. She felt between her legs and drew her glistening hand back with a start before realizing it was just her own wetness. Thank god, thank god, it was simply an even more vivid dream than ever. What else could it have been, anyway? Relieved, the thumping of her heart slowing apace, she collapsed back down on the pillow and willed her blood to calm its wild surging through her body. Then, as she turned her head, she smelled the unmistakable vestiges of rosemary and her veins turned to ice. Outside the window the wind howled in a brief gust, smashing the leafless twigs of the plane tree against the glass before they settled themselves into stillness once again.

Chapter Twenty-Two

"YOU'RE LOOKING A BIT TIRED" said Carlo as he opened his car door for her outside of Luke's apartment. "Have you been working too hard?"

"Very gallant of you to notice. I've been sleeping like shit." She nestled herself into the soft leather seat with a sigh. "I expect today will set me to rights, though."

"Worried about losing your job?"

"Some of that. But it's more that I've been having bad dreams."

"What about?" Sarah had never told Carlo anything about the dreams. It was beyond the limits of their friendship, and Gianluca was a relative of his, if removed. She wasn't going to bring them up now. It was supposed to be her day of freedom from all that.

"Dead people. Let's not talk about them, all right?"

"All right," he agreed cheerfully as he piloted them smoothly across Florence to the conference centre where the show was being held.

Sarah stared out the window. "It's nice that the weather's starting to break a bit. At least we won't be dashing through the parking lot in a torrent." The sky was showing promising patches of blue through the clouds. "This damp cold has been every bit as bone-chilling as an English winter."

"It's lovely in the mountains in winter," Carlo offered. "I'll be going on a skiing holiday the middle of February, in Cervinia. Why don't you come?" He glanced over at her and smiled. "Paolo's coming, too. He could be our chaperone."

Paolo was the man Sarah had met at the disco on her one dreadful outing there, and someone she had met again from time to time when she did things with Carlo. "I like Paolo but somehow I don't think chaperoning is his strong suit."

Carlo laughed. "You're probably right. But you don't have to worry: the idea of going skiing was a suggestion, not a proposition."

"I know, Carlo. I'll think about it. I haven't skied for years. And I really don't have the money for that kind of thing."

"We've taken an apartment, so you can stay with us for free, then all you'd have is your skiing to pay for."

It was tempting, taking a holiday with two charming men, doing something physical, enjoying the winter at its finest in the beauty of the Alps. Then it occurred to her that Luke was due to return somewhere around then. "Luke might be coming back at that time."

"Well, if he's delayed, the offer is open. How is Luke, anyway?"

"Fine. He's enjoying his project." Sarah paused. "We don't speak much, actually."

"Are you two OK?"

"As OK as you can be when you're miles away from each other, I suppose. It's hard. I feel the distance when we talk on the phone, and our conversations end up drifting into nothing as a result." *And he reminds me too much of the ghost who haunts me every night, but you'd never understand that one.*

Carlo nodded. "It's a difficult test for a young relationship."

She had never quite thought of their relationship as young, since she'd felt as though she'd known Luke forever when she first met him. As for their separation being a test, she wasn't getting very high marks so far, just as Luke had predicted. But didn't Gianluca provide mitigating circumstances?

"How's business going?" she asked.

"Sales are good. Excellent. But this government, they're robbing me blind. How anyone can make money in this country, it's a miracle if they do."

Sarah knew that much of his business actually ran on under-the-table deals, but it was a familiar rant and she let him him carry on, prodding him with just enough questions for the topic to last all the way to the fair. That was perfect, as far as she was concerned. Nothing to do with her life at all.

The conference centre was a vast, rambling, modern industrial building surrounded by parking lots. After a couple of wrong turns they managed to find their way to the right entrance, bought their tickets and entered. Carlo bought a catalogue and they marvelled at the extent of the show. There were three floors of paintings and sculptures in a series of small rooms, created by partitions, that appeared to go on and on. It would be easy to become totally boggled by the array of work on offer, so the first thing they did was to sit at the central bar and sort through the catalogue over coffees, trying to find the dealers most likely to be selling Sarah's type of work.

No prices were marked in the catalogue. When they started visiting specific dealers, however, they discovered that even small canvases were starting well above what her own work had sold for at Christmas, and soaring from there. Among the modern masters on sale there were many lesser lights who at least had developed sufficient reputations to hold their own. Sarah was both excited by the possibilities and thoroughly intimidated by the sheer amount of quality art that was out there. The competition was staggering.

They posed as buyers to get a feel for the banter of sales and why certain works were being held up as worth the price. By midday Carlo was looking seriously at a painting in sulphur yellow tones by a turn-of-the-century Italian impressionist, for which the dealer was asking about what Carlo must have paid for his Mercedes. If he was doing this as part of their buying act, it was very convincing.

"What do you think, Sarah?" he asked her. "Would it be good over the sofa in the sitting room?"

Incredible, she thought, but answered more carefully. "Well, yes, it would. But—it's a bit on the high side, don't you think?" The dealer launched into a diatribe as to why the price was, in fact, a bargain, turning to Carlo and excluding Sarah from the equation as an obvious damper on his possibility of a sale. The two men argued terms until, much to Sarah's shock, Carlo bought the painting. He arranged for its delivery and as they left the booth he looked highly satisfied.

"I'm very pleased," he confided to her when they were out of earshot. "That painting will continue to go up in value. The artist is quite popular these days."

Sarah was trying to overcome her surprise at the easy way her friend had just dropped a great deal of cash. "But it was so much money!" she blurted out.

Carlo raised his hands in a shrug. "I've received a small inheritance. I thought it would be a good idea to invest some of it in art and anyway, I like what I just bought."

Sarah said nothing.

"Would you paint me something as well?" he asked.

"When you can afford a De Pisis, why would you want something of mine?"

"Because I have more than one wall, and your paintings also please me," he answered sincerely. His tone made Sarah begin to warm to the possibility.

"What kind of thing did you have in mind?"

"How about a nude self-portrait?"

Sarah frowned at him.

"Just kidding. But something sexy, like the photos you showed me from your London show. Sexy, but subtle. And big. I want it for my bedroom."

"De Pisis in the sitting room, and Powell for the bedroom."

"You make it sound as though it's an insult to want your work for my bedroom, but it shouldn't be. It's a very important room for me."

"So I would imagine," Sarah answered with a smile. "No, I'm not insulted. It was just an observation. I'm in the midst of a series right now, actually, that will probably do the trick."

"Good! What would you charge?"

"Less than five percent of what you paid for the one you just bought."

"Then I'd be getting an even better bargain," he declared, and took her hand affectionately. "Let's go up to the restaurant for lunch; I'm starving."

They had a quick lunch and soon went back to their exploration of the show. By the end of the afternoon, they wandered listlessly, dazed by all they'd seen over the course of the day. Sarah was happy to get back to the car and off her feet by the time Carlo was ready to head back. She napped in the car, lulled to sleep by the soft luxury of its seats. They returned to Carlo's apartment and she occupied herself by reading magazines while he followed up on some necessary work, until it was time to go out for dinner.

As she slid into her chair at the tiny restaurant, Sarah felt thoroughly relaxed. The day, and Carlo's company, had been lovely. So entertaining and easygoing, with none of the terrible tensions she'd been feeling lately and none of the complications that had crept into her relationship with Luke. She looked across the table at her dinner partner. His handsome, angular face was particularly attractive in the candlelight, his white teeth flashing in a smile as he raised a glass of Champagne in celebration of his new acquisition.

"Do you still go discoing with the blonde girl?" Sarah asked him out of the blue.

"Rosa? No. Around Christmas she met someone she thinks might be more susceptible to marriage."

"Are you not, then?"

"Not with Rosa. But I plan to marry one day."

"To a nice virgin who can cook a mean ragù?"

"Do I seem that traditional to you?" he asked, genuinely concerned. "Virgins are not very much fun in bed, and I can buy the services of a cook. I hope for something more."

Sarah looked down at the table, embarrassed to have been so cavalier. Anyone would consider him a good catch. "I'm sure you'll find her," she said quietly. "What do you recommend for the *primo*? You've eaten here more than I."

"That depends on your appetite."

"Enormous."

He smiled. "That's good. You're feeling revived by our day out?"

"I am. Exhausted in a good way. Which feels like revived, to me."

"Then try the fettuccine with truffles. It's creamy, rich and very delicious."

The meal was splendid, each course a delight, and by the time they had gone through both the Champagne and a bottle of fine, deep red, Sarah was viewing all of life as very pleasant indeed. "Let's go to your place for a grappa," she suggested when they were done. "Since you're just around the corner. I don't feel like stumbling all the way back to Luke's place just yet."

"Great idea." He helped her on with her coat and they walked out into the crisp night air, the sudden blast of it refreshingly clarifying after the warm confines of the small restaurant. As they walked along, Sarah hooked her hand in Carlo's arm, liking the feel of his closeness when she did it. *This is delightful*, she thought to herself. *This is good, being with Carlo. He's been such good company today, sweet and attentive.* His presence beside her was comforting, compelling even. There was nothing of Gianluca in him. He was simple flesh and blood, attractive flesh at that, and unrelated to any of the mess in which she'd been entangled lately.

Emboldened by her happily tipsy state, she let herself consider what it would be like to sleep with him. Excellent, by Lily's expert account. Great sex, uncomplicated by any haunting past, with someone she knew well and liked well. The idea grew on her throughout the short walk back.

They entered his apartment and hung their coats on the rack, then Sarah turned to him, her hand on his arm to stop him from turning to go into the main room. "Carlo," she said, and saw how the tone of her voice confused him, his instincts understanding fully what was on her mind but his rational brain telling him that had never been on their agenda. She put her hands gently to his face. "Kiss me."

A dozen emotions passed over his face in the course of seconds as Sarah pulled his unresisting head towards her. He was tentative when their lips touched, still unsure, until Sarah opened his mouth with her inquiring tongue and pressed her breasts against his chest. His arms went around her then, his body responding to her invitation, their kiss gaining momentum as they sustained it. He moved one hand up her side. It was feeling its way to her breast, moving of its own accord with practised certainty, when suddenly he broke away, holding her by the shoulders and looking utterly muddled.

"Sarah, please. I don't know what you're doing. I think—I think this is not a good idea."

"It could be a good idea," she countered, her arms at his waist pulling his hips close to remind him that his body definitely agreed with her.

"It's not right. You and I...you told me yourself," he faltered.

"Oh come on, Carlo," Sarah cajoled him, surprised and slightly irritated at his reluctance after all the times he'd demonstrated his attraction to her. When his body was demonstrating it now. "You didn't have any qualms about Rosa. Or my sister. Why the high moral ground now? I'm a consenting, single adult."

"But you're not available, not the way they were, really."

The rosy glow of inebriation that had launched Sarah on this course began to fade in the face of Carlo's resistance. She struggled to hang on to the carefree abandon she had felt just moments earlier. "Can't we just...ignore that problem for now?" she ventured.

Carlo looked her in the eyes, weighing her comment. She thought, suddenly, that he looked tortured. She had done that to him. What was she thinking?

"I can't," he said. "You can't either, if you're honest with yourself. I've seen what you have with Luke. He's in America right now, but he's coming back. I'm not interested in being a substitute. And he's family, too. I can't do that to a cousin." He pulled her to him, holding her tightly, and spoke into her ear. "I think you can see that, in many ways, there's nothing I'd like more than to sleep with you. But we can't do this, to me or to you. You're not finished with him yet. It would be a mess, and I care about you too much to be part of a mess."

All the struggles of the past week came welling up in the safety of his strong embrace. She went limp against him and began to sob quietly but uncontrollably into his shoulder.

"*Madonna*, you poor thing," he muttered as he steered her to the sofa, grabbing a few tissues on the way, and sat there holding her until she had cried herself out.

She blew her noise wetly, then said in a small voice, "I've been very confused lately."

"I can see that." He stroked her hair as she cradled against him. "Would you like to stay here tonight? You can have my bed; I'll sleep on the couch."

"I'd feel guilty, putting you through all this, then taking your bed as well. I've been such a bitch."

"Don't be ridiculous."

"It would be nice," she capitulated without further encouragement. The fact was, the thought of Luke's empty apartment was a very depressing one. She knew that at least part of her sudden desire to sleep with Carlo was simply a desire to avoid the lonely alternative. Carlo took her into the bedroom, showing her where everything was and getting her fresh towels and a spare bathrobe. They shared his toothbrush. Once she had cleaned herself up and settled herself into his bed, he opened the door a crack to look in on her.

"Are you all right, then?" he asked.

Sarah smiled. "Yes, thanks. You'd make a very good mother."

"I'll take that as a compliment. Good night."

As she pulled the covers up tight around her, Sarah had a moment of imagining how her painting would look on the far wall, before she plunged into the void of an exhausted sleep.

◊ ◊ ◊

She slept late and woke with a pounding headache, but more rested than she'd felt for days. Pulling on the bathrobe over the T-shirt Carlo had given her to wear for the night, she peeked out the bedroom door to find he was already up and drinking coffee over a newspaper at a side table. He looked up when he heard the door open.

"*Buon giorno, tesora*," he greeted her cheerfully.

"Good morning," she replied as she came out into the room, pulling the robe around her a bit more tightly and feeling a little shy.

"Coffee?"

"I'm desperate for it, yes. And some aspirin, actually."

He laughed. "Medicine chest in the bathroom."

She went to the toilet and popped two aspirins while she was there, to return to a steaming cup of cappuccino. "You do know how to pamper a girl," she said as she sat down opposite him.

"Practice," he grinned.

"Look, about last night..." Sarah mumbled. "I'm sorry."

"Don't be. I was tempted."

"Well, I'm glad of your restraint."

He stared at her long and hard, an unfathomable expression on his face. "I thought you might be," he said finally. "What are your plans today?"

"I'll go back to the house at Guzzano, get back to my painting."

"*The* house at Guzzano," he quoted back to her. "Why don't you ever say *my* house?"

She looked at him, nonplussed. "I still find it hard to think of it as mine."

"Then why do you stay there, if it doesn't feel like yours? Why not sell it, and go someplace that's more to your liking?"

Why indeed? she thought. Because she was hoping it would feel like home if she hung out there long enough? Because she found it, somehow, irresistibly compelling, just as she found Gianluca, and Luke, or whatever joint entity they represented? Because she understood that she needed to fight its force and see the battle through, instead of running as she usually did, even though she wasn't sure exactly what it was she was battling? Because she felt desperate to prove to herself that she could accept her grandmother's gift without losing herself in the process?

Sarah stared at him dumbly. "You always ask me the most difficult questions," she said, and left it at that.

◊ ◊ ◊

Dear Sarah,

Lily came to visit me today and she had lots of things to tell me about you. First of all, I'm sorry about your Maestro. But at least you don't have to worry about paying the rent, since you have my house in which to live, and I always felt the restoration work was beneath your abilities. Lily assures me your art will easily cover your other costs, with several more paintings of the dreams already underway and that gallery fellow of hers wanting them to sell. If you do have any money problems, tell me. I have some to spare.

It surprised me to hear that you're not happy to be having the dreams, when I had understood from our conversation at Christmas that you enjoyed them. That Gianluca was attractive to you. They were something special for us to share, a gift to you along with the house. Here I've been envying you having them, only to find you wish you didn't.

Could it be you still don't understand their great value? For all that they're painful, the loving aspects of them kept me alive, literally and figuratively. The sorrow of losing him elevates the joy and makes us realize how precious the joy is. It's an excellent lesson for life, and one I thought you would find useful.

When I first started dreaming of Gianluca, I had to paint in the day what I experienced in the night, to communicate the feelings onto canvas, and I gather you're feeling the same. If you're hoping to exorcise them in this way, however, I can tell you that it didn't work for me. Only once I had embraced them as a positive thing did my need to paint them go away. The dreams, as you know, never did.

I hope you're not finding things too difficult with Luca away. He will return before you know it—which is more than I could ever hope for.

Call me! I want to hear from you.

Love,
Gran

Chapter Twenty-Three

SARAH CRUMPLED UP THE LETTER, with its wavering, spidery handwriting and its rebuke, and threw it in the fireplace. A gift! If she had important life lessons to offer Sarah, why didn't she just speak to her in plain English like every other grandmother, instead of using a spectre to carry the message? And that dig about 'my' house. Turning the screws to ensure Sarah didn't lose sight of who had bestowed her good fortune upon her. No wonder Sarah couldn't think of it as her home.

Then there was Luke. Be sure not to be stupid enough to underestimate his value, along with all these other lovely things I've sent your way, Gran might as well have said. Remember how lucky you are, to have all that I did not.

The letter had arrived in the Saturday post and was waiting for Sarah when she returned from her outing with Carlo. She'd barely put her overnight bag down before reading it, and that had been a mistake; it had put her in a proper snit. She stomped through the rituals of homecoming, lighting the fire in the hearth and poking at the burning letter as though she were skewering the devil, cranking up the boiler, throwing her bag up the stairs, tossing Beppe's food haphazardly towards his bowl so half of it scattered on the ground. Exorcising her anger.

By the time she plunked herself in the big chair with a glass of Ribena from the stash she had renewed over Christmas, she felt a little calmer. The cat crept up cautiously to brush against her leg.

"What are we going to do, Beppe? My grandmother is a menace." He sat at her feet and stared at her. Not my problem, he seemed to say. I only care about getting an invitation onto your lap. Sarah sighed. "All right, come on up," she said, patting her thigh. She scratched his neck. "A cat's life is so much simpler."

Call me, Katherine had commanded at the end of her letter. Sarah was disinclined. And if she took pen to paper it would unleash a torrent of anger and resentment. What good would that do, castigating a dying woman? Her best recourse, she felt, was to put the letter behind her and get back into the careful routine she had tried to set up last time, however pitiful the results had been. Practice makes perfect. Then she remembered she didn't have any food in the house to speak of, and that every store would be closed, it being Sunday. Not a good start.

She got up, drained her juice, and called Annalisa asking to be fed that night. "Of course" was the ready answer, and she could have some bread and milk to bring home for breakfast the next morning, oranges too if she wanted, to tide her over until she could get to the grocer's when it opened in the afternoon.

Satisfied that she was off to a good start despite the mood the letter had put her in, Sarah went into her studio to get down to work. She'd sent the first three paintings off to James and Geoff near the end of the previous week. When she viewed the canvas she'd started on Thursday, she was surprised to see what a sinister edge it had taken on. There was a greater darkness than in the previous three. That wasn't where she had intended to take the painting. It must have been because she'd felt so tired, she decided, and put it aside to begin a new one.

She looked through the blank canvases she had in stock to see if she had anything really large on which she could begin Carlo's project. Now that she'd seen where the painting was to go, she knew exactly what kind of thing she wanted to do for it. Unfortunately, there was nothing left in her stock except medium sizes. She should have picked up some rolled canvas while she was in Florence so she could make frames and stretch the material herself as she wanted it. Maybe it was a blessing to be missing canvas, she told herself. It gave her a good reason to go into the city again later in the week. There was no hurry to begin Carlo's painting. Instead, she selected a sketch from the wall and sat down to consider how she would make her next painting for The Mallet.

Later in the week, however, Sarah's plans for a canvas shopping-trip into the city were shelved when she woke to find she was aching all over with a debilitating flu that had been making its way around much of Italy. How could she possibly catch a bug when she lived in almost total isolation? She must have picked it up in Florence. She'd been an easy target, since the moment she'd come back to Guzzano her sleep was once again sporadic at best, leaving her immune-deficient and exhausted. When she eased her way slowly down the stairs to make herself some tea, after spending most of the morning dozing fitfully in bed, her joints creaked as though she were ninety.

She entered the kitchen and surveyed its neglected condition with disgust. What a tip. Even before she'd been laid low with the flu, she'd fallen into the lazy habit of only washing a dish as it was needed, having dirtied virtually everything as the week progressed without ever having found the will to fill the dishwasher, let alone scrub pots. Just as it had the week before, the same creeping descent into a state of obsession over her thoughts and paintings had befallen her, at the expense of personal care. She put the kettle on to boil and continued the pattern without thinking, rinsing out a stained mug that looked slightly less septic than the rest. While the kettle heated she creaked her way into the studio.

Half a dozen paintings in various states of completion were propped up haphazardly around the room. She hadn't managed to get to the end of any of them. Each time she got well underway with one, new images would force themselves into her head to distract her from what she'd set out to paint earlier. Even looking at her reference sketches over and over was not enough to keep the images she wanted to retain foremost in her head. With each new distraction, she had set the unfinished work aside and started new pieces or sketches based on whatever mental pictures were intruding at the time. The result was a dizzy array of thumbnails and the current collection of half-done paintings. She turned from it all with a sigh as the kettle began to whistle.

Crossing the hallway, Sarah caught sight of something moving swiftly across the kitchen floor, and she hurried forward to see what it was. As she passed through the kitchen door, it had just moved out of sight beyond the bulk of the table, but not before she understood what she'd seen: small, brown and furry, it was the dog from her dreams. She recalled the barking she had heard outside the week before. Her hair standing on end, she stooped to look for the creature under the table, but could see no sign of it anywhere. In the big chair, Beppe's hackles were subsiding back to flatness as he stood looking intently in the same direction. Feeling somewhat silly but needing to reassure herself, Sarah looked behind furniture and through cupboards. There wasn't a trace.

"Great," Sarah said to Beppe dully. "Now we're hallucinating about dogs. Both of us, no less."

She brewed her tea and laced it liberally with sugar to make it more fortifying, then hauled herself back up the stairs to run a bath. Two more aspirins safely in her stomach and tea mug in hand, she sank into the deep water with a sigh. The scent of the tea tree oil she'd added to the bath rose to her nostrils, faintly unpleasant yet somehow soothing as she imagined its medicinal effects working their magic invisibly through the pores of her skin.

Sarah leaned her head back against the pink, plastic, inflatable pillow that was attached to the bath with suction cups. It had been there when Sarah first took over the place, deflated but not broken. At first she'd thought it looked ridiculous, particularly in pink, one of those things she'd seen in bathroom stores but would never consider buying for herself. Once she'd tried it, however, she'd found it an indispensable part of a relaxing bath. Perhaps Katherine's most useful gift, she mused. Relaxation had been hard enough to come by lately, after all.

Gianluca had been with her so relentlessly in the nights that Sarah never recalled dreaming about anything else, although she supposed she must. She hoped she did. Once she had felt him in her bed again just before the break of dawn, in that semi-conscious place between dreaming and full wakefulness. She had sat determinedly upright, waking herself and forcing herself out of bed in the half-light, for fear of falling back to sleep and having him return if she stayed there. She wondered how long this was going to continue. Would he force her out of the house, finally, through sheer fatigue? It didn't feel to her as though that was his objective. What was?

Listen to yourself, she thought. *How can a phantom in a dream have its own objective?*

But even with the admonishment came a sudden burst of clarity. *Gianluca has probably been helping me*, Katherine's letter had read. It wasn't just Gran sending Sarah dreams by telepathy. She had sown the initial seed, perhaps, but somewhere along the way, Gianluca had taken on a power of his own. Katherine had only had four dreams; Sarah was well beyond that. Her grandmother had lost control over the dreams long ago, she realized with some fear. She finished her tea and her bath and put herself back to bed. Regardless of what might happen there, it was the only place her body wanted to be.

◊ ◊ ◊

A relentless pounding woke Sarah from a black and empty sleep. It took her a moment to sort out what was going on. It was light out, late afternoon she guessed, and she was still in bed. Then she moved and the aching of her body reminded her she was sick. What was that pounding? It had started again. Through the thick fog of her sleepiness she finally realized it was someone at the front door, and dragged herself downstairs to see.

"Annalisa" she said weakly as she peeked out of the house, then opened the door for the old woman to enter.

"*Madonna*, you look awful. How long have you been sick?"

Sarah shook her head slowly. "I don't know. What day is it?"

"Monday."

"Several days, then." She tottered into the kitchen. The fire had been dead for days, leaving the room chilly with only one small radiator to heat it. There were dishes everywhere and all the cupboard doors had been left open after Sarah's desperate scavenges to find the last bits of food without having to get herself to the grocer's.

"Your kitchen looks even worse than you do, if that's possible," declared Annalisa, then looked over at Sarah shivering in the centre of the room, looking lost. "God in heaven, put on a robe, you'll be in hospital if you stand there like that. You go get one now and I'll make up a fire and some tea."

Sarah nodded and walked slowly upstairs, stopping in the bathroom along the way to splash some water on her face. By the time she came down again, a fire was beginning to lick at fresh logs, the kettle had been put on to boil and Annalisa was up to her elbows in soapy water in the sink.

"Oh, Annalisa, please don't clean up my mess," Sarah protested weakly.

"You're not exactly in shape to do it yourself. Go sit by the fire," she ordered. "I'll bring your tea when it's ready."

The big chair was inviting, warmed a bit already from the growing fire. Sarah curled up in it and laid her head against the back wearily. "Why did you come? Did Luke send you again?"

"Does it matter? No one had seen you. And I called you several times but as usual you never answered. I do wish you'd answer once in a while, or listen to your messages. What's the point in having an answering machine if you don't listen to who's called?"

"Spoken like a Mama. I haven't listened to anything since I got sick."

Annalisa turned and looked hard at her. "That's why I came. And a good thing, too—why didn't you call me when you got ill? You haven't any food in the house at all. After our tea, I'll go shopping for you, and I'll bring some things from my freezer that are all made up, so you don't have to do anything in order to eat well."

It was no use protesting when Annalisa was in her mega-*nonna* mode. Sarah let herself be taken care of and was glad of it when a fresh cup of tea was placed in her hands. Once she'd consumed half of it and lost some of her initial grogginess, she began to feel almost human again, although she ached deep in her bones and could feel she was still running a fever. Annalisa finished cleaning up and heaved her bulk onto one of the small wooden chairs by the table.

"There, that's better. That looked like more dishes there than one sick person would accumulate over a few days. Have you been all right otherwise?" she asked suspiciously.

"I've had a lot of dreams again. Worse. Sometimes even when I'm almost awake, Gianluca comes to me and seems so real…" Sarah trailed off.

"You have too much imagination to live alone."

Sarah thought about this. "I don't think the dreams come from my own imagination. I'm just a conduit, not the creator. So many images, it's impossible to keep up with them. Even when I'm awake they come to me. The scenes flash into my brain when I'm painting something else, distracting me and begging me to notice them instead. It's like having a hundred children all demanding attention at once."

"As though you would know what that's like."

"So it's my worst nightmare of what it would be like to have a hundred children. The studio is littered with little sketches."

"I gather it's not normally like this when you set out to paint."

"God help me if it were! My art would kill me. Something else is going on here. Gianluca, or Katherine, or both of them are sending me all these ideas."

"You don't think it's possible that maybe you're feeding yourself the ideas?"

"OK, you tell me. Here are some details I don't know how I'd come up with." Sarah laid her head back on the chair and closed her eyes, seeing the images again clearly in her mind's eye. "There's an ancient bicycle, in black. In my dreams, I'm on that green one that's now broken out in the shed, and he's riding the black one. We cycle along rough dirt roads and look out over the valley." She stopped talking for a moment as the memory flooded her: the feel of the breeze in her hair, watching the muscles of his back as he pedaled, always stronger, ahead of her, along the rugged roads. "And a dog," she continued, "a puppy, brown with one white paw. I even thought I saw him in the kitchen the other day." She opened her eyes and looked at Annalisa, searching for her reaction.

The old woman sighed and shook her head. "I'd forgotten those things, myself. Yes, Gianluca had an old, black bicycle and that's how he got around. Scooters hadn't been invented yet. And the puppy was a present to Katherine, of sorts. Meant to keep Katherine company while she was at the house, then we took him back again when she went away. It was a problem, actually; he was always coming up here looking for her. It took ages for him to learn to stay at our farm after."

"So, it's true then. Gianluca's showing me things."

"Well I don't know about that. But you're seeing things from the past, however it's happening."

"Gran said they were meant as a gift, the dreams," Sarah said wearily.

"You've talked to her about them again?"

"No. She wrote me a letter. She made it clear I should be more grateful, that they were of great value and I didn't appreciate them properly."

"Very like Katherine."

"Do you think so? I always had this idea when I was growing up that she was the one adult in the family who wasn't judgmental. Who only had my interests at heart. I never saw the other parts of her because, maybe, I always did what she wanted. But now—"

"Now you're realizing she's human?"

"Worse. Now I'm realizing she has some pretty nasty aspects to her. And they're coming my way."

"Nastiness is part of being human."

"I suppose. But I always thought the idea was to spare your loved ones that part. You've been friends with my grandmother for decades; what's your opinion of her, really?"

Annalisa folded her hands over her ample stomach and thought for a moment before answering. "She's very compelling. So sure of herself, she makes you feel as though you'd be crazy not to go along with her. That's her real talent. And interested in a million different things. I've learned a lot from her over the years."

"Those are all good things," Sarah said.

Annalisa took a long sip of tea. "I would say she's careless about others. She has uses for each of us she keeps around her, but she doesn't generally consider the consequences of her actions for other people, even those she cares about."

"Lily says Gran's selfish."

"That could be said of her."

"But despite that, you've stayed close friends."

"No one's perfect, are they? I learned what I could expect from her, and I liked what she gave me enough to forgive the less attractive parts, as one must do in any relationship."

"Was she that way with your brother, too?"

"Selfish? What lover isn't, despite all protests that the loved one is, in fact, the most important? And careless. Passion is a reckless thing, an indulgence. It's not careful by nature—but I don't think Gianluca saw it that way."

"Wasn't he the same?"

Annalisa focused on some spot far across the room, as though seeing him there. "Generally, no. But when it came to Katherine, he was as selfish and careless as it's possible to be. He would have done anything to be with her. He even talked to me of travelling to England to claim her back. He didn't know about the child—your mother. Imagine what that would have been like."

"My mother would have changed everything for him, wouldn't she?"

"Who knows? The war came and he never got the chance to make his daring trip."

"Do you think that was sort of a blessing?"

"I do not," Annalisa said emphatically. "Death is too heavy a price to pay for avoiding life's complications. Better to cope with misery than to lose the chance to cope at all."

"So he died unresolved, still dreaming of claiming her. Maybe that's why his spirit is so restless: he never completed his big mission."

"And Katherine is about to die in the same state," Annalisa pointed out.

Sarah closed her eyes, suddenly very tired. Her head felt as though it weighed a ton. She couldn't keep it upright and settled for letting it rest against the back of the big chair once more.

"When, just in the nick of time, she and Gianluca spot the granddaughter Sarah, someone 'receptive' as Gran put it, and see a way of keeping the flame alive."

"Perhaps. Or perhaps it's just as Katherine says: that they are a great gift. It is a gesture of tremendous trust to give to someone else the images of one's most emotional, passionate moments."

"Unfortunately, they feel more like a burden than a gift. I have my own life to sort out. I don't want the weight of their sorrows, or even their joys. And I don't want a phantom as my lover."

"Then why have you embraced the dreams so?"

Sarah shook her heavy head slowly from side to side. "I don't. The dreams are inescapable. I have no choice."

"To be alive is to have choice."

"It rarely feels that way to me." Sarah sat forward in her chair and rubbed her face in her hands. "I'm tired, Annalisa. I need to go back to bed now," she said, ending their conversation, its weight having sapped what strength she'd had.

Annalisa rose. "I'll get your supplies and bring them here. Shall I just let myself in?"

"Please. Take the key, it's on the hook in the front hall. And thank you for your help."

"I'll bring you a pot of soup, and leave it on the stove. I want you to promise me that when you next wake up, you'll come down here and eat some."

"I wouldn't dare not to." As Sarah stood at the base of the stairs she had a thought.

"What happens if you get sick? Who takes care of you?"

"Costanza looks after me. Don't worry. She calls me every day to check."

After Annalisa had left, Sarah noticed the phone in its place in the front hallway. She sat in an unenthused slump on the little chair beside it and reviewed the messages on her machine: Carlo: reminding her they were going skiing the following week and asking if she was coming; her mother: why didn't she ever call or, for that matter, answer her own phone? She trusted all was well; Lily: checking in; Luke: calling to say he'd be delayed getting back by a couple of weeks and he hoped she actually listened to this message so she'd know. She rewound the machine. Nothing she wanted to cope with right now. *Nothing I choose to cope with right now*, she corrected, smiling thinly to herself. *And don't I just feel a hundred percent better for exercising my choices as a living person.* She hauled herself up the stairs with what was left of her energy and crawled back into bed and to sleep, healing or otherwise.

Chapter Twenty-Four

"COME WITH ME" she said, taking his hand. "I want to show you something special, something of mine." Outside the bedroom window the deep night sky shone with the brilliant sparks of a million stars. The faintest of breezes ruffled the sheer cotton curtains as it wafted slowly into the room, carrying a hint of lavender upon warm, August air, the scent following them as they made their way silently down the stairs. She pulled him through the kitchen, her footsteps light, dancing, her trilling laughter a siren song for him to follow, and he smiling, pleased at her eagerness to show him something special.

They emerged out the back door and into the welcoming night, under the stars that had witnessed the abandon of their lovemaking so many times throughout that hot summer. A full moon shone, pale and luminous, casting its silver light on everything around them. Up along the path they went. The scent of new-mown grass rose up from the meadow on either side, surrounding them with the rich, living greenness of its odour. Naked as a nymph she danced on ahead of him, her bare feet unheedful of the pebbly path, then she'd return and take his hand again, whispering to him to hurry as he teased her by going slowly, savouring her excitement.

At the top of the ridge the huge rock glowed surreal. "This is it," she told him breathlessly. "My rock, my magic place. You can view the whole world from here." She climbed up onto it as she had done a hundred times before and stood, conqueror of all she surveyed. Feet apart, arms spread wide and head flung back, she howled to the moon with a wild, thrilling joy, howled until she felt the heat of his body pressing along the length of her back, until his hands, deft on all the soft contours of her body, turned her howls to moans and sighs of pleasure.

They melted, sinking weightlessly to lie upon the heated rock. His mouth was on her, his angel mouth on every tender spot at once, her breasts, the moonlit velvet hollows of her neck, her deepest, secret folds. And then the heated thrust her hips rose eagerly to meet.

The wind, in desperate fury not to be outdone, rose out of nowhere to compete. It swirled, in celebration or in fury she couldn't tell, as she lunged and writhed against the sweet weight on top of her, her back unaware of the gritty stone beneath, all details of discomfort lost to the overwhelming feeling that swept her into a bright oblivion.

Then all was still. Slowly, like a silent, early morning fog lifting to reveal, bit by bit, the realities that lay beneath it all the while, the images of love and passion dissolved before her as she lay there, paralyzed with an awful, creeping certainty. She began to feel on her clammy skin the true coldness of the night air and the unyielding harshness of the rock against her back. The sky at which she stared unblinking held no moon or stars but just the dull, chilling greyness of a cloudy night. There was no new-mown grass, nor lavender, nor any vestige of the warmth of August, only the grim and inhospitable atmosphere of a rugged hillside in the grip of winter.

As she came to consciousness completely, she realized she was shivering, her teeth chattering uncontrollably as her fevered body made a frenzied attempt to counteract her exposure. Her feet and hands were numb with cold. She sat up quickly and wrapped her arms around herself, whimpering with fear and pain, then rose unsteadily to stumble her way along the sharp-stoned path, slowly at first and then running, running in terror to the shelter of the house.

Sarah sat in the tub and waited impatiently for the heat to rise around her and subdue her chattering teeth. She winced as the water penetrated the small cuts she had on her feet from the path, and the abrasion at the base of her spine. She had turned on the small heater in the bathroom to warm her bathrobe and towel as well the room itself, and had locked the door—against what she wasn't sure, but it felt better that way. The blood was slowly making its way back into her hands and feet until finally, neck deep in the water, she felt as though she could calm down enough, was warm enough, to think about what she'd just experienced.

How had she ended up at the rock in the middle of the night? She had been sleepwalking, lured there by her dream? *But no*, she thought as she recalled the course of the dream, *I wasn't lured, it was my idea to go there, I wanted to show Gianluca my special place.* She shuddered. That was worse. Could she blame it on her fever, or was she going mad? Would she be painting sunflowers and cutting off her ear next?

It was one thing to be haunted by dreams in the safety of her bed, but if they started driving her out into the February countryside in the nude, the situation was clearly dangerous. Maybe she should get out of the house, go someplace else. But where? Annalisa's? There were plenty of spare rooms there. Pride stood in the way, however, as she tried to imagine herself asking for refuge because she was afraid Gianluca was going to get her in the night, like a child fretting about a bogeyman. Or, even more ridiculous, that she was going to get herself, she thought, since Gianluca had never shown an inclination to bring her to harm. Quite the opposite.

She could go back into Florence, to Luke's apartment. The dreams never came there. But how would she drive all that way in the shape she was in? It was probably more life-threatening than her jaunt up the hill. She resolved to stay at the house for the day and see what transpired. It was almost five o'clock in the morning; she would simply stay up now, and not go to bed again for fear that sleep might bring about more wandering.

Wrinkled and pruney from a half hour in hot water, but feeling as though she might have just counteracted the effects of exposure in time, Sarah emerged from the tub, dried off and slipped into her toasty terry cloth robe. Unlocking the bathroom door, she peeked out into the hallway, then chided herself. What was she expecting to see, anyway? She shuffled down to the kitchen on slippered feet, flicking on any lights along the way that hadn't yet been switched on in her earlier flight to the bathroom, needing to obliterate the darkness. Beppe yawned widely and stretched as he emerged from the big chair.

"Show some heart and stop looking so completely unconcerned," Sarah snapped at him as she prepared herself some industrial-strength coffee. When it was ready she used it to wash down more aspirins, then ate a small bowl of sugar-laden cereal, hoping their combined effects would rid her of her insupportable headache and clear her foggy brain enough that she could paint. It was the only way she could think of to stay awake.

In the studio, she looked at the six unfinished paintings, contemplating which of them might be most easily completed. She wasn't in the mood, or the condition, to do anything complicated. Then a sketch among the many scattered about the floor caught her eye. It showed the top half of a man whose bottom half was being sucked down into a dark vortex. His arms were flung up, his expression resigned, his eyes fixed on some point far away, or on some picture in his imagination. She picked it up. *This will do nicely,* she thought viciously. *Perhaps I can encourage his departure by painting something that looks like he's being sucked into an abyss.* In sepia tones. Monochrome. No vivacious colours. She set up the second-to-last of her remaining blank canvases and sat down to sketch it out, laying down the first colours of the painting as the black night outside the studio window shifted to a shadowy near-dawn.

Costanza called late in the afternoon to tell her that Annalisa had fallen ill with the flu and to check if Sarah was all right, especially since there was a big storm brewing that would make it difficult to go anywhere. Sarah could come stay with them if she needed help. Sarah's skin prickled with tension, feeling her escape routes disappear as she listened. She didn't want to inflict herself on Costanza, whom she barely knew, when the woman already had Annalisa to look after. And any remote chance she had of successfully driving to Florence were gone now, too. Sarah reassured Costanza that she was doing fine, on the mend, wished Annalisa a speedy recovery and thanked her for calling.

"Damn," she muttered aloud as she put down the phone and walked to the window to look out. Over the course of the morning, she hadn't noticed how the wind had picked up. Every twig, branch and blade of winter grass was trembling in anticipation of the coming storm. On the horizon, bloated, dark clouds drifted ominously across the tops of the mountain peaks that cradled the valley. The first of it would be at the house in an hour or so.

Sarah went into the kitchen to warm the container of Annalisa's ragù she'd put out to thaw that morning, and set a pot to boil for spaghetti. Best to keep her strength up with some decent food. She was feeling achy again, and very tired; seven hours awake was twice as much as she'd managed for a week.

After her meal, with digestion sucking up any vestiges of energy she had left, she could no longer say no to sleep but wasn't prepared to risk lying down in bed. Instead, she set herself up in the big chair with a fire in the hearth, a blanket wrapped around her, and the light on overhead. As a final precaution she placed a teacup, saucer and plate on her lap. If she were to sleepwalk again, their crashing to the floor would wake her as she rose from the chair. Beppe, disgruntled at having been displaced from prime position by a few dishes, stomped off to sleep in the parlour. The sound of his paws plodding across the floor was barely gone from the room when Sarah slipped into inescapable sleep.

◊ ◊ ◊

The loose shutter from the upstairs window banged against the wall and the wind howled furiously at the house that stood in its path. Over them both, penetrating Sarah's sleep, another sound, a persistent ringing. The hallway phone. Something about the insistent sound startled her into wakefulness and she sat up quickly, sending the dishes flying to the ground with the resounding crash of china smashing against brick. The ringing stopped, then started again a minute later. Whoever was calling was ignoring the answering machine and redialling until she picked it up herself. Sarah got up, light-headed, and made her way to the hallway to catch it on the fourth ring.

"Hello?" she asked, her voice thin. She could hardly hear herself for the din of the storm. The line crackled. "Hello?" she asked again.

A tremulous voice, even weaker than her own, answered and she had to cover her open ear with her hand to hear.

"Sarah, is that you, finally, not your machine?"

"Gran? Yes, yes it's me."

"Good." There was a pause and more crackling.

"Gran? Are you still there? Why have you called?"

"That's the wind I can hear, isn't it?"

Sarah's groggy brain was trying to follow the reedy voice, barely audible. "Wind, yes. There's a big storm."

"I knew there would be." Sarah thought she could hear her smile.

"Gran, what's happening? Why have you called?" she repeated.

"You've been painting." A statement, not a question.

"Yes."

"They're wonderful. I can see them. Stunning."

Sarah was confused. "How do you mean, see them?"

"In my mind's eye. Very clearly. The pictures from your dreams."

"Yes." What was happening?

"More dreams than I ever had. Gianluca has shown you everything. He trusted me to keep my own memories, but he's shown you everything."

"Yes." Reluctant this time.

"That's good. Now we won't lose it." Her laboured breathing entered the receiver wispily.

"Gran," Sarah began. She wanted to say, *I don't want them anymore! Tell him to go away; I've seen enough! I can't possibly appreciate them the way you want me to!* But something made her stop before she could utter the words.

"Do you know why we gave you the dreams?" Katherine asked.

"To keep Gianluca alive. To keep your memories alive."

"That's very nice, but it's not the reason."

"What is, then?"

"How can anyone know how precious true love is, how profound, if they haven't yet encountered it? In their ignorance, they might throw it away."

"They might."

"But now you've seen love's power. You fought it, of course. I knew you would. It's terrifying, after all. But irresistible. And you embraced it in the end, took the dreams we gave you and made them your own, let Gianluca in and let him show you everything. That's why we gave you the dreams. So you could know what we knew."

"I'm not sure I wanted to know."

"You needed to, whether you wanted to or not. The knowledge will serve you well."

A thin thread of understanding filtered reluctantly through the silence of Sarah's stubborn refusal to accept the lessons her grandmother insisted on giving her.

"He's coming for me tonight," Katherine said at last. "I can feel it."

"Gianluca?"

"Yes. To take me with him. He won't bother you anymore."

"Gran," Sarah began, her voice more urgent this time. "No! Are you...?" She couldn't finish.

"I want you to do something for me."

Sarah couldn't help herself. "Another thing?" she asked wearily.

"One more thing. I know you'll do this for me."

A resigned silence filled the air between them.

"Paint me a happy ending," Katherine said.

Tears began to course down Sarah's cheeks silently. "Yes," she whispered, listening to the thin thread of her grandmother's breathing beneath the pelting of rain against the windowpane and the incessant banging of the upstairs shutter.

"And Sarah, this is most important," Katherine added.

"What?"

"Love Luca."

"That's two things," Sarah said in a tiny voice.

"Just one thing for me," Katherine told her. "The second thing is for you."

Chapter Twenty-Five

*A*N OBLIQUE RECTANGLE of brilliant golden sunlight had been angling its way across the worn bricks of the kitchen floor for several hours by the time Sarah woke the following morning, curled back up in her nest in the big chair. Beppe had opportunistically replaced the fallen dishes with his heavy warm body, purring in the hollow of Sarah's lap when he felt her stir. She opened her eyes tentatively. Awake, she confirmed, and alive. She raised her head off the back of the chair. Not quite well, but definitely improved. Her head no longer throbbed, and she felt truly rested for the first time in weeks. She thought back over the night. The raging storm, Katherine's call, a dreamless sleep.

Sliding the cat off her lap and into the chair, Sarah rose and walked on weak legs to the window. The downpour of the day before rendered every glistening colour vivid and alive in its wetness, the twigs and trees a richer brown or deeper grey, the winter grass in the meadow shimmering deeply green, the sky washed clean to a perfect clear blue. She went to the kitchen door and stepped outside. The entry stone beneath her slippered feet was warmed by the sun, and the air that filled her lungs was clean and sweet. A bird sang nearby in celebration of the promise of spring held in the silent landscape. A landscape fecund and waiting for a day such as this, with the first hint of warmth in the air and the fullness of the sun stirring it into life again.

The telephone rang and she went back into the house to answer it.

"Sarah, it's me."

"Lily, hi."

"Look, Sarah, Mum asked me to call you. I have—" Lily began, but her sister interrupted her.

"Bad news."

"Yes." Lily sounded startled.

"Gran's dead."

There was a silent pause at the other end of the line. "How did you know? I told Mum I'd call you myself, since she was so fried."

"Mum didn't call me, Gran did. She phoned last night to tell me that Gianluca was coming for her." An even more profound silence greeted her statement. "Are you still there, Lil?"

"Yes. But Sarah, Gran couldn't have called you. She was in a near-coma. Mum was with her the whole time."

"Mum must have gone to the bathroom for a moment."

"No, listen. Gran was in a coma," Lily repeated.

"She sounded weak. But she was talking to me," Sarah insisted.

"Maybe you dreamt it."

"It felt real."

"What did she say?"

"She gave me a gift."

"What kind of a gift?"

"Something wonderful and rare. Something I've been looking for, for ages."

"And that would be...?"

"My life," Sarah told her. "The whole rest of my life."

◊ ◊ ◊

From the moment she had woken that morning, Sarah had understood that she was now properly alone in the house. Gianluca's presence had always been palpable to her, a kind of tension, a sense of incompletion that penetrated everything about the place. Now that he was gone the atmosphere was serene, as though the house were finally at peace with itself. It was still filled with memories, but no longer host to unfulfilled dreams.

The relief Sarah felt at being liberated from Gianluca's grasp lent her a feeling of calm that turned her grief over losing her grandmother into something that was almost like contentment. Gran was where she'd wanted to be for decades. And all three of them—Gran, Gianluca and Sarah—were free at last. Sarah put on an extra sweater and opened all the windows wide to the fresh air, expelling whatever residue remained of fear and sickness. She packed the washer with the first batch from a mountain of dirty clothes, swept the floors and did the washing up before heading off to the bedroom to strip the bed of its sheets, grimy and stiff with the dried sweat of a week of fever. Once it was made up again with a sweet-smelling, pale violet set, she went into the bathroom to see to herself.

Under the hot blast of the shower she scrubbed herself with the dedication of Lady Macbeth and washed her hair twice. As the water poured over her, she let the tears come, not in a howling sorrow but in quiet recognition of a new void. Gran was gone. The woman who, for better or worse, had shaped so much of Sarah's life and given her so much opportunity. It was up to her now to use it well.

Once she felt sufficiently cleansed in body and spirit, she donned the jeans and sweatshirt that were her only remaining clean clothes and drove down the hill to Annalisa's house. Ill or not, Sarah knew Annalisa would want to hear the news of Katherine's passing.

Costanza came to the door to let her in. "I'm glad to see you really are fine after that big storm, and having been sick. Are you here to see Annalisa?"

"Yes. How is she?"

"She has the constitution of an ox. And the temperament, I'm afraid. I'm glad she doesn't get sick too often, because she's terrible when she does."

Sarah smiled. "I can imagine."

"Come along, she's awake at the moment—your timing is good. And she could use the diversion."

The news of a friend's death was hardly a diversion, but Sarah she didn't tell Costanza why she was there. Annalisa needed to hear it first. She was propped up in bed with a bizarrely flamboyant, furry bed jacket around her shoulders, some vestige of a more glamorous youth.

"I heard you at the door," Annalisa said, "so I thought I'd better make myself presentable."

"How are you?" Sarah came over and kissed her cheeks, then sat on a chair next to the bed.

"I feel even older than I am, and that's old. But I think the worst is over. You look better, yourself."

"I am. Annalisa," Sarah began, and took one hand in hers, "I have to tell you—Gran died last night."

Annalisa closed her eyes briefly and crossed herself, her lips moving in some silent benediction. She turned to Sarah. "Well, we knew her time was coming." Sarah nodded, eyes on the floor. "Did you speak to her?"

"Yes. She called me last night. I'm not sure of the time, but it was not too long before…"

"Mhm. That's good, that you got a chance to speak to her."

"Lily said it wasn't possible. She said Gran was in a coma—that I dreamt it—but I'm sure it was real."

"Did you tell her we were in the middle of a storm?"

"She knew. She could hear it."

"She would have thought it was all in her honour."

Sarah smiled. "Your brother's ghost whipping the heavens into a frenzy at the prospect of being reunited."

With her eyes closed again as though she were picturing them both in her mind, Annalisa nodded slowly. "And you? What do you think?"

"That anything is possible."

Now it was Annalisa's turn to smile. "Perhaps you're right. Do you think her passing will affect your dreams?"

"It has already. I had no dreams after her call, at least none I can remember. And I know I won't have any more of Gianluca. He's gone, I can feel it."

"So now you're free."

"Yes, I believe I am."

"Any plans?"

"I have a lot of painting to catch up on. All those images Gianluca fed to me. I still want to paint them. I no longer feel obsessed about it, but I do want to paint them, to complete the cycle." She didn't tell her about Katherine's request. That was personal, between the two of them.

"And Luca?" Annalisa probed, looking hard at her.

Sarah looked at her lap, suddenly shy. "He's not back for another two weeks or so. He's been delayed." Annalisa said nothing, waiting for the real answer to her question. "I have some fence-mending to do there," Sarah finally offered.

"It's worth it."

"You're probably right. I need to think about where he fits into my life, now that my head's clear enough to do so."

"Love doesn't bear over-analyzing too well."

"Advice taken."

"Are you going to take care of yourself now?"

"Yes I will. I still have quite a lot of the frozen food you gave me." Sarah could see that the old woman was starting to doze off, her sick body needing to rest again. She rose. "I'm going now. I just wanted you to know straight away."

"Thank you. When is the funeral?"

"Two days from now. I'm going back for it tomorrow."

"Buy her some purple flowers for me, please. Any kind you can find, so long as they're purple. She always loved that colour best."

When Sarah returned to the house she fixed herself a good lunch and had a nap, in keeping with her resolution, once again, to take care of herself. This time, however, she felt certain of maintaining her regime, now that she was over most of her flu and, more importantly, over her trials with Gianluca. There were other things to take care of as well. She reviewed the state of her studio and decided that as soon as she returned from the funeral in London, she would finish the existing canvases first, the ones she hadn't been able to bring to completion earlier. Then she'd start work on Carlo's commission and, maybe, she'd be ready to make good on her promise to Katherine. She organized everything neatly and cleaned her palette properly, scraping away the accumulated residue of paint in compensation for the shoddy job she'd done of it over the past few weeks. All the sketches went in a folder for future consideration; three were set aside as possible ideas for Carlo.

Sarah wondered if her paintings would have the same force now that Gianluca was gone. And what was she going to paint after she'd finished mining all the inspiration the dreams had given her? She shook her head. She had exorcised her obsession with the past, but it was going to take even longer to exorcise her self-doubt. Someday, she told herself. Someday.

She looked around the studio. It was satisfying to see everything nicely organized and ready for when she returned, ready for her to get on with her life. Her life. What an idea. It *was* hers again. Changed, certainly. Altered irrevocably and, possibly, for the better for being filled with the lives of others who came before her, others who were the reason for her existence and the reason that she stood where she now did. When the dreams, the images of their experiences, were hurling a barrage against her brain, she had felt there could be no existence for her beyond what they were feeding her. There could not possibly be enough room for both. But now that their relentless pressure was dissolved, Sarah began to see that there was, in fact, infinite room for experience and memory within her. Theirs and hers.

Sarah looked at the phone. There was an important call she needed to make.

◊ ◊ ◊

Her car was filled with canvas, gesso and fresh paints as she drove along the back roads from Florence back to Guzzano. Also tucked in among her supplies were the three fantastic Kolinsky brushes she had bought as an indulgence. *No*, she corrected herself, *they're an investment.* The new sweater she'd bought, and the expensive leather boots, were an indulgence. Katherine had been well off when she died and had divided the bulk of her estate, including the value of the house at Guzzano, between her two granddaughters. It was enough to give them security about the basics, if they were careful, while pursuing their talents.

She thought about her sister and smiled. Lily was finally going to be able to move out on her own. She was looking at buying a flat, but after seeing her together with James, Sarah didn't think Lily would be needing her own place for very long. They looked like a couple who were in for the long term, something Sarah had never seen in her sister before. Even their parents begrudgingly accepted him, his creative and, for them, incomprehensible occupation overcome by the fact he was very good at it.

The road Sarah took back to Guzzano ran high along the side of a long ridge, following the curves of the hillside on the right and with an unobstructed view of a broad valley sweeping away to the left. Sarah was driving with her window down to take in the fresh air, still brisk but with that hint of warmth that signals the coming of spring. The sky was a painter's dream: blue studded with pristine clouds of the fluffiest white to give it depth. She loved this landscape, the drama of its vast, open skies pierced in the distance by the Apennine peaks, the ever-changing patterns and colours that the seasons played upon the land, the heavenly quality of its light. Even when it wasn't the subject of her painting, its beauty inspired whatever else she chose to portray.

She began to sing the romantic little tune her grandmother had loved best, the one Gianluca and then Luke had always played. If it had come into her head a week ago, she would have thought of it as yet another of Gianluca's unwanted thoughts and would have swiftly moved to squash it. Now she sang it with pleasure, enjoying its sentimentality and unafraid of the memories it evoked. She thought about the first time Luke had played it for her and how astonished she had been at the quality of his voice. If she'd had any doubts about whether or not she was going to sleep with him, he had erased them with the first few notes—and rendered her weak-kneed with lust by the end of it.

That same quality of voice had hit her afresh when she'd called him from Guzzano after Katherine died. He had come on the line and her heart had skipped a beat just as it used to do, surprising her. Why hadn't she heard it when they'd spoken the other times? She'd called again, from Florence, and felt the same powerful draw, blathering on about anything just to keep him on the line.

The days surrounding the funeral had given her a lot of time to contemplate Luke. No one had begrudged her ample quiet time amidst the events and the stream of people wishing to offer their condolences. She had wondered, briefly, if Gianluca's final departure would result in the disappearance of his traits in Luke: the fear of Greece, his slack-hipped stance, the way he put his arm around her shoulders, his gift at the piano, his love of the house. But she knew they would remain, just as her own chin would always tilt upwards in defence, her laugh would always trill, and her hands would always paint. She was coming to see these similarities as blessings instead of impositions, as timeless reminders of one generation for the next, some genetic and some inexplicable, and some of which she and Luke might pass on in their turn.

When she arrived at the house, Sarah answered Beppe's pleas to be let in the door, but didn't enter herself. There was something she needed to do first. From the passenger seat she took the small urn that had been travelling with her and carried it up the path behind the house, past the meadows poised to stir soon with fresh green growth, and up the last little stony incline that led to the big rock. The day was perfect, with just the right amount of breeze coming from the right direction. She climbed up onto the rock and stood at its edge, her mind flooding with memories at the gesture, memories of the many things she had felt, and done, and been in that spot, as Katherine had before her. Tearless and tranquil, Sarah lifted the stopper out of the urn, raised the vessel high, and let the wind carry its contents across the silent, waiting fields.

◊ ◊ ◊

Glorious, if I do say so myself, Sarah thought as she stepped back a couple of paces from the painting and viewed it with a critical eye. Katherine and Gianluca embraced, their bodies melding together in a swirl of colour like a cloak wrapped around them, vertical and soaring, surrounded by a meadow filled with flowers. It was quite unlike anything else the dreams had engendered. There was no sinister edge, no tension, no threat. The colours were brilliant and alive, interpretations of the countryside rendered in tones more dazzling than the natural world: the gemstones of angels.

'*Angels*', Sarah thought. *That's what I'll call this one.* She had decided, contrary to her earlier plan, to fulfill her promise to Katherine right away. One of the things she'd received in her inheritance was the journal Katherine had written at the nursing home. The story of her love. Sarah had started reading it with trepidation but had finished it with joy, understanding through it the details of her dreams and Katherine's long-secret feelings. It had inspired Sarah to start on 'Angels' sooner. She'd found herself eager to express the purity of emotion in its happy ending.

The other canvases were being finished in turn. A large packing crate stood to one side of the room and she carefully wrapped each one as she finished them, setting them in the crate, where they awaited shipment to her one-woman show at The Mallet in June. Sarah was both thrilled and terrified at the prospect. There wasn't all that much time to get a full show together as well as seeing to Carlo's commission. But when she looked at the number of sketches she still had pinned up on the wall, she knew she had enough material there to pull it off. All the dream images would someday hang in other people's homes, but 'Angels' would stay at Guzzano, in the kitchen, an echo opposite Katherine's original painting of the two of them in the meadow.

She cleaned her brushes, finishing early for the day. As she walked through the kitchen towards the back door, her eye was caught by the envelope that had been lying, unopened, on the kitchen table for several days. Something from Roger.

Time to test this new-won sense of strength, she told herself, and opened it. Inside was a cheque for a reasonable sum, with a hand-written note on a scrap of paper attached. *From your Indonesian paintings. This is the last thing I'm going to do for you. R.*

Sarah laughed out loud. Little did he know she no longer needed him to do anything for her. For a mean moment she wondered if he'd deducted a commission for himself, then she decided that was unfair. This was his peace offering, his apology despite his fierce assertion that none was necessary. In her heart of hearts, she knew he would be pleased to find that she'd finally heeded his advice, even if it was only because it served to maintain his belief that he was always right. She left the cheque lying there and, grabbing her jacket on the way, walked out the back door towards the ridge and her rock.

The view from the top thrilled her as it always did when she reached it. She sat upon the rock and gazed out across the two valleys, the extent of ridge between them, and the peaks of the higher mountains, still white with winter's snow beyond. How often had Gran done exactly this after a day of painting, she wondered, and with the thought came the realization that it would always be like this, that she would continually find vestiges of her grandmother in much of what she did herself. Her life would forever reflect Katherine's influence, because her legacy was inescapable from the day Sarah had been born into the world as her descendant.

It was dawning on her, however, that what she made of that legacy was her own. Her inherited talent she had tried to disavow, only to find it was the one thing in her life she could never abandon. Her inherited house was hers because she loved it so. Even when its memories grew into nightmares she had always returned, drawn by some invisible thread.

Then there was Luke. Her own Moretti. If all had not happened between Katherine and Gianluca so long ago, Sarah would not be here to run into him. And what errant twist of fate had made him seek the land his father had left behind? She had made her choice about him the first evening she met him. Then fought it hard, just as she had fought her talent and the lessons Katherine had wanted her to learn through Gianluca. She'd fought because believing in herself and in her heart, and bringing out the best in both those things, took far more courage than the alternative.

Down by the house, sunlight glinted on a car as it made its way up the gravel drive. She stayed in her place on the rock while she watched him get out and go to the house. She wasn't worried; he'd know where to find her. A minute later he appeared on the path below, climbing towards her unhurriedly. Her heart beat a little faster as she took in his familiar lanky frame and slow, swinging stride, his hands in his pockets. So like Gianluca, and so unalike.

She sat on the rock and waited, while the sun shone warm in a simple, blue sky.

The End

Born in Canada but global by nature, Shelagh has lived in Canada, England, the United States, and most memorably, Italy – the land of great food, gorgeous landscapes, and handsome people. Her previous books include *Pearls in the Ashes*, a novel that arose from a chance encounter on the Mongolian steppes, and *Gumption: The Practical Woman's Guide to Living an Adventuresome Life*, a six-step program that reflects her own passion for living fully. Shelagh is also a popular blogger at practicalwomansguide.com and a guest contributor to Huffington Post, among others.

www.ingramcontent.com/pod-product-compliance
Lightning Source LLC
Chambersburg PA
CBHW071459170626
46811CB00007B/2634